Wicked Kind of Love

Prairie Devils MC Romance

Nicole Snow

Content copyright © Nicole Snow. All rights reserved.
Published in the United States of America.
First published in August, 2014.

Disclaimer: The following ebook is a work of fiction. Any resemblance characters in this story may have to real people is only coincidental.

Description

WICKED LOVE: UNDENIABLE, DEEP, AND RELENTLESS...

Emma Galena thinks moonlighting as a medic for the Prairie Devils MC is tough, and then she meets Tank. No job is supposed to be this hard, this dangerous, this insane. Neither is her attraction to the tattooed giant who upends everything.

John "Tank" Richmond has taken more beatings than anybody for his club. Bullets, knives, and brawls were never half as painful as the dagger Emma twists in his heart. Tank wants this chick *bad,* but he won't have her in his brutal world, knowing it's a one way ticket to suffering.

If only he could forget about claiming the angel who won't leave his head. If only he could stop the crazy lust boiling his blood every time he imagines her wearing his brand and nothing else.

PROPERTY OF TANK? Not so fast.

Tank's right about how vicious the underworld can be. Soon, a broken heart is the least of Emma's worries when a Fed with a grudge ropes her into a scheme to bring down the Devils for good, testing her loyalty to the outlaws she's sworn to serve and the man she can't stop loving.

Will chasing an impossible, wicked love cost Tank and Emma everything?

Note: this is a dark and gritty MC romance with language, violence, and love scenes as wild as they come. Outlaw love is merciless!

The Prairie Devils MC books are stand alone novels featuring unique lovers and happy endings. No cliffhangers allowed! This is Tank and Emma's story.

I: Fractured (Emma)

Did I have regrets?

Not until I saw him behind the glass and heard the chains rustling on his huge arms. For a man his size, handcuffs weren't enough.

The bastards put two hulking sets of medieval looking irons on his wrists, and it still looked like he'd break right through them if he flexed his arms. His legs were just as anchored, bound as his wrists, but not in any way that would really be able to contain this giant. If he'd wanted, one kick would've snapped the rusty links scraping the floor between his ankles.

But what would've been the point?

Tank was done running. He'd proven that in spades last week when he killed to protect me.

The guilt stung, and I lowered my eyes, focusing on my hands before his eyes could focus on me.

He'd reached the end of the line. Just like me.

Lust made us lovers, and murder made us more, bound together in a pact of blood I thought was only meant for Tank and his brothers.

Wrong? Hell yes. Regrets? No, no, *fuck no.*

Nothing but one. I signed myself to him in blood and sin, and I'd do it all over again just for one more crushing taste of his lips.

The sole thing I regretted was seeing those chains bulging around his rock hard muscle and the ratty orange jumpsuit one size too small for his skin.

We'd reached the end of the line, but at least we were here together. Now, there was nothing left to do but face justice. For him, it was the dingy prison and the solemn faced judges. My justice was all *him,* a heavily tattooed god who'd broken my world and pieced it back together again as he damn well pleased, harder than anything I'd imagined but oh-so-worth-it.

The thick glass between us felt like nothing. It was no match for the raging fire in his eyes. I looked up, trying not to see my own guilt inscribed on his gorgeous ink, the same massive arms he'd used to split a monster's skull open.

I was the reason he killed, the reason he was in here now. And if things were really as fucked up as they seemed, I was the reason he'd be stuck here until he was old and gray, too withered to ride a Harley.

How could I even begin to speak? It would've been better to rip out my heart out and sling it against the glass, savage beating proof that I owed him my life, my love, my soul?

If only it were so easy to pull it out! My heart throbbed so tight in my chest I thought the surging blood flow up my head would cause me to black out in front of him.

My words were obliterated, and they didn't start to return until he was fully seated. I swallowed hard. The bruises and scrapes on his face were still there, only halfway faded, brutal reminders of the damage he'd suffered, a sacrifice that said more than a thousand *I love yous* ever would.

Of course, he'd never flinch at physical pain. Dents and scratches never fazed him, and I wasn't sure mortal wounds did either. Hell, he was so fearless and hard headed he probably didn't care about the real punishment that was only beginning, the imprisonment away from everything he loved.

I wasn't so strong. The crappy orange jumpsuit wrapped around his muscles burned my heart a thousand times worse than my eyes, turned it to ashes when I wondered how much life he'd forfeit in a shoebox cell.

Jesus. Why, Tank? Why?

I shook my head. The answer came a second later, sparking in his eyes.

Because murder doesn't come cheap, and neither does love.

The cop near the door behind him stepped through it and continued to watch us through the little glass pane.

Hell didn't do anything to dampen the way I got lost in his eyes. When he stared at me, I froze, instantly forgetting all the scripted sorrows I'd been practicing to myself in the waiting room.

"Emma," Tank said, breaking the tomb-like silence. "Why did you come?" He turned his wrist, showing off the eagle with the Devil's head in its talons inked on his forearm, two symbols that wrapped up his whole mad world.

Just tell him the truth. Perfect words aren't worth a damn. Honest ones are.

"I had to, Tank. I needed to thank you. He was unstable. He was going to hurt me if you hadn't –"

"They're listening," he warned. "Prisoners got no right to privacy, babe. Especially guys who're part of a club the Feds are trying to brand domestic terrorists."

The damned club! His whole life was folding, and still he stayed loyal, giving his brothers the same grim sacrifice he'd given me.

My whole mouth tasted bitter when I thought about it. If it weren't for the Prairie Devils MC, neither of us would be suffering like this right now. We wouldn't be here with this shitty glass between us instead of in each other's arms.

Then again, there was plenty of blame to go around. I couldn't pin it all on the club, however tempting.

If I hadn't gotten myself into a cash grab I didn't understand patching up their wounds, I wouldn't have met him. If I hadn't met him, he wouldn't be here, and a man's blood wouldn't be on both our hands – and the selfish fucking psycho who deserved everything Tank gave him wouldn't be having the last laugh from beyond the grave by bringing down my man and his brothers.

"That isn't going to happen. No one's going to take down the club." I shook my head, desperate to shake the unpleasant thoughts. "The lawyers are working on it. They'll get your guys off the hook and get you home."

Tank snorted and flashed me a smile. It wasn't a smart ass gesture, though. More like an old man marveling at a child's innocence.

"Blaze's lawyers have got some fancy tricks up their asses. Yeah, the club'll be fine, but nobody's gonna spring me free. Shit doesn't work like that, babe. I'm gonna be cooling my heels in this shithole a good long while. Thank fuck those tours in Afghanistan taught me all about patience."

I took a good long look at his face. Killing hadn't changed a damned thing. Why would it? It wasn't like my kill was his first.

He was beautiful, through and through, a living, breathing contrast to the black heart within. My grandmother used to tell me I had big friends in high places when I was a kid, but her silly little saying never meant anything until I met Tank. And right now, it meant the whole world, my overly logical brain's attempt to justify this mess and prevent myself from breaking down into a weeping pile.

My guardian angel was behind that glass, paying for my mistakes.

"You didn't come to talk business, babe." He leaned forward, close to the glass as he could get. "We both know why you're here. Listen, Emma, whatever may or may not have happened last week – don't ever feel a flap of guilt about it. Not for me, and certainly not for that motherfucker who tried to kill your sweet ass. What's done is done. And I wouldn't have it any other way. I did everything to keep you safe. Nobody but you and my brothers matters worth shit."

Damn! The tear sliding down my cheek burned like lava.

It wasn't supposed to go like this. Maybe if he showed something besides the cool and collected intensity beaming out his eyes, it would've made this easier. I couldn't reconcile him accepting surrender with the fact that it looked like he could get up, break his twig-like chains, bust through the glass, and walk right out of here.

Whatever, just as long as he didn't warn me again. I wouldn't be able to take it. Not after he'd warned me about this life, trying to nudge me away from it, and far away from him.

Couldn't he see there was no going back? I was already tainted, in too deep. At this depth, a girl couldn't have those regrets, or else she'd drown.

I wasn't going to walk away, dammit, no matter how much he aimed those perfect honey eyes in my direction. He was paying the ultimate price for me, but I'd suffered for him too!

Pleasure made walking through pure hell a whole lot easier. I couldn't forget the months I'd spent heating up like a rocket in his presence, let alone the perfect nights when I traced those sexy tattoos with my fingers, my tongue, my everything.

"No, Tank, you listen! It's my turn to talk." I reached up and tapped the glass. So cold against my palm. "We were going to have something new and wonderful before all this crap hit. I still want that, and I don't care one bit how long I have to wait. If it takes you ten years to come home – even twenty! – I'll be waiting. There's nobody else but you, and there never will be. Just thinking about another guy makes me want to throw up. Nobody'll ever fill your giant damned shoes. They can't."

For a second, his eyes went bright, glowing with the same addictive fire I saw when we were alone together. Then it went out, and my heart dropped like a rock. He was determined to turn me away.

"I fucked up, Emma, and I'm not talking about the reason I'm in here. I fucked myself when I decided to go after you. Trapped your heart when I should've set it free. Should've stuck to my guns. Should've kept you away. Should've had the Prez turn you right out of the fucking clubhouse and found a girl half as beautiful and smart to play doctor…"

"Shut up!" I was shaking now, losing more tears in hot, painful streams. "You can't regret this! I have mine, but they're all about the time we've wasted. If we weren't too stupid, too slow, playing games on both sides, we would've had more to remember. But I don't care how much or how little there is. Everything I've had with you, I'm holding onto. I'm not going to let it go just because someone tells me to – even if it's you."

His smile was gone. He moved slow, never taking his eyes off me, never showing the tiniest crack in his rock hard armor. My hand was trembling, splayed out on the glass.

It was hard enough to look at him like this, but I couldn't see a damned thing after he mirrored my little hand, eclipsing it in his huge palm behind the glass. The whole world went blurry, sprouting painful thorns.

"We had our time, babe, but the motherfucking clock's run out. I'm gonna cherish every fucking second we had 'til the day I die." He paused. "This shit cuts both ways, you know. I know it's gonna take some time to get your head and heart fixed. You'll tell me and my advice where to fuck off to, and that's your right. But I'm not gonna let you waste the rest of your life circling the skies for me, wasting your best fuckin' years. Gonna make you listen, and listen good, because it'll make sense someday when days have turned into weeks and weeks have become fucking months."

No, no, no...

Why did my eyes have to fail me like this? Why couldn't it be my ears? Hot, painful tears jerked at my vision.

"Walk away, Em. Pack your shit up and leave Missoula. You can land a nursing gig in Seattle or Portland or Eureka and start all over. Forget the Prairie Devils and my stupid ass too. What went down happened because I couldn't let you get hurt – same damned reason I'm saying this shit now. If you really care about me, you'll do exactly what I say, and do it as soon as you fucking can." He inhaled slowly. "My life's fucked, babe. Yours isn't. Fuck, you were the victim here. Nobody disputes that. I can't drag you straight to Hades like a goddamned boulder strapped to your back. Look at me, Emma…"

He waited. Slowly, I did as he asked, clearing my eyes. If he was really this determined, it might be the last time I'd see him, and I wanted this to count.

"Please. There's got to be another way." My words were faint, weak, defeated because I knew damned well there wasn't.

"There's only one way, and I'm pointing to it." His hand was gone from mine, and he stuck a finger out, pointing toward the exit sign down the hall. "Go. You got strength and beauty, babe. That's gonna make this whole fucking thing easier with time. You wanna talk about regrets? Only one I got is breaking your heart. But if that's what it takes to keep you safe, then I'm game. One day, everything'll make sense, and I'll be nothing but a distant fucking memory. Get the hell out and go live enough for both of us."

I jerked up. I couldn't listen to anymore of this heart wrenching shit. He was right about one thing: the man had a knack for shattering my heart and piecing it back together so many times I'd lost count.

He wanted to confess regrets? Then so did I.

I regretted ever losing my head and falling for this stern, violent, beast of a man. I regretted re-wiring my head to the point where I *knew* I'd never love another man as much as Tank, and I'd keep loving him against all the terrible odds.

I wasn't going to stop. I couldn't. If prison bars or his stupid high ideals stood between us, I didn't care. Not one tiny shred.

He'd keep hammering my heart to pieces – that much was given. But as long as I still had a single beating ember left, I couldn't shut it off. If he blew my love to pieces, the tiny cinders would just keep beating for his dumb ass, and *only* for him.

He owned it all – every fragile piece of me – and he'd keep it if we never laid eyes on each other or spoke again.

II: A Miserable Arrangement (Emma)

Months Earlier

"Linda, what's wrong?" I hadn't seen my lead RN so pissed since a patient beaned her at Christmas with the cafeteria's nasty pea and red lentil soup.

She burst into the break room, hands up in the air, heading straight for the coffee pot like it was filled with something a lot more potent to take the edge off.

"You wouldn't believe the nerve of those bikers," she hissed.

"Bikers? You mean the big guys in the leather hanging around the ICU's waiting area?"

"Yep. Those are the pricks," she hissed, leaving me shocked and stupid at her rare curse. "Put a man on a Harley, and he'll walk around like his dick owns God's green earth plus everything on it. Stay away from them."

She shot me a severe look. I practically expected her to wag a finger at me, clucking like the grandma she was. I shook my head to suppress a smile.

Okay, now the guys out in the waiting area *really* had my interest. The two big badasses caught my eye that morning when I walked through. Their muscles and tattoos would've sent the buff dudes who delivered supplies at the hospital's loading docks running. I honestly couldn't tell who was rougher. The pair looked like they could've been brothers.

They definitely *didn't* look like any bikers I was used to seeing around here. I'd been a Montana girl all my life, and everybody with a brain in their head stayed the hell away from the greasy, vicious criminals who wore the Grizzlies MC patch.

These guys, though...they were a clean kinda rugged. Not just clean, but *ripped*, big boys who'd built themselves up without letting drugs and booze whittle down their muscles. Either the Grizzlies had some hot new recruits, or something else was going on here.

"Emma! Did you hear what I said?" Linda cocked her head, eyeing me suspiciously. "Don't get any funny ideas. These are men you don't want to mess around with. Even a simple hello can lead places you'd never imagine..."

I shook my head, breaking the trance. "Sorry. I don't understand...what happened? What did they do to you?"

"That freak named Maverick..." she gritted her teeth. "Not only did he try to slip me cash for supplies, he wanted to know if I wanted to *work* for his stupid club. Can you believe it? *Me,* working for a bunch of brutes like them? Ha!"

She threw her hands up. "It's so ridiculous it isn't even funny."

I bit my tongue, suppressing another smile. Linda was so damned uptight, but she was a good boss just the same. Everybody said she'd been wilder in her younger days, and now she did overtime playing the perfect grandma to make up for it.

"How much cash are we talking about, Linda?"

"More than any of us will make this year with overtime. If crime didn't pay, there wouldn't be creeps like them." She shook her head, dashing a little redness in her angry cheeks. "Bastard had a whole stack of hundreds ready. He called it 'good faith' money."

"That's...that's terrible. I'm glad they walked away when you showed them the door."

"Those boys are scum, Emma, but they aren't stupid. I stopped just short of spitting in their faces. I wasn't afraid. They aren't going to lay anybody out here. Thank God for the cameras." She sighed, gathering her wits. "Just hope that's the end of it. We've already got enough rogues coming through town without these Prairie Devils stomping fresh blood all over Montana."

I nodded. We talked about other crap that wasn't so heavy and infuriating.

But when I got back on my shift, the wheels started turning in my head. Wheels made of bills. Lots and lots of hundred dollar bills.

Holy crap, a voice snapped inside me. *You're not really thinking about this...are you?*

Not quite. I was thinking about bills. I was up to my neck in overdue notices aplenty and those damned student loans I hadn't put a dent in since the payments came due. I'd only been on the job six months, and if I didn't toss them something soon, they were sure to go to collections. After that, they'd threaten my RN license.

Gotta love the logic: *pay up, or we'll make it so you'll never pay for anything again.*

By the end of my shift, I couldn't get my mind off this strange new opportunity. My old acquaintance, Tracy, was pulling double duty at the Dirty Diamond strip club, plus another new one that had opened up several towns over. If anybody knew where to find these guys, it would be her.

It was late by the time I left. A quick phone call later, and I was on my way to Python, just south of Missoula, where the Devils had landed from North Dakota.

"I'm Maverick, and this is my VP, Blaze. You're the nurse?"

I nodded. The men were even more dangerous up close, and pretty damned hot too. Not that I'd ever admit it to these hardened wolves. They looked like the type who'd eat a girl alive if they caught a tiny whiff of interest – or, who knows – maybe they didn't need a whiff at all to sink their teeth in.

"Course she is. This girl's got the body for it, bro." Blaze looked me up and down, smiling the whole time. "Fuck. Maybe we can have her pulling double duty at the bar. I wouldn't mind looking at that little outfit while she's serving drinks. Just gotta make it a little tighter."

I folded my arms, trying not to go ruby red. Were these guys so out of touch they thought ordinary scrubs were sexy?

Maverick slammed his fist into Blaze's side. Obviously a hothead, he glared at the President, but never so much as rubbed the tender spot.

"Knock it off, man. This is serious shit, especially with the Grizzlies breathing down our necks."

My eyes widened. So, the two clubs were at odds. I started to think this was a big fat mistake if I was about to wander in between two warring motorcycle gangs.

"You showed me your license," Maverick said. "Far as credentials go, that's all I need. I'll have a brother dig into the dirty details to make sure everything's as spotless on your record. Now for the interview."

Blaze opened up and stepped close to me. "How do you do under pressure, nurse? You gonna run off scared the first time some brother needs fresh blood while we're fending off fuckers circling this clubhouse on their choppers?"

I couldn't imagine it. I really couldn't. He was describing crap that supposedly died with the old West. But my eyes were all filled with green, and I wouldn't let seeing red get in the way of what I needed.

"Absolutely not. I think I've seen more bodies torn up than you have, Mister VP. These mountain roads aren't kind when it's icy. Neither are the grizzlies – the real bears, I mean."

I glared at him. Blaze had a stare that shocked me to the bone, exciting and dangerous, but he also had a rough edge I didn't like. Still, it was easy to see why some girl was going to get her panties melted off.

"You wanna put money down? I'm a betting kinda man, baby. And right now, I think you're full of –"

"I believe her." Maverick stepped between us, spreading out his hands. He turned to me. "Don't mind my fucking brother. I'm not just calling him that because we share the same patch. I inherited the brains, and he got all the hot fucking blood."

"Don't forget I got the goddamned looks too!" Blaze locked eyes with his brother, clenching his jaw.

"He'll learn to appreciate you, Emma, and so will I. You've got spunk. I like that. Congratulations. You're working for the Prairie Devils now. I'll have Tank bring out your retainer."

I waited with him by the bar while Blaze stormed off looking for the third guy. Maverick filled me in on their tension with the Grizzlies up in Missoula. He also told me he might need a checkup for a girl he'd picked up at their strip joint, some woman named June.

Blaze returned a few minutes later, and my eyes nearly popped out when I saw what was behind him. If these two brothers were built to kill, then the man behind the VP was made to end whole worlds without breaking a sweat.

He was huge, and handsome. A little younger than the other two. Clean cut. Eyes that hung like delicious dark diamonds, glowing in the dim light. I imagined they were little windows that let me have a glimpse at whatever crazy furnace underneath his skin powered the mountain of muscles.

"You got it?" Maverick asked.

"It's all here, boss. Every cent." He drew a thick stack of bills from his pocket wrapped up in plastic and pushed it forward.

"It's not mine, brother," Maverick shook his head. "Give it to her. Emma's gonna be taking real good care of your clumsy ass from now on. Everybody else's too."

Tank pushed forward and reached out. His eyes were all on me now. I'd never been melted by a man's glare before. I thought that was only the kinda stuff that happened in bad comedies and cheap romance novels, but right here, before me, I was turning to mush.

Make that sizzling, tingling, smoking mush.

I had to focus real hard to make my hand move and push toward his. My fingers brushed his as he laid the stack in my hand. The weight was a big surprise.

Jesus, Linda hadn't been kidding about the bribe. It was at least a year's salary. Hazard pay, Maverick had said, as well as a retainer to make sure I wasn't going to walk away without the club's permission.

But it wasn't half the shock I got when I lost myself in his big brown eyes. Tank exhaled, lips moving just slightly on his concrete jaw. He towered over me, nearly a foot and a half taller, shoulders that could've swallowed me up several times over.

An irresistible urge shot through me. I had no clue lust and curiosity could get together and dance, but they did, throbbing until I couldn't imagine anything but reaching for his shoulders, climbing him like a tree, and planting my lips on his, perfectly even and so damned hot.

"Hey!" Blaze snapped, jerking me back to reality. "Stop gawking. Both of you. Tank, walk the girl out to her car. It's fucking dangerous around here."

Maverick laughed. "You heard him. See her out and then come on back. We got a lotta shit to unload before Throttle's crew starts coming here on runs."

I stumbled after him, clutching the money dumbly in both hands. We were outside, heading for the place where I'd parked by their garages, when Tank finally offered his first real words.

"Stuff that shit in your purse. It's not just assholes in the Grizzlies we need to be concerned about. If you get robbed by some local fucking yokel or a cop sniffs around your cash, it'll be club business. That money's yours to spend, but it's a gift from this MC."

"Of course!" I could've smacked myself in the head. Instead, I shoved the money away, tucking it between two old pay stubs.

Suddenly, those crappy loans and the other bills didn't seem so bad stacked up against my *new* salary.

"Don't worry about it. You're new to this, same as me not so long ago. You'll learn quick, babe."

"I'll do my best."

I flipped the button on the remote to unlock my car. Tank beat me to the door and opened it, resting his hand on the top while he waited for me to climb inside.

"It'll be different having a professional lady around here." A thin smile pulled at his lips.

"Oh?" I slid into the car and looked up. Damn, sitting down below him, it was like he reached up to the sky. A total redwood of a man, and just as glorious.

"Yeah. Most of the other bitches who hang around here are whores." He saw the surprise in my face and his smile faded. "Uh, club whores, I mean. All part of the lifestyle. Not used to having girls around who aren't here to fuck."

Fire licked at my cheeks. Even the silly boys at my old campus hadn't talked about sex so casually.

"Got it. I'm not judgmental."

That was rich. Compared to these guys, I was just as big a prude as Linda, fearful and sadly inexperienced. For some reason, I hated being like that. Hot jealousy shot through me when I imagined him with some faceless skank.

"Thank you, Tank. I appreciate the advice, and I'll take the rest from here."

He nodded and stepped back after closing my door. As I pulled away, he was still watching me. If he were a dog, I had a feeling his tail would've been wagging, eager to chase me down and keep me from leaving.

What the hell was I thinking, anyway? Hanging around these hardass bikers had gotten me so dizzy I'd nearly lost my senses in a blink – especially to him.

"It's just a job," I told myself, driving back to the tiny house I rented.

I reached down and patted my purse, reminding myself what this was all about. I didn't care how hot those bikers were, or how fast Tank made my pulse thump between my thighs.

Men like that weren't dating material. They fucked strippers and prostitutes and then threw them away. I shuddered, wondering how many STDs I'd end up treating for these boys.

God, what if I had to examine *him?*

Tomcat or not, Tank was polite, and I'd be kind right back. Nice and professional. Nothing more.

I'd already done a crazy thing. No damned way could I afford to get any deeper into this – even if it was a sin to think about any girl but me climbing all over his walking perfection.

My phone went off while I was winding down my shift a few days later. Not the little mobile I'd had for years – the *other* one. Blaze called it a burner, and told me to keep it on me at all times.

I flipped open the cheap device and felt my heart stop when I saw the text.

NEED YOU RIGHT NOW. TANK'S BEEN SHOT. CLUBHOUSE.

I wrapped up, grabbed my bag, and nearly bowled over Linda on the way out. She threw her hands out to stop me.

"Whoa, Emma, where's the fire?"

"It's my mother's place. Seamstress stuff. She forgot to drop off a rush job and really needs my help. Business hasn't been so awesome lately. I'm trying to keep her afloat."

White lies never did any harm, right? Surely not, especially when they were mixed with dark truths.

Linda narrowed her eyes. "I need you to look over some files with me tomorrow. The admin's been complaining about inventory mismatch. Supplies missing. I've talked to everybody but you and Katie."

"Of course! Anything you need." My phone buzzed again, rocking my whole purse. "Didn't know that was a problem. We'll sort it all out, Linda, I'm sure it's all in the files."

Shit! Shit! Shit!

Great. Now I had two nightmares staring me down. I roared out of the parking lot and took off before Linda took the notion to follow me out and saw me driving like a maniac.

I thought I'd been tracking everything I took for the club's infirmary without missing anything. I must've slipped up, and now someone had noticed.

I pounded the steering wheel. Whatever. It wasn't time to worry about that until it was staring me down. I had to focus on the patient, and nothing else. Saving a man's life mattered more than my slip ups – especially if that man was Tank.

Worry churned in my stomach, the kind I didn't get over most patients at the hospital.

Why did it have to be him? I wondered, pinching my bottom lip between my teeth.

Perfect. First real job for the club, and I was already coming apart at the seams. How could I be so stupid and weak? I was letting myself get weighed down by worries, and it wasn't going to get any better when I had his blood on my scrubs.

When I got to the clubhouse, Blaze waved me to the rear. Tank was sprawled out on the table they'd set up in the little storage room, way too small to contain him. His cut was off and his shirt was rolled up.

I grabbed the shears off my supply table and clipped the rest off. God, if it wasn't for all the blood, his muscles would've held me transfixed, lost in the violent world of ink on his chest. The huge Devil's face on his breast watched me the whole time as I worked on the wound.

He'd taken a direct hit. Some surprise attack on the road, Blaze told me. They were lucky he hadn't hit the pavement at full speed, or else there would've been a whole lot more than this hole in his side to worry about.

The VP stood in the room, watching for a long time. I expected more infuriating bullshit out of him, but he held his tongue and let me do my job, standing aside while I cleaned the wound and patched him up.

We were low on anesthetic. Hadn't pulled enough from the hospital's stock, and shipments to the clubhouse were getting wrecked by the Grizzlies attacks.

My hands were so hot on his body they went numb. Tank groaned once during my crude surgery, bristling like a doped up tiger.

I finished the job in a haze, only coming out of it when I noticed how pale he'd gotten. The new bag of blood pumping into his system was almost depleted.

I walked to the refrigerator I had the guys fit and calibrate at just the right temperature. "Oh, shit!"

"What the hell is it?" Blaze ran up and stood at my side.

We both looked inside and saw the gory mess. Some bag on the top shelf had gotten pierced and bled all over everything, its thick contamination was smeared everywhere. No blood bank in their right mind would use anything it had touched, and neither would I. There wasn't time to wait around and try to disinfect the rest.

Unfortunately, that meant the whole shelf marked with Tank's blood type was toast. I felt *my* blood draining and slammed the freezer with a grunt.

"What!" Blaze demanded. "It's a fucking spill. You telling me all that shit's no good?"

I shook my head sadly. Thoughts of creeping into the hospital and trying to slip out blood under lock and key flashed in my head. Or, worse, letting Tank languish without the stuff he needed to fight his shock.

I couldn't let that happen. Everybody needed the right balance to heal, even this giant who'd taken a blow that would've sent most ordinary men to their graves by now.

"Hey!" Blaze grabbed me by the shoulders, pushing his elbow toward my face. "Take mine, nurse. I know him and I got the same damned type. I set this place up myself. Same fucking tags for Tank and I on that shelf. Give him my blood."

Wriggling away from his grasp, I stood up, shock and awe spreading across my face. "It doesn't work like that! There's no time to test for disease or alloantibodies..."

"Bullshit!" he roared. "This is fucking war, Emma. You got the equipment to hook my ass up and draw out what you need. I'm fucking clean. Haven't had a goddamned sniffle in years."

"There are lots of other germs –"

"Look at him – he's white as a fucking sheet!" Blaze pointed, fist shaking in fury. "Fuck it! I'll do this myself if you're not gonna do your job. No bro's gonna crash out and die or fuck off into a coma while we've got the stuff to stop it."

He marched toward the shelf where all the equipment was stored. I pinched my teeth and sighed. Blaze was right.

When I tried to push my way past him, grabbing for the old transfusion machine we'd gotten shipped in, he didn't fight. His anger melted into a kinda smug satisfaction, happy he'd forced me into this medieval procedure.

In less than an hour, it was over. I watched three hundred milliliters of Blaze's fiery blood slide through the IV into Tank.

"Hey, one more thing," he said, just as he was about to leave me in peace. "Don't tell him about this shit."

I looked at him, raising an eyebrow. Blaze just shuffled his feet.

"I'd give any brother a kidney or a fucking lung if I had to. Just don't need him knowing we're literal fucking blood brothers, though. I don't want anyone owing me special favors. I just need them to fall in line and listen." He tapped the V. PRESIDENT tag on his leather cut, and then took off, leaving me alone.

Another hour, and Tank opened his eyes. The anesthesia was wearing off. I swept his huge hand off the table and pressed it to me, clutching it tight between my fingers.

"It's a miracle!"

Not really, but I said it anyway because it sure as hell felt like one to me. It wasn't my skill or modern medicine I was staring at totally amazed. No, I was gawking right at his rock hard body as the poor dumb mountain of a man tried to sit up and throw his legs off the table.

"Hold on! You're not going anywhere. Let alone getting on your feet! Lay back down please."

"Club's been hit. I need to see the Prez." Rage flickered in his eyes. The flesh under the gauze had to be hurting like hell, but if it was, he didn't show it. "You did your part, Emma. I need to take over from here and help my brothers skin some bears for what they've done."

"Look, you're just barely getting enough blood into your system to keep you conscious. You're still not out of the woods for infection. If you go galloping off right now, you'll collapse the second you get down the hall. And I *really* don't want to drag you back here myself."

Crap, crap, crap.

I was trying to talk serious, going into full RN mode with an unruly patient. Too bad he was no ordinary patient. Bratty kids and cranky old ladies were never this imposing, this massive, this gorgeous.

He locked those honey eyes right on me, and I fell right in. Jesus, I could've gotten lost in those eyes again, if he wasn't naked from the waist up. My eyes kept traveling along his rock hard hills and valleys, flesh lined with pitch black tats like Celtic runes smoothing wild ground.

If I were a religious girl, I would've been scared. The club's devil symbols were everywhere, mixed with small skulls, scythes, and screaming eagles. The chain around his neck bounced when he moved his head, clanking his dog tags against raw tattooed muscle on his chest.

"You don't understand, babe. I'm damned grateful for everything you've done here today, but I need to get up and fight. I'm fucking useless laid up like this."

"You want to help your club?" I said, forcing my eyes back to his, flushing like an embarrassed schoolgirl. "Then let me help you get well. The facts don't lie, Tank. You were shot twice and lost a lot of blood. You're too weak to go charging into battle. You can't run, can't ride, and can't shoot straight when it's taking all your energy just to sit up. You want to help your brothers? Then get well. Not just my opinion. I'm sure Maverick or Blaze would say the same thing."

He gritted his teeth and lowered his face. Slowly, he nodded, accepting the grim reality.

I held my relief in my lungs. Thank God for small favors. Weakened or not, it would've been hell trying to hold his bulldozer body back if he tried to walk through that door.

My brow furrowed. The drive burning him to pieces surprised me.

I was just barely starting to understand this strange club life, but I could see a man hurting, torn up inside because he couldn't do his duty. I wanted to say something, wanted to reach out and soothe him.

Curling my fingers, I reached a tentative hand to his shoulder, and stopped halfway when the knock came at the door.

Crap. Perfect timing.

Maverick. The MC's President stepped inside, looked the room over, and asked me about Tank's condition. I quickly debriefed him. He was clearly on edge, hungry to strike back at the men who'd done this to Tank and still threatened a whole lot more.

"Listen, we got ourselves a situation. We've got to take the fight to the Grizzlies *now,* man down or not. If he's not ready to move out on his own, then I need you to move him. Tonight." Maverick leaned against the wall.

My heart skipped a beat.

"Move him? Where?"

Tank looked up from the table and mumbled a few protests, insisting he could walk. Damn! Crazy, determined, *and* persistent. And I was supposed to drag this insane giant – where, exactly?

"Don't fucking trouble her, boss," he grunted. "I got this. Just gimme a couple more hours and –"

"Bullshit. Listen to the lady, Tank. You've already done plenty for this club and landed yourself a quick dance in hell. All I want you to do is follow this nurse wherever she says. She's gonna keep your ass out of trouble while you rest."

A cold realization prickled at my neck. I eyed Maverick, afraid to seize the question I kept chasing in my head.

Fuck it. Here goes.

"We both know he can't go to a hospital," I said slowly. "You mean you want me to bring him…"

My words still failed me. For the first time since he'd appeared, bowed up and snapping orders like a good President should, Maverick smiled. Tank watched the whole time as Maverick closed in on me and nodded.

Home.

The single word out of Maverick's lips ripped me in half.

My home. That's where Tank was going to recuperate. I knew right then and there this was more than just a part time gig for ridiculous stacks of cash. No, now my whole stupid life would never be the same.

If only I could've known then how bitter, magnificent, and intense it was going to be having this sexy hulk at my side.

III: All Kinds of Damaged (Tank)

Laid out on her little sofa, I was stressed as all fuck. I'd been at Emma's place for more than a day, and I couldn't stop thinking about the attack.

Why didn't I see it coming? I survived a dozen hit and runs just like it on the road back in Afghanistan, courtesy of the Taliban, only to end up with hot lead going through my guts right here in Montana. Or damned close to them, anyway. Emma said I'd be laid out in a hospital or a body bag right now if the shit had really hit my stomach.

The girl claimed problems like that were beyond her abilities. Didn't believe it.

She worked fucking miracles, and nobody was gonna tell me otherwise. The girl was beautiful through and through: an hourglass blonde with tits and legs I would've carried right off if I found her in a bar, never believing for one minute she was a nurse – and a damned good one.

Beauty and brains. That was rare, especially when I'd spent my whole life hanging around army sluts and biker whores who were always missing one half of the equation.

The thing I didn't get was why the fuck she had so little to show for it. Near as I could tell, riding in Em's car with the rattling tailpipe and laying on her rumpled sofa, civilian life left a lot to be desired – especially money.

Nothing else explained it.

What was this talented, hot ass nurse doing in this shitty little house? What was she doing with me *here*, working for the club?

With her beautiful fucking looks and brains, she should've been in Paris or something, one of those specialty docs doing chin lifts and sucking out lard for rich assholes. And where the hell had she been before? If she wasn't homecoming queen before putting on her scrubs, it would've fooled my ass.

Loved her damned body, every sexy inch of it. When I walked her out to her car the first time I laid eyes on her, I didn't want to let go of that door and watch her drive away.

Fuck no. I wanted to climb inside that car, take her long blonde locks in my fucking fist, and smash her to the seat 'til my lips smothered hers. My cock raged like a bull when I thought about those sleek long legs wrapped around my waist while I rocked between them, thrusting deep as hell. And if I got my hands on those tits, that ass, that perfect pussy waiting where her thighs fused together…shit!

I'd be done. Over. All fucking over.

Hell, I already was, and it hadn't even started. I couldn't let it.

I couldn't get too close, even if my greedy cock had me by the throat, shrieking orders through my blood. If I did something so fucking stupid, Maverick would beat my ass. Blaze too. Hell, both brothers would probably take turns thumping my skull like a goddamned basketball, and I'd deserve every damned blow for scaring off this healer chick.

But damn, some things a man can't help. My horny, evil thoughts wouldn't do any harm if I kept them under lock and key.

After all, I was sick – not dead – and being cooped up here was turning into one bitch of a tease. Felt as guilty eating her hot ass up with my eyes whenever her back was turned as I felt about being laid out, away from the front lines with my brothers.

I should've been at the clubhouse or in the mountains helping poach bear patches off dead bodies. Not here, an overgrown burden on this host who made my cock pulse each time I looked at her.

"Tank? How're you feeling?" Emma came through the door, wearing the same bright smile I'd quickly learned was her trademark.

Didn't have a fucking clue how she stayed so upbeat through all this shit. All the brothers were starting to crack with the Grizzlies popping in and out, drawing blood and then disappearing like fucking ghosts.

I sat up, feeling the fire in my side. "Could use a few more pain pills. Or else a whole bottle of Jack."

She laughed and shook her head. "The last thing you're doing under my care is mixing booze and drugs. You blow out your liver, you'll be here a whole lot longer, buddy."

I nodded glumly. The girl wasn't wrong, even though I hated every fucking truth coming out of her pretty little mouth. Having those lips making different noises crushed against mine was way more appealing.

Pain pills and a big glass of water landed on the coffee table in front of me a minute later. I looked up and caught her staring at my chest again.

Shit, I'd be staring too if I had a dude right next to me who needed a shower this bad. "I get it. I fucking stink."

Emma's face went white and she feverishly denied it. "No, it's not that bad. We'll clean you up this evening. You're lucky it's not summer."

Why was she wearing so much red on those cheeks? If I had all my senses, I would've sworn she was into me, but I didn't trust a damned thing right now. Whenever I sat up and tried to focus, my brain wanted to slip back in the fog, threatening to go blank and numb when the fire bit.

The girl told me it would go away in a few more days. Fuck if those days could come soon enough.

"Where's your shower? I'm ready right now." I stood up, way too slow for my liking.

Next thing I knew, Emma's little hands were on my chest, holding me up. That only made me stiffen up harder. Shit, I had to get control back. If I toppled over like a goddamned tree, the last thing I was gonna do was fall right on her.

"Wait, wait, wait!" Her eyes flashed angry, melting into a smirk of concern on her face. "If you're so damned determined to do this now, let me help. You can't shower alone. Not for a few more days. Too much risk of you falling or getting crap into those wounds before they close all the way."

My jaw nearly hit the fucking floor. "What're you saying, babe? You mean you're gonna shower...with me?"

Her face went bright red. Must've been the wild laughter pouring out her lips heating up her blood. Whatever the hell I said, it sure caused her to giggle. No surprise, the girl had a great laugh, beautiful as the rest of her. I stood like a dummy listening, music to my ears after all the shit that went down the last couple days.

"We'll get you rinsed off good. Come on. There are more ways to clean a guy up than standing him in the shower."

A few minutes later, she had a hot basin of soap and water ready next to me. I sat on the toilet, back turned, a throwback to boyhood.

Humiliating as shit. Hell, the nurses working for Uncle Sam didn't do this when I took a piece of shrapnel outside Kandahar...

"Hold still. Just take it easy, Tank." Emma talked to me slowly, like she was trying to keep a skittish horse in line. "If anything seeps down near the bandages and starts to burn, you let me know."

I didn't know shit. I was clenching my jaw 'til I thought my teeth were gonna pop, hating every second. A grown man should be able to clean himself, injuries be damned.

No need for this pretty thing to be running her hands and suds and a rag all over me. Except, much as I hated to admit it, it really wasn't half bad. I stopped flexing at every stroke and relaxed, my muscles going slack beneath her calm, smooth touch.

Having the hot water trickling down my back was nice. Didn't have a damned thing on her fingers, though, especially when she ran them right over the ink beneath my shoulders.

"What's this all about? What does it mean?" She poked gently, right in the middle of the ring of fire.

I had a whole maze sketched around my spine. The ink whorls were black flames that opened up near the middle, breaking up into stars surrounding an eagle with a pitchfork in his claws.

"Story of my life, babe. Skin's just a canvass. I did three tours for Uncle Sam. One in Kuwait, two in Afghanistan. That's what the eagle and the stars are for. Same as these tags." I reached up and gave my chain a jerk.

"And the flames? The pitch forks?" She sounded uncertain.

"The rest of my life since discharge. My whole fucking future's right there. Only full patch members in this club get to wear symbols on their skin. I've got plenty, and I'm not done yet either. The club's the alpha and omega. Makes everything that happened before I was a prospect for the Devils seem like a dream. Don't know what's coming next, but I'll be there for my brothers, thick as blood. In this MC, you put everything on the line: life, limb, fortune. Fucking everything."

She made a little sound like she was surprised.

What the fuck? Maybe she didn't think bikers were so deep, same as the other civilian assholes who thumbed their scorn at us on the road.

I was all soaped up, and she switched to rinsing me off before saying anything.

"I think I'm starting to see why these clubs are around in the first place."

I turned a little and looked at her, reaching up to grasp her hand pressing the warm cloth to my neck. "You're gonna start to figure out a lot of things the longer you hang around, Em. Don't doubt it for a single second. Everybody under the MC's protection gets what they deserve. Same as any assholes dumb enough to cross us."

A couple days passed in a haze. One day, I woke up feeling a hell of a lot better.

My brain didn't instantly try to black out when I hobbled to my feet. I seriously contemplated hitching a ride to the clubhouse and hopping on my bike, but the Prez or VP would beat my ass for sure if I showed up without Emma's clearance.

Later, I was glad I didn't go anywhere. Something was totally fucked up the second she walked through the door that night.

The usual sweet smile on her face was completely gone. I bolted up. First time since getting shot when I didn't want to flop back down and clear my head.

"What's going on, girl? Tell me." I took a step forward. Didn't like the sharp wrinkles in her perfect face one bit.

"I screwed up, Tank. It's the supplies."

"You mean the shit you used to fix me up?"

"No, *everything* I snuck out to help the club set up the infirmary. We took too much, too fast. My lead's onto us, and so is the administrator. There's going to be an investigation once she gives the go ahead."

Fire shot through my brain, different from the raging pain. This inferno was just rage period.

"Christ! How do you know? Is somebody threatening you?"

I didn't care if it was just her job on the line. Bloodlust flowed to my fists, and my heart began to pound. If anybody fucked with Emma in *any* way, I'd slam their ass into the ground so hard they'd need metal hips to get up again.

"I'm one of the girls being looked at." She looked down, shaking her pretty head. "Shit, Tank, what if I get fired? What if they take my license?"

Poor girl. She looked so fragile standing there, so fucking lost in heavy, dangerous seas she'd plunged into without understanding.

I stepped up, closing the distance between us. Only had one thing on my mind when my hands wrapped around her and pulled her close, shoving her face into my chest. Didn't have a clue where this was gonna lead, but one thing was clear: I wasn't gonna let her suffer for helping the club.

"Nobody can take away your skills, babe. If that happens, you'll be working for the MC full time. I'll hound Blaze and Maverick all goddamned day 'til you get what you need. And when things settle down and this shit with the Grizzlies blows over, you're not taking more risks like this. I'll drill it into the club's skull that we're getting drugs and tools elsewhere from now on. *Not* from your fucking job."

She looked up at me, bright eyes flicking from side to side, trying to see if I was telling her the truth or just blowing smoke.

No way she couldn't have seen it.

I was dead set on protecting her. I'd do that for any girl with an ass like hers, but *this* girl saved my life too, so I owed her double. Fucking with her was fucking with the club, and when anybody did that, we broke their fucking dicks so the last thing on their minds was...you-know-what.

I smoothed my hands down her back again and again, trying to keep the fires beating through my veins in check. My cock was an ill mannered SOB, and he wanted to claim her right now. Good thing I was man enough to use my head.

When she stopped crying, I took a few steps back, reaching for my wallet. I pulled out a wrinkled fifty and pressed it into her hands.

"You're not making shit for dinner tonight, Em. Go buy something nice and bring it home. You know I'm not picky. Whatever it is, I'll eat it. Beautiful night out there. Get some fresh air."

It took her another minute to gather herself. Then, smiling, she took off.

A short drive always set my stewing mind at ease, and I had a feeling it'd do the same for her too, even if her little two door didn't surround her in a Harley's soothing growl.

Now for the important part. I'd given her a happy distraction and bought myself some time to think, to plan, to make sure her problem went away for good.

I waited until after dinner, a high end pizza and some fancy gelato, to make my move. Not exactly my standard grub, but it made her purr, and that was all I cared about.

The dinner helped, but it didn't fix a damn thing. No amount of food in her belly would totally mend the sadness coursing through her system. Emma turned in early, just like I thought.

When I was sure she was asleep, I walked into the kitchen, eyeing the list of contacts she had plastered to her fridge. My finger stopped on Linda Barrow, the boss she'd mentioned. Carefully, I opened the door and stepped outside.

The pain in my side didn't start to bitch until I got to the bus stop. It was a dull throb, hot and angry, like all my damned frustrations collected together in one spot. This shit wasn't gonna do anything for my temper when I reached my destination.

I had a good feel for this town since I'd arrived and done scouting duty for the club. It was only a ten minute ride to the neighborhood where the bitch putting the heat on Emma worked, conveniently behind the hospital, which towered over everything.

The neat house was all lit up. Good. I'd give her an hour or so to stick her head out before I went in.

Tonight, luck was on my side.

A woman in her fifties with faded blond hair stepped out on the porch for a smoke. I let her get in a few puffs before I showed myself.

Fuck, all the pain on the walk and the bumpy bus ride had been worth it. I could feel my devil tats grinning as her eyes bugged out. She was just like all the others my brothers and I met in the civilian world, too damned scared to do anything sensible like run or scream.

"You Linda?" I asked, stopping just behind the banister.

Took her a few seconds to process the question, to process *me* standing on her fucking doorstep. Too damned long, and my patience was in short supply. The lady's eyes bugged out. Looked like she'd seen Satan himself coming up from the ground.

"Look, I know you're shitting bricks over missing supplies, wondering where the fuck they went. You're the one who bitched out my brothers when they came to you about a job." I rounded my way to the stairs, taking one more for every step she took backward.

"Bastard! Get the hell away from here! I-I'll call the cops. No bluff."

"I'm not bluffing either, lady. I'm here to help your ass out. You stop worrying about the missing shit because I'll tell you where it went: *I* took it."

Her eyebrow wrinkled and she dropped her cigarette. "You? That's such bullshit! Nobody gets into the supply rooms without a security clearance."

I let out a long breath. "You really think key cards ever held back this club when we decide to take what we want? You see this patch?" I tapped the red 1% diamond on my cut. "You know what it means?"

"Yeah. You're outlaws. I've danced with your kind in my younger days, boy, and I know what you're all about. Same reason I want all your asses *out* of my town. All you do is murder, kill, steal…"

I stopped. The shit coming out of her mouth surprised me, and so did her about face from shock to anger. This old bird knew how to play defense, I'd give her that.

"Great," I growled. "Then you realize we play by our own rules. Not your laws. I don't need to tell you a damned thing about how or why, but yeah, we took your fucking supplies. We were gonna buy 'em off you. Too bad you were too damned stupid to take the money and run. You turned down my brothers, and we had to do shit the hard way."

Linda shook her head, faded hair bobbing on her head like a nest. "So what? What now? Are you going to hurt me if I don't do what you want? Hurt my grandkids?"

Kids? Fuck no.

My stomach churned. Whatever experience she had with bikers in the past, I had an ugly feeling it was all with the Grizzlies MC, fucks who had no boundaries this side of hell.

I took one step back, giving her a little space – but only a little.

"I'm doing you a courtesy. The club sent me here to let you know we're done. No more offers for your stuck up ass and no more pawing at your precious medicines. We've got other sources for the shit we need." I paused, taking a step forward again, turning my face to dead stone. "All we need you to do is *forget*. All of it, Linda. You're not stupid. Obviously, you know a thing or two about MCs. What I'm telling you is to shut your fucking mouth and never breathe a word about this shit to anyone. Doctor the damned records if anybody sticks their nose in our business. You wouldn't help us out the first time, I get it. Now, by doing you a favor and leaving you out, you're gonna help us seal the deal and walk away clean. We'll never hit your old ass up for anything else."

Her face was beet red, shining through the dull darkness. Half-expected her to spit in my face or take a swipe with her long green fingernails. Whatever, I was ready, as long as she kept those old claws away from my wounds.

"Okay!" she shouted at last. "I'll do two things: wind down the investigation and keep quiet. You came to my house and talked up a storm. Now, I want *you* to understand something, Mister Badass…"

She stepped up to me and stabbed her finger in my chest. If she were a man, I would've broken it right off. I held.

Fuck it. I let the old bird take a little jab. She was giving me exactly what Emma and I needed, and nothing else mattered worth shit.

"You ever come to this home where I live and my grandchildren sleep again, I'll kill you myself. I was too stupid, too complacent. I wasn't ready for you, so you're going to get what you want. Just this once. Next time, I won't even call the cops. I'll bring out my own heat and shoot your ass dead."

"Don't waste your bullets, bitch. Fucking with old ladies and kids doesn't make us hard. We're the Prairie Devils MC. Not the fucking Grizzlies."

I turned and walked off. We had our understanding. If this wound up crone lived by her word, then Emma's career was safe.

By keeping her from getting dragged deeper into this shit, *she* was safe. Only thing that mattered. I wasn't about to go against my club's officers, but every minute I spent with her told me she wasn't cut out for blood and death. I wanted her sewing stitches, handing out Tylenol for hangovers, and then going home.

Emma saved my ass. If I could save hers by preventing her from doing double duty for the club and winding up in a world of shit, then maybe I'd sleep at night without drowning myself in pills and Jack.

The next day, everything went to shit.

I missed three frantic calls from Blaze and picked up on the fourth. The clubhouse was gone. So were the Missoula Grizzlies. Worst of all, so was my fucking bike!

I couldn't believe it. They'd used the bomb idea I floated to Maverick while I was laid up. Just not any way I ever imagined.

The brothers rigged up our bikes, invited the bears in with a mock surrender, and blew our own headquarters to kingdom come. The boys barely made it out in time, and everybody was heading to Bozeman to regroup. Throttle, our national Prez, was on his way from North Dakota to see if the bastards would take a truce after we beat their asses raw.

My medical leave was over. Blaze was coming for me right now, and I was gonna leave Emma's place behind.

I started to scrawl out a note for her to leave on the kitchen table when the door burst open. She was home early, eyes wide, mouth hanging just a little. The girl looked like she'd seen a fucking ghost, and she was looking right at *me.*

"What's wrong?" A terrible jolt slammed my skull. "Don't tell me they're fucking with you?"

"No, Tank. It's the opposite. Linda and the admin are dropping the whole thing. I don't know what the hell happened."

"Shit! That's fucking great!"

Mission accomplished. I walked to the door and pulled her inside. Threw her over my shoulder, not giving a single shit about the pain. I squeezed her until she stopped laughing.

When her feet were on the floor again, she looked at the table, then at me. "What's going on?"

Shit. Time to drop another bomb.

"I've got to go. Right fucking now, unfortunately. Blaze's orders. I was gonna leave you a thank you note, babe. I appreciate everything you've done for me, and I mean it."

The happiness drained from her face. She looked clouded, confused, as if the whole world just dropped out underneath her.

"What? Why so sudden?" Her eyes snapped down, and then right back at me. "Will I see you again?"

Fuck! Those eyes. Those beautiful, glistening, desperate green eyes. They called me like sirens, and wouldn't let go. Every part of me mutinied against leaving her, especially without a single taste.

I said the only thing I could. "It's club business, babe. All of it. No promises, but I got a feeling we'll be back after the bears are cleared out and no longer breathing down our necks. This town's gonna be Devil's territory before too long."

And you too, Emma. I don't give a shit if they make us settle in Billings for the new charter. My dick won't let me stay away from this town.

She'd retreated into her shy, shocked little self. The clock was ticking too. Fuck my thoughts and fuck caution.

I stepped forward, throwing my arms around her all over again. This time, I didn't let go. I reached low, clasped her ass. She gasped, barely able to keep up as I pushed her several steps backward, straight to the wall.

I wasn't gonna let it end with her gawking at me like I just put down her dog. She was gonna remember me, damn it, and remember me right. And I was gonna take something on the road to remember her, something savory and sweet I'd never, ever forget.

My hands squeezed her perfect ass while I leaned in. Her lips were so fucking hot when they hit mine, and bombs went off at every junction in my blood. I saw fucking stars.

Fireworks. White lightning.

Hot, churning lights urging me to kiss her harder, deeper, shoving her back against the wall. Back, back, 'til there was nowhere else to go but plush against my torso.

Emma moaned into my mouth and I sucked her lip. I pulled it tight, pushed my tongue through the gap, and wouldn't let go before I gripped her with my teeth. I dove, twisting, stroking, exploring her wet, warm heat, searching to find her tongue.

I broke. My breath was steaming out all over her, hotter than a fucking sauna, and I still hadn't let up on that kiss for a single second. She was shaking in my hands, hips making little circles on my hands.

My cock was about to bust through my jeans, especially with her body screaming *fuck me,* same as her heavy breath.

No, I thought. *Fuck me. Fuck me for doing this without wanting to admit how hot it would be just to have my tongue against yours. Fuck me for thinking I can kiss and walk away like nothing. Fuck me for imagining I'll be anything but a cold lost wolf every second I spend away from this town, away from you, Em.*

We locked lips, teeth, and tongue. I wouldn't let go 'til it was too fucking much.

She tried to break for air, and I still wouldn't let her. I pushed her head with mine, slamming her against the wall, catching her hair in one hand. Fisting those sweet gold locks was even hotter than I imagined. I wound them tight around my fingers and pulled, wishing that was all I needed to keep her here, forever up against my ink.

Mine. I held her in place while my tongue danced against hers, pistoning in and out her lips, fucking them with the same rough motion I burned to throttle between her legs.

Several seconds more seconds of that was all she needed to stop struggling. Em melted beneath me, burning up in my hands. The need for air wasn't half as bad as the lust cutting through us both.

I held on so tight I didn't expect her to jerk away. She tore hard against my hand and I let go, caught by surprise.

Her feet tumbled to the floor. I gave her a few inches of space, letting her breathe. Fuck if I didn't need air after all.

I'd screwed my share of whores all over the world in the club and in the Army. No woman – *none* – had been able to keep up. Now, I stared at the girl who *finally* matched my heat, and knowing I was about to be a lone furnace on the road made me want to flip my shit and put my fists through the nearest wall.

"Tank!" she panted, swiveling and bracing herself against the counter for balance. "What the hell?"

I took a good, hard look at her. My cock pulsed in my pants, rumbling like a goddamned jackhammer, but I wouldn't give in.

Asshole! a voice snarled in my head. *You're supposed to be giving her some distance. If you want to keep her safe, then do it. Doesn't matter if you're here or five hundred miles away.*

She can't be your woman and a safe woman.

Let her go. Do it like a man.

"Little going away present," I said, trying to gather my words. "Damned good chance I'll be coming back sooner or later, babe. But listen...I can't come here."

Those words hurt like hell. They tasted like ash, bitter ice splashed against her sweetness bubbling on my lips.

I stabbed my finger at my chest. "I'm the one who had a little talk with your head nurse, Linda. Told her to lay the fuck off, and she agreed. I did it to protect you."

"What?" Her hair was a beautiful mess, and it rippled on her shoulders when she shook. "They told me it was a slip up…a mistake…somebody took inventory all wrong."

"Then they lied through their fucking teeth. Exactly what I wanted. I told her myself to forget about the club and the hospital." I paced backward, hating the way the hot red I pumped in her face was fading to white. "I know that look, babe. You're pissed, scared, wondering if I threatened her. I didn't hurt her. I did what I had to – just words – and I'd do it all over again. I did it to keep you safe, Emma."

"Maybe I don't need your help." She swallowed, her soft voice on edge. "You could've fucking talked to me first, Tank. I told you what happened because I wanted your support. I didn't ask you to go out and solve my problems yourself!"

"Damned right you didn't. I don't need permission when it comes to doing what's right."

Shit! Why didn't she understand? I had to make her.

I took a step closer. She recoiled, throwing herself against the wall, dismay tearing through her eyes.

"How can you kiss me like that and then turn into such an asshole?"

Damn, those eyes were beautiful, even when they were lit with anger rather than lust. I shrugged. Good fucking question.

"Take it as a reminder, Emma. You work for the club. Not me. As bad as I'd love to tear off those scrubs and finish what we started up against the wall, I'm gonna put *you* first, your safety and sanity. We've got to keep this shit professional. Big fucking chance you would've lost your job if I hadn't stepped in and saved it. If that had you worried – and it did – then just imagine how stressed you'd be if we'd fucked. You couldn't handle all the shit coming your way after my dick's been inside you. You almost took a spill for this club, for *me*. Now I'm helping you up before you get hurt, understand?"

"No!" She gritted her teeth. "You're right about one thing: this is a job, and I *am* a professional. You're not my boss. You don't get to tell me where I go or what I do with my body."

Fucking shit. She still didn't get it!

"I will, babe," I growled. "Especially when you don't have a fucking clue –"

"And fucking?" I never should've let her cut me off. "Forget about it. I don't know what I was thinking..."

Ouch. She knew how to go for the nuts, and not how I wanted.

She jumped when the horn started to blast outside. It was Blaze, and the asshole slammed his fist down on the horn and didn't let up, rocking the neighborhood with one long, jagged note.

"It's time for me to go, Em. Take care of yourself, and I won't have to do shit for you." I walked out the door and slammed it behind me before she could say another word.

I got out and hopped in the big ass van, taking one of the last empty seats. Everybody was jammed in except Maverick and his old lady. We were on our way, speeding halfway across the state, putting distance between me and her.

It feels like shit because it's right, I told myself.

Not very convincing. Whatever was about to come down, it wouldn't stop me from thinking about Emma. And anytime the patches on my skin ached where the bullets bored into them, I was gonna taste her lips, crude reminders of the heat and need I tasted, everything I wouldn't forget 'til I was six feet under the goddamned ground.

IV: Boomerang (Emma)

The bastard was right.

Tank left me shaking with rage on the day the Devils fled. At least he wasn't around to see the tears.

My purse was heavy on the counter with the last cash they'd given me, bundled up in stacks. I picked it up and flung it against the wall, screaming like a little girl who'd just been through her first bad breakup.

For all intents and purposes, I *had*.

Tank was the first man who acted like he was really interested in me for ages, and he fascinated me with more than just his body. But like a typical man, the calm mask fell off when it was time to run, time to discard me like the piece of ass I'd nearly become for him.

As much as Tank pissed me off, I only needed to look in the mirror if I wanted to boil over.

It was my fault. All of it. By signing on with them, I'd opened myself to this. In just a few weeks, I'd lied, stolen, and risked my whole career for thugs and killers. Maybe they were cleaner than the Grizzlies, but there was no denying the cold, cold truth.

I'd signed onto a deal with the Prairie Devils, and I wanted out. I wanted to forget their stupid club, forget Tank, forget the fact I screwed over Linda and probably scared the hell out of her too.

I stared at my purse on the floor, crisp bills halfway spilling out of it. I went down, slumping against the wall, the same one he'd forced me up against and leveled the kiss of my life.

Tank, damn him, was right again. I really *didn't* understand this world I'd waltzed into, but its harsh realities were starting to hit me in the face. Worse, I was starting to understand things about myself.

My greed and stupidity did this. Every one of those leafy green bills in my purse was a prison building block. So were the ones I'd already spent paying down debts.

In too deep? I couldn't believe Tank missed the glaring realization I was already there. And even if the club stayed away from Missoula for awhile, there was no walking away. Not while I owed them a single penny or a drop of blood.

Weeks went by. I kept my head down at the hospital. Linda avoided me outside direct job duties, as if she knew he'd showed up to right my wrongs. Or else make new ones.

As spring turned into summer, I had my own life back. I was able to forget, ignoring the faint whispers I heard around town about the Devils returning, this time to Missoula proper instead of Python. The Grizzlies were nowhere to be seen. Montana changed hands, passing from one gang to another, the one I was afraid to acknowledge I belonged to.

I was relaxing after a long day with crabby patients one evening, when I heard the dull roar fading in my driveway. My heart was beating out my chest by the time I ran to the door.

I stopped in front of it, hand on the knob. I closed my eyes, unable to bear looking through the peephole.

Jesus, no. If it's you, Tank, I swear I'll –

A fist banged on the wood. My eyes snapped open and I saw Blaze through the glass, stern and impatient as always.

He pushed on the door before I had it open, but the chain caught. I looked out, eyes narrowed. This man wasn't coming in my house like he owned it. I didn't give a damn how powerful he was.

"Emma, what the fuck?" He grabbed the door's edge. "Need to talk to you."

"The only thing I want to talk about is what I need to do to repay you. I made a mistake, Blaze. I don't want to be your club's nurse anymore."

I moved back, expecting him to kick down the door. Instead, he laughed.

"You gotta be fucking kidding me. I heard about the shit that went down with your job. Tank filled me in."

Wonderful. I made a sour face.

"Hey, if you're worried, don't be. We've got a nice new clubhouse here in town. No more dragging yourself down to Python to take care of business. Bigger infirmary too. All the supplies are coming in from our brothers out in the Dakotas, so we won't need a damn thing from your hospital. There's no more need for stupid fucking risks, woman. Understand?"

Why was I still listening? Because the man was an ass, but he had the gift of gab. I wondered how many helpless girls he'd talked into his bed or onto his bike over the years.

"It's gonna be different this time! You got my word." He paused. "Now, open the fuck up so I can pass along the new address and this checklist to go over. It's your infirmary, Em. Anything you need, we'll get it shipped over. Just say the word."

"Different? How? Will I get blown up instead of losing my license?"

Blaze snorted. "Fuckin' please. The Grizzlies aren't at war with us anymore. We got ourselves an understanding. Besides, I'm the goddamned President of this club now. Maverick rode off into the sunset with his new old lady. That's what Nomads do."

I rolled my eyes. He was seriously trying to tell me that having his hotheaded brain on top was an improvement?

For some stupid reason, I turned, reaching for the chain. It clipped off and Blaze stepped inside, looking me up and down.

"We really need you back, Em. I don't give a fuck if I have to pay you more exorbitant stacks of loot. Shit went wrong the first time because we walked into a damned trap. That isn't gonna happen again on my watch. The biggest things you'll be dealing with are hangovers and handing out condoms. You got my guarantee."

He flashed a grin. Anybody in the right mood would've smiled back, but I just felt my intestines knot, tight with confusion.

"All right. Fine. We can work something out either way," he said. "I'm not interested in having anybody working with us who's there against their fucking will. This club doesn't roll like that. We're not into slaves. Take a good look: you got an offer here for more pay on a part-time gig than anything you'll make in a year at that damned hospital. Think it over and call me back. I won't force you to do shit. But I still hope you choose wisely."

He slammed the paperwork down on the counter and walked right out. He didn't wait a single second before starting his Harley and roaring away.

I wasn't sure what was worse: seeing him and instantly being reminded how hot and unstoppable Tank looked in the same colors, or grappling with this brutal decision he'd dropped in my lap.

God help me, I took the bait. I wanted to believe things would really be different. Maybe the Devils would settle down and stop killing. Maybe they'd be satisfied running their strip clubs and black market goods out to the Pacific.

For awhile, the club lived up to Blaze's promise. I made myself scarce around their place, always trying to avoid Tank.

The first few calls were easy: a checkup for their new club whore, Marianne, prescription antacids for big bearded Moose, Reb's tooth infection. That one was beyond me, and I referred him to a dentist.

Otherwise, I only stopped by to check inventory and make sure the new prospects were cleaning the room to proper medical standards. There was a new girl I saw from a distance working the bar, a former stripper named Saffron.

Never bothered approaching her because she seemed so caught up in her own turmoil with Blaze and some other drama I wasn't sure about. I saw Tank once in two weeks, and only from a distance.

He'd been voted in as Sergeant at Arms, a perfectly dangerous position handling the club's defense and internal order. I was walking to my car after dropping off Moose's refill when I saw him. He was right outside the garage, perched on his Harley, engine revving.

Damn! I'd forgotten how sexy he was – and that was before I'd seen him on his bike. Welded to his machine, he was a coarse barbarian with a wicked charm designed to send panties soaring over the mountains.

He looked up, a beautiful tattooed hulk on a steel rocket, black ink rippling on his arms as he gripped the handlebars. The Harley sputtered, new and loud like all the other bikes the guys had. He didn't need to yell at me. The machine did it for him.

I smelled oil in the air, the same gritty scent welded to his masculine richness up close. I wasn't sure how I moved my heels and got my ass in the car, but I did.

My shaky hands steadied on the steering wheel. I drove like an idiot, desperate to get the hell away before the gate closed, scared to death he'd follow.

Don't lie, girl. Part of you wants him to.

"Shut up!" I snarled at the sardonic voice in my head.

I was so damned tired of everybody else telling me what I wanted, or what was best for me. Now, even my own head and heart deserted me. The fight when he left seemed like a lifetime ago.

Did it really matter anymore? Or was I going to listen to the nagging urges, the ones that screamed at me to spin the car around and return to him?

I managed to ignore it, but didn't relax until I was almost home. Tank didn't follow after all. My heart sank like a stone.

Why? was the only thing on my mind that night.

He could be a dick, but he was serious about his word, just like Blaze.

Was he staying away because he was hellbent on protecting me? Or had my inner bitch driven him away for good?

The phone I hated woke me up the next morning. It took me a groggy minute to realize it wasn't my usual alarm. I lazily tapped the key and pressed it to my ear.

"Emma? Get your ass down here for the club. Stab wound." Blaze's voice barked over the line.

"Tank?" His name came out of my mouth without a second thought.

"Yeah, it's him. Again."

I gasped. Now I was completely wide awake, jumping out of bed. "I'll be right there! Move him to the infirmary if you've got something on the wound. But be careful!"

What crappy luck. Poor Tank. Poor me!

The full realization I was going to have my hands on him hit me on the drive over. I didn't let it slow me down, even if it nearly paralyzed me. Whatever had gone down before, I was his nurse first, and *only* his nurse.

When I got to the clubhouse, Moose pointed to the infirmary. "He's in there. Sneak attack. Bastards almost got the Prez and we had to roll to defend the clubhouse right outside our own fucking gate. Did our best to stop the bleeding, and I hope like hell it was enough."

I wandered on past. No time to slow down for idle chatter.

When I got inside, Tank was conscious, groaning on the table. His pants were off, leaving nothing below the waist but tight black boxers. A steady trickle of blood surrounded his huge thigh, leaking past a crude tourniquet someone tied to stop the bleeding.

Blaze, Reb, and Roller were gathered in the tiny space. I had to nudge my way past them to get to my patient.

"Well? Is he gonna be okay?"

"Give me some space and I'll work on it!" I snapped.

Blaze bared his teeth like he was about to strike back, but he trusted me, and waved the other two guys out of the room. It hadn't taken long to figure out bikers were the most demanding pricks around when they needed to be.

"Just lay still," I whispered, my first words to the man I hadn't spoken to since he stormed out of my house. "Here's something for the pain."

I moved to his healthy side and pushed a syringe deep into his flank. With any luck, the stuff would put him down and keep him still for a few hours, giving me ample room to do my work.

Blaze watched the whole time. I sliced off the tourniquet, examining the cut. It was nasty. A long, jagged blade had slid right across his thigh, possibly tearing through several major nerves. It was bad, but it could've been even worse.

I grabbed alcohol and antiseptic, splashing the whole area generously. Good thing the morphine worked fast. If he were awake with all his nerves, he would've been throwing me and Blaze around the room, going mad with fire arcing up his hip.

"Come on, woman. Throw me a fucking bone here," Blaze said from the corner as I was moving for stitches.

"He'll live." I shot him a stone cold glare.

The intimidating President didn't scare me at all with Tank hurt. Work was more important than egos, and I had to stuff mine too, keeping my eyes on the injured flesh. I couldn't let it wander across his boxers, not to the huge lump straining there.

I'd seen it on male patients a hundred times. Anxiety, adrenaline, and red hot blood makes for some scary erections at the worst times, and Tank had it all storming through his system.

I chewed my lip. Stitches were usually left to the doctors unless they were very minor. I'd never patched a wound so big, but I worked my fingers fast, stuffing it with medicated gauze before I began to close the threads.

The stuff inside would dissolve as he healed. I hoped the knife wasn't dirty, or else he'd be in a world of hurt when infection took hold.

Blaze leaned on the wall, arms folded, glowering at me impatiently. When I cut the last thread and looked up, letting my tools clatter on the big steel cart, I mimicked his stance.

"Don't you have something more important to do, Prez?" God, I wanted to make him choke on his title. "He'll be okay if the thing that sliced into him wasn't too dirty. We'll keep a close eye on that. I can take it from here...all by myself."

Blaze's eyes narrowed. He stepped forward, circling me like a hungry shark, all bowed up because I'd called him out on his crap.

"Yeah, I've got church to call. Gotta round up all the brothers and figure out how we're gonna gut the motherfuckers who did this. Fuck, that easily could've been Saffron there on that table. Tank saved both our asses." Blaze's arm shot out, pointing at Tank's huge body on the table. "Listen, I'll let your bitch tone slide this time because you did your job well and I know you two are real tight. You're all he's fucking thought about since we got our shit together here."

Hot redness licked my cheeks. Anger, shame, embarrassment. The man really knew how to push a girl's buttons.

"But you trot your venom out on me again, and we're gonna have a real close chat. Just you and I. This isn't a fucking game, Emma." He tapped the PRESIDENT patch on the front of his cut, and then a small red patch beneath it that read SATAN'S SYCTHE. "You give respect in this club, you get it. You start fucking with me, and I'll take your damned head off. I'm a fair boss, but this isn't the fucking hospital. Only gonna say it once."

He turned sharp, walked straight, and flung open the door. It clattered against the frame, slamming loudly.

With a heavy sigh, I looked at Tank. It took forever to lift off his cut and open up his shirt. When I finally did, I hooked up the monitors I needed to keep him safe while he was out.

A flicker ran through me when I brushed his chest with my fingers, applying the sticky pads connected to the wires. Had I really taken my time on these bulging muscles before, smoothing his evil looking tattoos with a wet cloth in my own little bathroom?

I had. It just seemed like half a lifetime ago.

Everything about him screamed trained killer. All the brothers were. He obviously hadn't gotten stabbed in the ambush doing charity. Angels didn't wear demons on their skin, and they sure as heck didn't mold patriotic symbols with skulls that Gengish Khan would've smiled at.

Touching the canvass on his rock hard chest should've reminded me how crazy this all was. But of course that would've been too sensible.

His chest, his face, his world enveloping shoulders did the opposite. They started a mud fight in my head. Crazy, mischievous, salacious thoughts beat through my brain, heating up my blood, making me feel sweaty and soaked.

The need was there. It hadn't gone anywhere. And I was in deep, deep trouble.

I snorted, pushing my hand away. His warmth was too much. So were the visions I had of myself perched on his great big body, naked and raw, filling my wetness with his rigid fire. I wanted him to burn me deep, fucking away whatever disagreements we'd had. I wanted it *bad,* and if I didn't put some distance between us right now, I was going to drown in my own sticky desire.

Christ, I needed something to take the edge off.

The next hour passed in a haze. I left Tank alone, carefully monitored by the instruments. Saffron was working the bar, and she served me a tall glass of water and some beer.

I drained both fast, eager to get fluids into my system to wash away the shock and awe, all the wild spell that came over me when Tank and I were together. We exchanged a few words. All the men were in the meeting room, a proper war council plotting their brutal revenge.

It was nice to have someone to talk to. Saffron was on edge too. I even prodded her about Blaze, and saw the shameful blush in her cheeks I'd felt countless times.

I was contemplating another beer when the door to the meeting room banged open. All the brothers came filing out, filtering through the clubhouse like soldiers who'd received their orders. Blaze came to the bar, walking right past me. He was going straight for Saffron.

I tried not to listen, but it was impossible not to hear it. He was talking candidly, close, and intense in the way a man only talks to *his* woman, an urgency in his tone about protecting her that seemed to go way beyond his duties as MC President.

My head buzzed pleasantly now, lightweight that I was. I cocked an eyebrow. Whatever was going on between those two, at least I was in good company.

I wasn't the only dumb girl who'd stepped into this world and fallen for one of the badasses here. Too bad I couldn't tell whether Saffron and I both were just chasing our tails.

I looked back at the infirmary while Blaze and Saffron danced around their passions.

Loving these men was an either/or proposition.

No matter how many times I went over the complicated possibilities, I didn't see a happy ending. If Tank ever relented and let me in, I was bound to lose everything.

Becoming an old lady meant embracing this world, and nothing else, watching the other one I'd known my whole life sink into the shadows, lost forever.

Later that evening, I slumped in the little chair next to his bed. Tank woke up late, sometime after midnight.

The craziness we'd been through today drained my energy. I'd already called in a sick day at the hospital tomorrow, but it wasn't much consolation.

"Emma? Emma?" Tank repeated my name, his smooth baritone voice echoing off the ceiling.

I rushed up and was at his side. "I'm right here."

"Fuck. Can't believe we're right back where we started. Sorry, babe. It all happened so fast..."

Right back where we started, huh? Does that mean more than just me working on his flesh wounds?

"Tell me what happened. The club's been so crazy today nobody bothered to fill me in." I swallowed hard.

I wasn't sure I wanted to know if it meant more ruthless trouble, more people getting hurt. Maybe even me.

"Fucking Grizzlies. They chased down Blaze and Saffron while they were coming to the clubhouse this morning. We rolled out to fight 'em off, but the bastards had the numbers. It was a fucking melee out there with blades and hammers. Fucks were smart enough not to come in blazing and shoot off guns where any neighbors could hear. Nobody wants any badges involved."

"Grizzlies? I thought you had a truce?"

Tank shrugged. "Blaze says it's a rogue charter. Loose dogs who aren't listening to the old heads of their pack further west anymore. Whatever. All I care about is getting the fuck out of here and breaking their heads."

He shifted with a groan. Next thing I knew, my hands were flattened on his chest, trying to hold back a mountain.

"You're not going anywhere! That leg needs to heal for a few days before you can walk. We need to make sure there's no infection too. Already gave you a booster for tetanus while you were out, plus some antibiotics."

"You're kidding me, babe. How many days?"

"At least two or three. And then the only walking you're doing is with this." I pointed to the corner.

He followed my finger. When he saw it, his whole chest jerked against my palms.

My stupid, sick brain wondered if it was the same way he heaved for air when he spent himself during sex. Jesus, what would it really feel like to make him lose control?

"Fuck! No. No, Em! No way in hell am I gonna use that fucking thing."

My hands swept up, landing on his shoulders. Fat chance of soothing him with words and a gentle touch, but I was going to try.

"It's only for a little while, Tank. I don't think you'll be away from riding and doing your business too long. It's temporary. I promise."

He turned, locking his angry eyes with mine. "You really expect me to stagger around the clubhouse with a *fucking cane?*"

I nodded. "You can't put too much pressure on your leg while it heals. If you want to walk, you'll be doing it my way. If you don't, you could rip the cut open and do a whole lot more damage."

His muscles heated up like hot stone slabs. I could practically feel the rage steaming through him — cursing the Grizzlies, cursing his luck, cursing *me*.

"It's not like I'm enjoying this," I whispered. "I'm trying to help. Please, listen to your doctor and you'll be back on the road in no time."

"Doctor?" He snorted. "You're a fucking nurse, babe."

I bristled at the insult, even though it was true. I wanted to slap him across his stupid handsome face until he looked up again, the storm settling in his eyes.

"And a damned good one," he said. "I'd be way more fucked up without you. The whole club would be toast. I'll listen this time, shitty as it is."

Nice save. I almost laughed.

My heart did a cartwheel. I couldn't believe I'd managed to get some sense through his thick skull.

I relaxed a bit, but only a bit. "I'm glad. You've got a good head on your shoulders, Tank. You just like to hide it." Smiling, I paused, resisting the urge to massage his shoulders again. "Tank. What kind of name is that, anyway? Is it from the army?"

The tension in his face eased. I was staring at the man who'd made smile before our blowout. Still hadn't touched *that* crap. It wasn't the time or place.

"That's what everybody thinks. Actually, Throttle laid it on me back in North Dakota. I just got my prospect cut after being a hangaround for fucking forever after my last tour in Kandahar. His old man, Voodoo, Prez at the time, had a big fucking tank of some explosive shit that needed to go up to our friends in Winnipeg. The drunken idiot welding on the supports for transport on the truck knocked out one of the stands. Fucking thing crushed his leg and landed on the blow torch." He stopped, raising his hands. "You're a nurse. What'd you think about these hands?"

He held them out to me. They were thick, strong, enormous. The skin was a little irregular.

"They're...holy shit. So smooth. You lost your fingerprints?"

"Prints, lines, everything. Nothing's barely come back in three years too. I rushed in and held up that hot sonofabitch while the brothers came running to get it propped up and rip the torch away. The knife in the hip today doesn't have shit on feeling your hands melt on hot metal. If the fire burned for a few seconds longer, the whole damned club would've blown itself sky high. There wouldn't be a Devils charter west of the Mississippi left."

"Wow. You're a hero, then." I didn't let myself gush all over him, but I really was impressed.

"Did what I needed for my brothers. Same fucking thing I'll do a thousand more times if I have to. I put this club first and everybody in it. Brothers, business, all our supporters." He fixed his eyes on me and wouldn't look away. "I appreciate you fixing me up and looking after my ass all over again. I know some bullshit went down between us last time we were together. One thing hasn't changed: I'll keep returning the favor. If you ever need anything, babe, you know where to find it. You come straight to me."

I nodded. Damn. He'd stolen my energy, my desire, and now my certainty. He insisted everything he did was for the club, but this offer was for me, and it wasn't just club business. I could feel it.

Smiling, I reached for his dog tags. He didn't stop me.

"So, that's your road name. Guess you wanted me to work to find out what you're really called…" He shrugged as I held the one metal tag up to the light. "John Richmond."

I blinked. Tank cleared his throat.

"I like it," I said. "It's a good, strong name."

"Momma never got real creative naming her boys. Whatever, I'm not complaining." He nodded, as if to reassure himself. "Simple name like that helps a man blend in. It can be useful with the places I've been."

He had a point. I let the tag slip back in place, listening to the metal chime on its chain.

"You'll be okay here for the night? I can bring you a few more blankets and pillows to keep you comfy."

Tank smiled. "Forget it. You've already run yourself stupid picking up after my clumsy ass. I've slept in the fucking dirt. This table is a big improvement over mud, not to mention those army bunks too."

I laughed. On my way out, my heart was skipping. All the fear and anxiety I had about crossing him was gone.

If he had a clue where this was heading, he wasn't showing his hand. But for the first time since he blew town, there was some hope, a gentle optimism I hadn't known I wanted before I saw him laid out on my table.

There were no guarantees Tank would open his heart or his bed to me. But at least he wasn't afraid to open his hand in friendship, wiping away the awkwardness and hostility I feared. We had a new understanding.

Of course, friendship wasn't half of what I wanted. Not really.

My heart, body, and soul wouldn't be satisfied until he wrapped those gigantic, mean looking arms of his around me and took us to a private place for a deeper, fiercer understanding I'd never forget.

V: Duty's Torture (Tank)

My body took a fucking beating. Nothing pissed me off more than the limits of my own skin, especially when it was too damned torn up to make me useful to my brothers.

Then again, nothing would've made a dent in the grim, heavy shit suffocating the clubhouse the past couple weeks. Would've needed magic to lift this storm.

The rogues on our asses were out to kill us, and skullfuck our minds in the process.

They made their point crystal fucking clear when they killed Saffron's mom. The girl was plenty shaken up by the tragedy, and Blaze was all over her, dead set on bringing their asses to Devil justice. Throttle was all over him too, riding my boss hard.

If we didn't show the rogues Satan's Scythe, and soon, the real Grizzlies were gonna come rolling in to deal with these imposters wearing their patches and running goddamned circles around us.

When the heat's on in this club, it's never just a little pressure. It's like fucking comets raining from the sky, exploding in molten lava, burning up the whole damned world.

I walked with my cane. Felt good to get out of the infirmary once in awhile, especially when Emma wasn't there. She still insisted it was the safest place for me while the damned tear in my hip healed.

I gripped the cane tight, wandering past the empty bar, past the whore's room. If I'd pressed my ear close, I would've heard Stinger cussing his guts out, pumping another load into Marianne or Sangria. The two girls were lonely without as many visits from the brothers.

Guess all this stress killed the hell outta lust, except for Stinger's. I knew I wasn't feeling shit. Except when *she* was around.

When Em had her little hands anywhere on these bones, it was like lightning. I wanted to grab her palms and turn them over, make sure she didn't have an electrode attached. Every bolt that went raking through my system always spiked down, straight to my cock, vaporizing the cool I damned well wanted to keep.

Fuck! Look at you, boy. You can't stop thinking about her, especially when she hasn't been by for more than a day.

I shook my head, fighting nasty thoughts. I stopped at the door to the room where Blaze had Saffron under guard. She hadn't stuck her head out since her mom's funeral a few days ago. I lingered, thinking about Em, and feeling my heart sink when I thought too long and hard.

Bad fucking karma in here. Real bad. The door didn't do shit to block out the suffering behind it.

Saffron's pain was a cold splash of water that iced my fire for the hottest girl alive who had scrubs hugging her sweet ass.

Blaze's girl was a living, breathing warning about what waited for any woman who got too deep in this business, too deep for their own damned good one with any brother. So was June, Maverick's old lady, a chick who would've been killed or raped herself without a lot of luck. Sticking her sharp fucking claws into anybody who fucked with her helped too.

Shook my head again. I practically heard rocks rolling around, all the broken, heavy dreams that collided with reality and shattered it to pieces.

If this world was a cold SOB, then mine was a fucking glacier.

Soon as a man puts on his patch, he's got his freedom and his family, men who'd lay down their lives for him. The road forges bonds thicker than blood or money or piddly little hobbies.

I understood that much perfectly. This life gave me the camaraderie I never got overseas. I put my ass on the line for ungrateful bastards who'd signed up to dodge Taliban mortars and bullets for a dental plan and a college education. Me, I came looking for something greater, some higher purpose.

No, it wasn't God and country. I wanted to find more men who didn't fit the world's nice smooth edges, jagged fucks whose worst nightmare was squeezing into a suit and tie for punching a nine-to-five clock.

I'd found them in the MC, my brothers. Not in the military. Everybody who shared Satan's patch took their duties on the nose, the price of wearing these colors and enjoying all their privileges.

Brotherhood came easy, without hesitation. I was ready to pay my ton in flesh if it benefited the club. I'd offer up my hands, my body, my blood. Knives and bullets and burns didn't have shit on dishonor, the one bitter thing I'd never tolerate.

I knew my job and understood what I had to do to keep my boys safe. Too bad Em was a whole different game.

Why wasn't it so fucking clear cut with her?

I watched Blaze twisting himself to pieces, desperate to hold onto the flame he'd lit with Saffron and keep her safe. Really, he was bending over backwards to marry two worlds that were never meant to be.

It was obvious. And yet, I didn't call him out, didn't climb up and get all high and mighty. I understood what he was doing because I had the same crazy temptation rampaging in my skull. I wanted Emma so bad I was gonna put her at risk, even if things seemed rosy when some assholes weren't snapping at our heels.

But I wasn't like Blaze and Maverick. There was no damned way I was gonna let the angel who'd saved my ass twice wrap herself around me while I had a target on my back.

Or, worse, drag her into mourning me when I took a direct hit between the eyes instead of a glancing blow.

Soon as I was able to ditch the cane, I'd be back in the field, riding with my brothers to take the motherfuckers who'd hit us straight to hell. And it might be one battle where my luck finally ran out.

I couldn't do that to her.

Fuck, I couldn't do it to myself, couldn't stand to rip her heart to pieces. I couldn't be the man for her when she deserved so much fucking better than the pitch black violence strapped to my shoulders like bloody stones. Especially when I couldn't hold those rocks forever, so heavy and unwieldy they threatened to roll right off my back and smash her if she got too close.

My half-healed cut pulsed angrily beneath my bandages as I hobbled back to the infirmary, a white knuckle grip on the cane. Blaze was in his office, spewing muffled, intense words at somebody on the phone.

My stomach knotted, and the wound throbbed again below the belt. This wasn't an infection. I didn't need any med school degree to know it stung because pushing Em away was gonna be a bastard.

Like it or not, I had to get this shit over with so I could get on with club business, and she could get on with hers. No other way around it.

I had to tell her. Had to spell it out in a way she wouldn't question, wouldn't doubt, and wouldn't come crawling back the next time she had to kiss my bruises.

The only way to protect Emma was to smash her pretty heart.

The door to the whore's room wasn't locked. I pushed my way inside and found Marianne stretched out on the big bed. Stinger was passed out face down next to her, bare ass up.

Fuck. The atmosphere here was so shitty everybody was drowning their sorrows in Jack or pussy.

I reached into my wallet and crinkled the crisp bills loudly to get her attention. Her eyes lit up when she saw me in the corner. Marianne slid off the bed, cat-like and fluid, reaching for her robe on the floor. She barely closed it as she approached, a saucy smile on her fat lips.

The woman was a little older than girls like Sangria. Already had herself an ex-husband and a couple kids, but she was one of those hot blondes who couldn't resist the danger and sex the brothers offered. *Hot* and blonde, yeah, just the way I liked 'em – but she didn't have one damned flame to Emma's perfect ten.

"What's up, Tank?" she purred. "You looking for another massage today? Sleeping on that shitty table back there must be hell while you're healing."

I pushed the bills into her hands. "I'm giving you a down payment on service rendered. You fucked me this fine afternoon. Not Stinger."

I pointed, narrowing my eyes. Shock and confusion flickered in her eyes.

"I don't understand. You know the brothers get whatever they want, and they don't have to pay for it." Her smile was back, and her long red fingernails brushed my chest, coming closer. "Don't tell that sexy head of yours isn't working like it should? They said the spill you took when you got stabbed was bad, but I didn't know –"

"I'm not retarded. Haven't forgotten shit either. I know how my own damned club works. That money's to keep your mouth shut except when somebody asks if you've been with me. Anybody asks you that question, bitch – *anyone* – then you tell them I got this cock rode like nothing else. Understand?"

"Not really…but I'll do it. Thanks, Tank. I can use the extra scratch." She flashed her perfect white teeth.

I turned, eager to get the fuck out of there. Had to step over a half-dressed Sangria on the floor.

Stinger chuffed in his sleep, smacking his lips when the bed creaked with Marianne returning. My VP took his R & R seriously, and he liked to hog both girls to himself to fuck the stress outta his system.

I wished a simple brainless fuck would've been the answer to my problems. Slowly, I closed the door, a couple hundred bucks poorer and ready to slit my own throat in front of the girl I really adored.

After this, she was gonna hate my ass. If the hatred kept her away from me, then I'd done my job.

A quick look at my phone made me pick up the fucking pace. It was almost time for my check up. I wanted to be settled in before she showed up – not looking like a flustered asshole who'd just lied through his teeth.

Because that's exactly what I was, and I wasn't done either.

"It's looking really good. Fresh bandages, healing solution…how's the walking coming?"

I looked into her eyes. Fuck, she looked innocent.

Her hand was still on my side, lingering above the wound below my abs. Her touch was always warm, soothing, tempting.

"It's fine," I said. "Barely feel anything when I'm up and about. Hope you'll tell me I can workout again soon."

The snake in my head hissed, tempted to spout a more devious lie. It wanted me to tell her how badly I needed her, how much I needed to fuck. But the real snake was between my legs, aching to keep her hands on my flesh, begging for just one fuck.

Shit, it had been so long.

Last romp I'd had was back in North Dakota, long before we landed in Montana. Hadn't been able to do a damned thing since I'd laid eyes on her. If I could've fucked this all away with one of the whores or some stripper, then maybe I wouldn't be all wound up, ready to fold whenever she was close.

Bastard, I thought. *Stay focused. Got to get this brutal shit over with. You fuck her and then throw her away, and you'll make this a thousand times harder.*

"You need to keep using that cane, I said. Did you hear me?" Emma blinked, a shallow smile on her face.

Fuck me. All this terrible desire and duty was making one hell of a distraction.

"Yeah, I understand. Need to help my brothers pay back the rogue charter. It's a lot more personal since they fucked with Saffron. Can I ride if I'm not a hundred percent?"

I didn't say shit about fighting because I knew that would really set her off.

Her face lined with concern. "Maybe short distances. Only if it's *absolutely* necessary."

I nodded. "Won't be going anywhere too far past city limits."

Our intel told us the fucks were hiding around here somewhere. With the way they kept popping up like spiders, they had to be hiding right under our noses. Soon as we found them, Blaze was gonna bring the hammer down, and I wanted to drive the fucking nails in as Sergeant at Arms.

"You shouldn't be going anywhere at all. I hope you're not about to get yourself into more trouble." A worried smile crossed her lips. "It's somebody else's turn. I'm tired of seeing you on my table."

I looked past her at the door, trying to pull the pin at the right chance. Something was hanging there on the hook.

"What's this? Someone got a new cut?"

"Special order for Blaze," she said. "Mom's a seamstress. She ordered it and put the patches on herself. It's...supposed to be a secret."

That got my attention. I wondered what the boss was up to. Standing up, I grabbed my own shirt and leather, and began to roll them on. Couldn't ignore the disappointment in her eyes as my bare skin was covered.

"Okay, okay. You really want to know?" That perky ass smile on her face turned mischievous. She leaned in and cupped her hands around my ear. "He had it custom made for Saffron. He's taking her as his old lady. That's a big deal for the club, isn't it?"

I was too lost in her hot, sweet breath to acknowledge what she was saying at first. Then it hit me like a bullet.

Fuck! Is this whole MC losing its goddamned mind?

Blaze and Saffron's drama wasn't gonna make this any easier. Steady adrenaline dumped into my blood. I tightened my fists instinctively, more determined than ever to finish this shit.

"Listen, babe…" I peeled away from her and crossed the room, giving us some distance. "There's something I gotta get across."

She cocked her head. Undeterred, Emma walked toward me, all tits and bobbing hips. If I didn't have a demon in my head, I would've lost it, hypnotized by the minx in the nurse's outfit.

"What?" She reached out, hand up high, lacing her fingers over my neck. Studying my face, she could see the bad news before I said a damned thing. "Don't disappoint me again, Tank."

Her perfect lips parted, wet and hot and wonderful. All I could think about was occupying her heat with my tongue, discovering how those lips would look wrapped around my cock.

Fuck, fuck, fuck!

It all came down in a storm raging in my blood. I lost it, every fucking thing, smashing her steaming lips with mine.

Everything was lost. The discipline, the buildup, the tension, the lies – all gone to shit in one fucking kiss!

I kissed her long and hard, ripping her off the floor and slamming her to the wall. My whole body built up like a bomb, realizing how bad I missed this kinda pure throbbing sex since I'd owned her lips weeks ago.

Fuck, maybe I was getting myself ready for how bad I'd miss it when I did the inevitable.

I kissed her 'til she moaned, picking her up by the ass, throttling my hips against her. The greedy bastard between my legs was energized, straining like mad. I sucked her bottom lip into my mouth and bit down. Hard.

My dick almost had me in a death grip – almost – until she jerked back and rubbed her lips.

"Ow!" Surprise brushed the fire in her face. "What the hell was that?"

I let go, my senses flooding back. The shit hit so fast and heavy it slammed right into the lust. The stormfronts clashing in my stomach nearly made me sick, two powerful forces trying to tear my ass in two.

Sex. Lies.
Sex. Lies.
Fuck!

"We can't do this, babe. I can't." I shook my head, sucking in a great big breath. "I took a damned oath to keep you safe, and I'm living up to it."

The lust in her eyes turned to anger. "Not this again! Aren't we past this, Tank?"

"No, this is something else. It's not just the danger, Em, even though that shit's real and deadly fucking serious. I'm protecting you from me." Snarling, I took a step closer, anger lashing me inside. "You don't get it, babe. I'm not the kinda guy who's ever gonna take you to the movies or put a ring on your finger. You deserve that, and you sure as shit don't deserve to get wrapped up in knives and bullets. Look, I don't give a shit what you do with this club. That's between you and Blaze. But you need to get over this stupid fucking crush and find a man who'll give you the happy ending you're looking for."

I reached for her and she jerked away, explosive and repulsed.

Idiot! This is what you wanted, isn't it?

Tears pricked at her eyes. When she looked up, her head was shaking. I wasn't the only one in the room about to go off like a goddamned rocket.

"You keep telling me I don't know shit, Tank, but *you're* the one who doesn't understand. I'm choosing *you*. Beneath that crazy buff exterior and all the scary tattoos, I know you've got a good heart. I can't pretend it isn't there. I can't pretend I don't want it."

She took a step forward. "Why? Why can't you close your dumb mouth and give this a chance?"

I balled my fists, trying to force some of that red hot anger into my chest. I needed a fucking shield to survive the a-bomb I was gonna have to drop next.

"You don't know shit," I said, switching to enforcer mode. "You don't know me either, babe. I tried to be nice and set this aside the easy way. You think I'm a good man? Fuck! How the hell would you know? You've only seen me when I'm laid up like a kitten on your fucking sofa or in this little room. You haven't seen the shit I do when I'm solid."

I raised my fists, folding them across my chest. "These fists have killed for Uncle Sam and the Prairie Devils, and I don't regret shit. You want a soulless killer to love? Don't fucking lie and tell me you do!"

Shock flashed in her eyes, but slipped just as quickly. The girl was determined as all hell.

If only this was a fight with a dude. I was bowed up, breathing hard, ready to fucking strike. But I couldn't. Fists wouldn't do shit with this gorgeous creature closing in.

"I want you. Tank. John. The man I see in front of me. If I have to deal with the rest, I will."

"How 'bout the women?" There. I fucking said it. "You ready to deal with that too?"

The defiance was blown apart as soon as it was out of my mouth. Emma balked, stumbling backward, the light and need and warmth leaving her eyes.

Fuck! This isn't what I wanted. But it's too fucking, late isn't?

Only one way forward. One way to end this and drill some damned sense into her.

"What? You thought we all sat around sipping beers when the day's done and talking about our stocks?" I stepped forward, a nasty edge creeping into my voice. "Every brother here who isn't chained up with an old lady heads straight for the whores, or else the bitches who show up at our parties. We fuck them senseless and wipe our dicks without a second thought. That's all I want, babe, and I'm not gonna do it to you."

She was moving her head from side to side, trying to bury her disbelief. "No..."

"Yeah. Marianne sucked me off this morning. Go talk to the slut if you don't believe me. She knows how to do her job like a good whore and walk away without pining over any brother's ass. You, on the other hand..."

I was about to reach out, clasp her shoulder, and drive the stake all the way into her heart. She covered her ears. Never saw a girl move so fast.

Emma whipped around, tearing the cut for Saffron off the door, and yanked it open. I caught a glimpse of Blaze standing outside. The door closed slowly.

I had time to hear Emma's pain stricken sniffle and see the spark in Blaze's eye. *What the fuck have you done now, asshole?* it said.

Fuck if I knew. I was still asking myself that question long after the voices outside the door disappeared, leaving me to my shitty, miserable self.

Ever since I ripped out her heart, the dreams were the same. And smashing her love to pieces was just the beginning of the shitstorm too.

Before I knew it, Saffron and her dumbass brother were picked up by the assholes at our throats, and Blaze sent us into battle.

A man never forgets a knock down, drag out fight. No matter how many he has to live it.

My dreams recalled the club's big blow out showdown with the rogue Grizzlies at that shitty makeshift clubhouse in the Montana wilds. Men screaming, bullets flying, grasping that big fucking auto in my hands and riddling the dilapidated building with suppression fire.

Then the real Grizzlies showed up. Worrying about whether or not Fang and his crew were gonna stab us in the back was just as bad as mopping up the rogues.

By the time it was said and done, Blaze saved Saffron's ass at the last second and exacted his revenge. We hauled ass away from that God forsaken place, listening to Fang and his boys finish them off. The Grizzlies boxed the imposters in their own clubhouse and torched it. I'll never forget the screams of those bastards roasting alive, howls like the shriek and groan of my fucked up life.

That was what really happened. We made it. Blaze got his old lady home safe.

But dreams wanted to take on their own life, and anytime I closed my eyes after the battle, things were different.

Blaze was too late. Saffron was dead, torn up, raped, all my worst fears about Em coming to life in darkness. I watched Blaze lean over his girl's limp body and let out a scream that ended the whole fucking world, a scream so much like the savage catcalls of Taliban fighters hitting my convoy on the road outside Kandahar.

They loved to nail our asses with mortars when we weren't expecting it. I hit the ground with other men in desert brown fatigues, all of us desperately seeking a target to let loose. Then a shell came screaming through the air and exploded on top of me, breaking everything apart.

Why did a bomb strike feel like some asshole's hand on my face?

Fuck dreaming. Fuck sleep. Fuck me.

"Wake up, brother! You're gonna be in a world of shit if you don't." Stinger hit me again on the jaw, letting his force resonate through my bones 'til I opened my eyes.

"Huh? What the fuck's going on?"

"You forgot church today, you drunken asshole. Second time this week." His lips twitched and his boot kicked at something on the floor next to me. "Look, Goliath, this is the last time I'm doing you this fucking courtesy. Next time, I'll let Blaze start shit without you. And when he asks where the fuck you're at, I'll point him right back here so he can see for himself."

"No!" I jerked up, pulling my pants up straight. "I'm sorry, boss. Just overslept."

Total bullshit, and he could smell it on my breath. The traces of Jack I'd knocked down last night poured out my mouth, sour as the burn in my skull.

Fuck, I had to find some other way to drown out Emma. Ever since our last big fight, I took up the bottle, using it to numb lips that still remembered her kisses. Didn't help that I had to hear all about Blaze and Saffron's big wedding coming up in Reno, or watch the brothers gallivanting off with club pussy and not a care in the world.

"Wash up and take a swig of Listerine. You've got five minutes. Try to show up to the table looking like you respect the patch." Stinger reached over his shoulder and tapped the back of his cut. "Christ. You're living like a damned Grizzlies asshole in here."

Without another word, he walked out, slamming the door to my sparse room. I wanted to rush his ass after the insult. VP or not, nobody in the Devils ought to take that shit lying down. Nothing worse than being compared to a bunch of sloppy fucking drug dealers and rapists.

Trouble was, he wasn't totally off the mark.

The empty bottle I stepped over wasn't the only one on the floor. My corner trashcan overflowed with glass and paper plates. I hadn't gotten around to repairing the cot I'd ripped up weeks ago in my crazy dreams, and I'd been sleeping right on the dirty floor ever since, wrapped up in nothing more than a cruddy blanket.

Just like the old days at war, days that should've been long behind me. No fucking way to live when I was supposed to be taking care of my club, an MC that was finally at peace after a rough start forcing the Grizzlies over the Cascades and cleaning up our home turf.

I grunted, staggering into the dirty bathroom outside, my single fresh shirt and my cut thrown across my shoulder. The morning was off to a shitty start, but it went to the cesspool when I looked in the mirror and saw my reflection.

There was nothing worse than staring at the fucked up liar I'd become, tortured at every goddamned turn by my own bitter choices.

They say there's no rest for the wicked. I was living proof.

At night, the dreams did my ass in unless I got lucky and marinated myself in so much Jack I couldn't see a damned thing. During the day, it was Emma's turn to torture my ass, her ghost filling up my brain and taking over the more sober I was.

The faucets squeaked loudly in my hands as I let the water run. Damn, that hurt. The squeal drilled straight into my damn head and fed the hangover humming in my temples.

One more piece of the vicious nag in my head that reminded me every single day I'd created this hell. But hell was a place I could deal with as long as it kept her safe.

Shit, I had to. I couldn't let this all be for nothing.

I'd rather die with my own demons a thousand times than see Em take a bullet or a knife or a burn like poor

Saffron did before Blaze caught her. Especially if that hurt was intended for me.

Blaze gave me the evil eye when I dropped into the seat next to him. "What the fuck's going on around here, Sarge? Late night?"

My eyes shifted over, ready to take a beating. Stinger sat on the Prez's other side, waiting for the other brothers to file in for church. The VP's face didn't reveal a damned thing. I wondered if he'd ratted me out after all.

I nodded. "Something like that."

"The boys tell me they've been sleeping like babies since we had the engagement bash." Blaze reached over and clapped me hard on the shoulder. "Couldn't fucking believe it 'til I rolled in at the crack of dawn myself. None of your workouts shaking the exercise room like a goddamned rhino. Did that knife take one of your nuts off, or are you just getting lazy?"

I forced a weak laugh. "More interested in getting my beauty sleep, boss. Still recovering from the big fight."

Another minute passed in awkward silence. Blaze and Stinger chatted about Nevada plans, while everybody else assembled around the table.

My eyes flicked down the ranks. Us three officers at the front, and then the full patch members: Reb, Moose, Roller. Smokey and Stone, our two prospects, stood near the opposite wall, invited into this meeting. Probably because Blaze was ready to test their asses one more time before we voted on their colors.

"All right." Blaze picked the gavel and spun it in one hand, a signal to everybody else to shut their mouths. "First thing on the agenda, like half you boys know, is making sure our territory stays neat. Haven't had any more bear trouble the past month. That's good news."

The men nodded. I mimicked them like a mindless puppet. What was good for the club was normally good for me, but I wasn't feeling anything except lifeless ash today, turning my insides to dead mush.

"But we're not all finished yet. We got ourselves a couple more clubs to patch over to the Devils, little crops of local good ole boys. Luckily, they're not inclined to give us any shit after the way they saw us drive the Grizzlies across the state line." He looked at Stinger. "You wanna fill us in on the first one, Sting?"

"Sure thing, Prez. Me and Roller rode out to Bozeman last week to take care of the Black Seeds. Patching them in went smooth as silk. Can't say they'll be much use to business. Mostly a bunch of old farts who like to smoke and fuck their whores. Their Prez told me nobody's fired a gun since the Grizzlies first came over in the eighties. Checked his background. All clean. They had a nice, easy gig with the Grizzlies, and I expect it'll be the same now that they're wearing our support patch."

Blaze nodded. "Damned well better be. We don't need to go chasing after a bunch of goddamned rogues who won't follow orders – especially after the meat we just sent to the grinder."

"Don't you worry, Prez." Reb looked up, sucking on a mouthful of chewing tobacco. "I'd be surprised if these guys can even get their dicks wet. They won't be giving us shit for trouble."

Stinger's trademark grin appeared. The VP always looked like a fucking Cheshire cat when his amusement crested. Everybody laughed.

"Okay. We'll put the stags stay out to pasture, long as they stay the fuck in line. Next up, closer to home, we got other bastards to worry about. What the hell were they called again?"

"The Rams," Moose cut in, stroking his beard. "Pagan Rams. I remember running into those fuckers about twenty years ago in Sturgis. Block, the President, is a fucking blockhead and a real asshole. Bastard nearly started a firefight in the middle of a crowded bar when he hit on another club President's old lady. Good thing old Voodoo was there, same as me and the other old timers. He stepped right between 'em and defused the whole thing before it erupted."

"Throttle's old man was a good one," I said, nodding.

Voodoo was the man who gave me my prospect cut when I started with the mother charter in Cassandra, North Dakota. He died just a few months later during our dust up with the Raging Skulls and that asshole mayor. Throttle took over then, and he'd been national President ever since. Also the first man since the army to knock some fucking sense into me, shoving me off onto Maverick and Blaze when I got into too many fights over a club floozy.

Fuck, what the hell was her name? Sure wish getting over Em was so easy.

"Tank!" Blaze snapped his fingers, clearly irritated, running me right off memory lane. "What do we know about security here? These assholes agreed to take the patch, but I'm not taking any goddamned chances. Their history's a helluva lot muddier than the Black Seeds."

I stared at him. Stinger cleared his throat, the goofy smile on his mug long gone.

"Uh…it's a good idea to send the whole club in if you wanna make sure they don't try anything. They've only got a few guys, all past their prime. We've got the numbers and the edge on firepower. If we want to keep 'em in line, then we better flex." I clenched my fists on the table, trying to focus. "Not that I expect anything. These fucks are a buncha old mules, boss. They won't do shit if they see us packing and remember how bad we fucked up the Grizzlies – twice."

"Hope you're sure about that, brother." Stinger's voice had a skeptical edge to it I didn't like. "Bikers get unpredictable when strangers start rifling through their home turf. That's what we plan to do. Search and seizure at their clubhouse. Gotta make sure they're not holding anything we should know about."

"What? You don't think I know how to do my job? I'm the fucking Sergeant at Arms, for Christ's sake."

Bang! Blaze rapped the gavel. The easy going expression on his face that started the meeting turned into piss and vinegar.

"Come on, bros. Knock this shit off. Everything Moose said was dead on the nose. The Pagan Rams are a tiny little shitstain of a club, but they're dangerous motherfuckers. At least, they were, before their hair went gray. The Grizzlies would've wiped their asses out if they hadn't shown balls big enough to get a truce all these years. Montana's *our* territory now, and that means we need to run a tight ship, or the fucking thing will run circles around us."

Stinger and I looked at each other. We both nodded. I was fucked, but I wasn't so far gone I was gonna sacrifice the club's order for a pissing contest with a brother.

"Okay, let's vote and lock this in. If anybody's got a better plan, put it forward now or keep your mouth shut." He paused, waiting for any options. Nothing. "All in favor of patching in the Rams as soon as possible with the full force of the Montana charter?"

A chorus of hands and ayes shot up. I added mine to the mix.

The gavel came down, quickening the tempo still pounding in my head.

"All right, good," Blaze said. "Now let's talk about that weekend pig roast…"

I zoned out during the rest of the meeting. When Blaze closed our business with a final slap of wood, I was out the door first. Didn't catch Stinger right behind me 'til his hand was on my shoulder.

I whirled. Anger pulsed through me the instant I saw his stupid rat face.

"I know you're heading for the bar, brother. Might wanna re-think that after this morning." He spoke slowly, carefully. "Give Saffron a break, and brother Jack too. We're gearing up for a possible fight and the whole club needs you sharp and ready to go."

"Fuck off, VP. When we deal with those assholes, I'll be ready. 'Til then it's not your concern what the hell I do in my free time, long as it isn't hurting the club. I'm not the big stupid animal you think I am, boss. I can handle a few shots to take the edge off."

I broke from his grasp. He didn't come after me.

Bullshit. Pure bullshit.

Stinger acted concerned, but I saw right through it. He was just trying to stay in Blaze's good graces after the constant strategic disagreements between them. Blaze let him get away with mouthing off and challenging his judgments, like any good VP with a brain should do, but Stinger knew letting any cogs in the club machine go to hell was unforgivable.

It was my job to keep the brothers in line as club enforcer, and Stinger did the same with the club officers.

My old wounds pulsed. Both of them, one near my guts and one on the hip. Always happened when I was pissed and dehydrated.

Shit, I needed something, and water wasn't gonna do it. I slid into the nearest stool at the bar and waited.

"Jesus, Tank, you look like hell."

"Good morning to you too, Saffron." I smiled. "Looking for the usual today. A great big shot of Jack. Then you just stick around and keep it coming."

She stared at me, her lips twisted. The girl was a damned good bartender. She hadn't abused her place since Blaze claimed her as old lady neither. She did her job, kept her head down, and understood where club business ended and the fiery shit she had with Blaze began.

"Okay, big guy, but I'm giving you a huge glass of water too. Drink up before you ask for any refills. I'm no nurse. But I know damned well when somebody needs it." She started to walk to get my order, and recognition filled her eyes.

Nurse. Fuck. She really said it.

She mumbled an apology and continued to walk off.

Saffron was the only one here who understood what went down with me and Emma. I'd staked my position damned clear to her over and over.

Emma and I were finished. I knew Saffron didn't like it one bit, but what the hell did it matter? Her opinion about it mattered as much as everybody else's – it was fucking worthless.

Shit, she was living proof what kinda toll this life took. Just a couple weeks ago, before Blaze proposed to her, I inked his name on the one good thigh she still had left. The assholes in the rogues had done a number on her before Blaze got her home, burning the shit out of her other side, destroying all the old ink she had going up her hip. They would've done a lot worse if Blaze had been ten minutes too late.

The drinks landed in front of me. When I reached out, one hand was shaking, and I snapped it back 'til I was sure she wouldn't see.

Fuck me. Damned good thing neither Saffron nor anybody else asked me for a tattoo lately. I doubted I'd be able to fucking do it in the fried state that was quickly becoming the norm for my sorry ass.

I banged back those two shots like lightning. Each splash of venom burned deep, ripping through the dull darkness inside me, if only for a few seconds. I needed hot amber light like I needed a hole between the eyes, but there was one thing to say about it: the shit did its job and it never talked back.

The warm, soupy buzz it layered around my brain never judged. It never piled on new responsibilities or split my skull open with painful fucking questions about right and wrong, life and death, love and hate.

I didn't need Emma's cures anymore. I just needed Doctor Jack. Long as I followed his orders and took my daily dose, I was gonna be all right. No more worries about –

Her.

I had to set my second empty shot glass down and rub my eyes. Christ, no, I wasn't just seeing things.

Emma was really standing right there in the doorway, out by the garages, talking to Moose. Some brother had left the door open. I watched through the hole, eyeing her up and down, loving the way she moved. Even when she just tore a little slip off a paper bag and pressed it up to Moose's chubby face, carefully running her fingernails across it, she looked absolutely fucking fine, blonde locks shining in the sun like golden threads spun to perfection.

Next thing I knew, I was hard as nails, every fucking inch of me. Staring at her sweet ass was like looking at the sun. She turned my blood to kerosene and lit me on fire from the inside-fucking-out, hotter and hornier than hell itself.

That babe looked so damned good she blinded me, and I still couldn't look away, eyes anchored to her curves. She was a bonafide fucking Medusa, and every inch of me turned a little more to stone the longer I stared and gawked and marveled at her fine, ripe shape.

My cock jerked, pure need throttling its veins, pounding in my head with one brute command.

Forget your mission, you drunken bastard. Forget it and go claim her. Work all this bullshit between you out with sweat and skin and screams.

"No," I muttered to myself, reaching for the water. Practically had to reach out and steady my fucking hand to keep it from shaking again.

Saffron was on the other side of the bar, tidying things up. When she saw me take a drink, she smiled, and gave me a tiny nod.

Whatever. I wasn't drinking for her. I was sending that ice cold fluid through my guts because it was the only goddamned thing I could take to keep from going up like a wicker chair on fire.

Glass drained, I reached for my wallet. I laid the crisp bills on the counter with a stupidly generous tip and moved toward the door.

It looked like she was finishing up with Moose. After a nod, a smile, and a loud thanks, my bearded brother marched away, heading for his bike while he stuffed the medicine bag in his pocket.

Emma must've had a sixth sense. The girl turned her pretty face right toward me. Naturally, I locked up, turned to pure granite by her fiery stare.

There was no love for my greedy, lying ass in her eyes. Not like before. It was gone, all gone, all because I pissed it away.

And fuck, why would it be any other way?

A shock ran through her. I saw her tremble slightly, and then cold hatred lined her face. She turned, stomping off to her car as fast as her little feet would carry her.

Shit! I waited. It was all I could do to keep from embarrassing myself. Jack hammered at my head, mixed with anger and confusion, desire and nauseating want.

You asked for this, asshole, a gruff voice screamed in my head. *Let her go. You can't keep teasing her when you're too dazed and confused to shit or get off the pot.*

That vicious little weenie on my shoulder was right. My conscience grabbed me by the balls and put a muzzle on my dick. My boots began to move, and I sulked back to the bar for another round from Saffron, more fiery rockets to blast away any crazy thoughts about chasing her tail for the umpteenth time.

We both knew how this story ended. There wasn't any reason – not one – for repeating it.

Damn, if only I believed that. Because if it was true, then why was it so fucking hard to keep this brutal song off shuffle?

By nightfall, I couldn't fucking stand it. I'd downed so much Jack I saw stars before the blackness took me on the hard floor.

When I woke up, my head was pounding something fierce. I ran to the bathroom and gulped big handfuls of water. For the first time in days, I'd downed so much poison I didn't dream.

It was a clear, dead, dreamless sleep. Would've been comforting any other time, but not today. Not when I'd been so damned close to Emma, when she was still the last thing I saw in my head before I crashed out and the first thing in it when I woke up in a fever.

I've got to see Emma. One more time. Even if it's from a damned distance.

Yeah, I knew what I was getting into. I was about to go full on stalker, pining after her like a lovesick little boy. Well, fuck it.

Nobody would ever call me little. They'd never tell me to keep my ass away either.

If Emma caught me dropping by her place, she'd get pissed and tell Blaze or Stinger. I could handle hell from my brothers. Taking one more second of feeling like a brain dead rock, forever ripped away from her...

No. No goddamned way. I was doing this, and nothing was gonna stop me, not even my bitchy conscience I'd drunk into a coma.

As soon as I was good to drive, I stepped outside and got on my bike. She purred to life in my hands, cool and comforting, the one reliable lover I still had.

Summer was over. Missoula was turning to autumn. The cut was starting to be more than just a uniform. It kept me warm on the ride through town, dampening the chill gusts on the open road.

I slowed way down when I blew into Emma's neighborhood. It was a nice neighborhood. Blaze ordered us to play nice with the locals, and I was gonna respect that instead of letting my fucking engine rattle their squeaky clean windows.

Leaving my bike parked along the side, I walked the last block, stopping to scope out her house, watching at the end of the street.

Never expected to hear her voice. But there it was, high and angry, as if she was having a heated debate over the phone. My curiosity went wild.

I came closer, closer, and hit a dead stop when I saw she wasn't alone.

Emma's curvy silhouette was on the porch, just a few inches from another tall man. Anger exploded in my blood. My guts tightened.

What the fuck? Had she decided to tear me out of her head with a new boyfriend?

Obviously not a very good one if they were fighting. The man mumbled more calmly. I picked up my pace, trying to make out their words. The damned neighbors had a radio going loudly in their garage, and it drowned out any hope of figuring out what they were saying without being right fucking there.

Just when I crossed the sidewalk in front of her house, the man walked right past me, heading for a sleek black car beneath the tree. The dude was only a couple inches shorter than me, but he had almost no muscle, lanky as a frigging skeleton.

"I don't care what you want, asshole!" Emma yelled after him. "Don't come near me again. I'll come to you."

The tall man smiled and nodded. He was starting to stoop down to climb into his vehicle when he saw me.

His eyes flashed recognition. He didn't stop, didn't smile – just nodded like a fucking idiot before he was in and the door clicked shut.

I wondered if all the bullshit coursing through my system was making me hallucinate. He looked like he knew exactly who I was, and his eyes had the sick kinda glint I'd seen on a dozen different predators before, jackals ready to take a big steaming bite outta your skin when they know you're cornered.

No, it wasn't my fucked up brain deceiving me. Emma's red, puffy face didn't lie. I was on fire now, and I rushed up her steps, closing the small gap between us.

Shock and anger exploded through her, the same evil reaction I'd seen earlier. "Tank? Go away! You're the last person I want to see right now…"

In a huff, she slapped her thighs, and quickly walked toward the door. I caught up just in time. Nearly tore the damned thing off its hinges when I swooped in to keep it open.

"What the fuck's going on here, Em? Who is he?" I got her attention, locking a long, close stare for the first time in a small eternity. "Don't look so surprised. You think I'm gonna walk away when some asshole's left you on your own doorstep bawling your eyes out?"

Confusion boiled in her gorgeous bright eyes. So did pain. Whatever the mystery man had done, I was the asshole who'd put ninety-percent of it there, a special kinda wildfire for burning my selfish ass.

I reached for her shoulder. Soon as I touched her, the spell broke, but not the way I hoped.

She jerked violently, retreating further into the house, shaking from head to toe. I seriously thought about following her in, too damned crazy to do anything else. Then she opened her mouth and spat daggers.

"Don't touch me, you fucking asshole! Leave now or I call the cops." She took a step forward, bowed up like a pissed off cat spying an intruder. "Better, I'll call Blaze! I don't need your help. I don't need the club's. This is all personal. And you, Mister, haven't got any right to step inside my life and blow it all to pieces for the hundredth time."

"Emma…"

Speechless. Totally fucking speechless. Where the hell was the nurse with the sweet laugh I'd been in knots over? Who the hell was *this* in front of me?

"No, you listen! I want you out. Don't ever set foot on my property again. I'm telling Blaze to drag your ass to the hospital if you ever get hurt. I can't do it. I can't be anywhere near you. You don't understand."

"What?" My fist tightened on the door's handle, ready to tear the fucker off. "What the fuck are you hiding?"

"Everything that's none of your fucking business!" She jerked her head, more like she spat at my feet than a proper nod. "We're through, Tank. No, we never got started, and I'm glad."

She stepped up to the screen. Her whole face was beet red now, eyes blinking like they were trying to drop more tears, but didn't have the fluid to do it.

"You want to know where you stand? Let me clear up any confusion." Emma sucked in a rattly breath. "I am not your girlfriend. I'm not your co-worker. I'm not even your friend. And I'll sure as hell *never* be your old lady."

I couldn't listen to a second more. Two choices pounded on my skull, howling to break out: suck it up and walk away, or break down the fucking door and spank her ass raw for all the things she said.

My cock knew exactly what he wanted. My asshole conscience did too, returning after a long vacation, drowned in whiskey and mean as all hell, pissed that I'd been so stupid to come here.

I slammed the fucking door in her face and turned around. Em gave it back to me just as good as she got. I heard the big wooden door behind the screen pound into its frame like a fucking gunshot.

On the way to my bike, demon energy seethed in my veins. I was wrecked because I lost her and pissed because I couldn't make sense of it. I *knew* why she hated my ass, and despised it with a vengeance. She'd made that crystal fucking clear.

What I couldn't figure out was whether or not she was in some kinda danger. And now, like a jackass, I'd made the one irreversible fucked up mistake that would stop me from protecting her ever again.

"Fuck!" I slammed both fists on my handlebars before I took off, not giving a shit if my coarse pain and the savage beat of my engine woke up everybody in the whole damned city.

VI: Drowning (Emma)

Hours Earlier

As soon as Moose called for his prescription, my heart sped up. Every visit to the clubhouse since the day Tank broke my heart meant a chance of seeing him, like an unwelcome ghost I'd tried so hard to forget.

It was a miracle I hadn't run into him during all the craziness that went down. Checking up on Saffron's burns meant daily visits to the club for a time. As always, everyone expected miracles and didn't want to listen to real medical advice.

Saffron shouldn't have been back at the bar so soon after what she'd suffered. She definitely shouldn't have gotten the new ink. When she told me Tank was the one who'd done the tats, I quietly fumed, hoping the art had at least hit him where it counted.

The womanizing, string pulling bastard had done a number on me. I couldn't believe I'd been stupid enough to nearly invite him into my life as a lover. Never thought for one minute he was just after a casual fuck.

But casual, meaningless trysts were the norm in this life, weren't they? Maybe men like Blaze and Maverick were the exceptions, claiming their old ladies like proper wives. Or else they'd just grown up a lot faster than all their rougher, rowdier brothers.

I couldn't ignore the whoring. I never saw Tank do it in front of me, but how could he possibly keep it in his pants at those crazy parties I only caught the very beginnings of?

Shit, the two whores who came to me for STD checks every couple weeks *lived* in the clubhouse. Then there were other girls, local floozies and travelers who looked like they'd lick the dirty ground for one chance at wrapping their mouths around a biker's cock.

I'd gone completely cold and clinical around that whore Marianne. She was the one Tank said he'd fucked. It hurt even worse because she looked like an older, sluttier version of *me*. Whenever she came to me, I ran her tests and slipped the results under her door, never stopping for any idle chit-chat.

If I started to talk to her, then asking the question that still ripped me to pieces would be inevitable. Tank was an asshole for spilling the awful truth, but one thing I couldn't stand was hearing it from her overpainted lips, imaging all the filthy things this creature had done to him.

I was lost in my thoughts as usual on the pharmacy run. With Moose's antacids in hand, I was returning to my car, head starting to throb at the painful whirlwind in my brain.

I never saw the black sedan roll up to me until it was perfectly parallel, cruising at my exact walking speed. When the window started to go down, I turned my head. A strange balding man in his thirties smiled at me from the driver's side, weird recognition in his eyes.

What's going on? Do I know you?

The unwanted escort continued for a few more steps. I was about to pick up the pace and high tail it away in case this man was a creep when he shouted.

"Hey! Is that really you, cousin Emma? It's Mark. Mark Ward!"

I stopped and stared. Running into my distant cousin here in town was the last thing I expected. I hadn't seen him for years, not since the old family reunions as a kid when his parents drove over from Washington.

"Sorry for dropping in on you like this. I should've called first." His face lit up with a long smile. "Listen, I'm hanging out in town for a little while and I thought we could get together and catch up. What do you say?"

"What brings you to Missoula?" I stared dumbly, feeling surreal that this long lost minor piece of my life had suddenly come tumbling through like a blowing leaf.

"Got a little business here." He stopped, reached low, and struggled to pull something out of his hands. "Come here. I want to let you in on my little secret. Did you ever hear about me joining the force from Aunt Mavis?"

I shook my head. My mother barely mentioned him after we lost touch, though I suppose a long estrangement with her sister over my grandmother's inheritance had something to do with that. I stepped up to the car as he moved his hands around something thick, grinning like a kid who'd snuck an extra cookie.

Mark's smile broke wider as he flipped open a wallet-like leather square.

Time stopped. Hot blood began to roar in my ears, and I had to grip the flimsy paper bag in my hands tight to restore some balance.

Jesus. Is this some kind of sick punishment? I wondered.

I was looking right at Mark's clean photo, and above it, a big golden eagle surrounded by the words Department of Justice: ATF. US Special Agent sat in the middle, razzing me like the speechless idiot I was.

ATF. Alcohol, Tobacco, and Firearms, I repeated from memory. *Holy shit.*

"Shit, Emma. Nobody's taken a good long look like that since graduation. Pretty awesome, isn't it?"

"How long..." I cleared my throat, dry and scratchy as hell. "How long have you been in this line of work?"

"Just passed my one year anniversary. The pay's not bad and the benefits are fucking great. Took me years to work my way in from the Seattle PD. Nothing beats the travel, though. The ATF is fucking great with sending me all over the country. Interesting places, interesting people. Now, I'm right back here with you."

He looked at me. I couldn't bring myself to smile back, too shocked to do much of anything but stare. After a few seconds, his grin melted. He cocked his head.

"You busy tonight? I'd love to get some dinner and catch up. It's been way too long, cuz."

"I'll let mom know you're back in town. We'll set something up."

He raised a hand. "Nah. I mean, I'd love to see Aunt Mavis again. But I was thinking you and I could catch up by ourselves tonight, cousin-to-cousin. I'm sure you've got some crazy fucking stories about being an RN you can't tell in front of your mom."

I nodded, forcing an uneasy smile. Something about the way he was looking at me said this was more than just a family talk.

A dozen possibilities flooded my head. Did he know about my role in the Devils? Jesus, did he have some super secret info he was going to lay on me, a warning about getting out before the Feds descended and tore the club apart?

I knew one thing: if there was something going on and I tried to shrug him off, he wouldn't go out of his way to do me any favors. We were virtual strangers, all shared DNA aside. If I didn't cooperate and he wanted to put the squeeze on the MC, then I'd get caught in government claws just as easy.

I had to find out what he wanted.

"How about coming by my place at eight or after? I'm only working a half-shift today, but I've got an early one tomorrow…"

"I'll be there." He winked.

"Oh! Do you need the address?"

He tapped the phone resting on the stand in his car. "Already got it, cuz. Rental off Ellway street, right?"

I didn't want to admit it bothered me that this man had my house number down, and probably a whole lot more. This was no time or place to lay out my cards, especially when he was only showing me one of his.

"Awesome! Say, why don't you serve up some of that pomegranate lemonade you used to make when we were kids? I haven't had any of that shit for years. Bet it tastes great with a splash of vodka."

"I'll see what I can do…"

"See you at eight!" Mark put his car into drive and began to roll, taking flight down the lonely street.

His exhaust kicked up the crisp autumn leaves near the gutter, showering me in dead brown confetti. I hadn't realized how tightly I was pinching Moose's poor medicine bag until I looked down. My knuckles were bone white.

I'd wanted something to take my mind off running into Tank at the clubhouse.

Don't just be careful what you wish for. Fear it, and fear yourself too.

Whatever business Mark had in mind, it promised to turn some lives upside down. I just hoped it wouldn't be mine.

Later, I was mixing the sickly sweet crap he asked for with vodka, trying to forget the run to the clubhouse. Tank was watching me the whole time while I passed along Moose's medication.

So, it was true. Everything Saffron said about him turning into a real bar fly and drinking himself stupid wasn't just something she'd made up to try to get us talking.

When I noticed him through the open door, the brightness in his eyes was gone. The strong, kind redwood of a man I thought I knew looked more like a soggy log. But the longer he stared, the more that spark returned, even if it was desperate and weak.

I almost felt sorry for him. Almost.

Maybe he regretted what he'd said to me. Hell, I didn't know.

Regrets didn't erase what happened. Any man who had his dick in someone else while pulling my strings wasn't the man for me. And I vowed I'd never become a whore for any man to pump and dump, including badass bullshitters who could probably do far more evil things with their tongues besides twist them up in lies.

I was done with him. I had to be. Anything less and I'd be crawling back to a cheater and a drunk.

My little meeting with cousin Mark was about to show me how badly my life was fucked. I just knew it. Still, it wasn't so crashed to pieces I was going to go running to *him*.

The doorbell rang just as I dumped the vodka into the pomegranate lemonade and gave it a good stir. I licked the spoon. It was tart, stupefyingly sweet. A bitter aftertaste crawled on my tongue when the sugar faded.

I shrugged. It would do. I hoped he sucked it down and got enough alcohol in his system to forget about any confrontations tonight.

The doorbell chimed again. I quick stepped through the house, pinching my arm to force on the biggest smile I could manage.

"Cousin!" False enthusiasm rankled my ears. "Come on in..."

Mark greeted me and followed me into the kitchen for the pitcher and some glasses. I guided him to the cool porch. If anything got too wild, then at least we were outside, where I could yell and put an end to this.

My cousin watched me drain the huge glass while he sipped at his gingerly. Damn, not much of a drinker after all, or at least not tonight...

"So tell me, cuz, how do you like working at the hospital?"

"It's a good gig. Gets a little stressful at times when the work really piles up. It's almost flu season, and they're telling us this year will bring in a lot of cases. Mostly old people and kids. Guess I'll be pulling double duty close to the holidays or I'd invite you back if you're heading home for Christmas."

He smiled. "I understand. How about the pay? Medical school must be expensive, yeah? I was reading an article the other day about how many poor bastards are up to their necks in student loans."

He clasped his hands and leaned forward. Those bright green Galena eyes were always a fearsome thing when they zeroed in on their target. I hoped I'd given Tank a look he'd never forget.

"Uh, I'm doing okay," I croaked. "Things were a little rough for awhile. I'd like to have a nicer place than this with a roof that's not five years overdue for a re-shingling. Lazy slum landlords, you know."

"Sure. One thing I'm not so sure about is how a girl like you paid off fifty four thousand in debt on a fifty one thousand annual salary. Pre-tax."

Holy shit. My heart plummeted, and the delicious buzz starting in my head from the vodka became a claustrophobic haze.

"What're you talking about?" I had to ask, had to stall, had to collect my wits.

He's got balls. Is this really happening?

"Got your credit report before I rolled into town," Mark continued. "It took a few favors with other bureaus, but you'd be amazed how easily personal data flows through the pipeline anymore. Listen, cuz, I hope you're planning to report that income on next year's tax return. The pitbulls at the IRS make most agents in my department look like poodles."

His smile was back, nastier and knowing. Slowly, he unfolded his hands, reaching for the lemonade and taking a long sip. He was waiting.

I realized I'd already made the worst mistake: having this asshole anywhere on my property without a lawyer. Well, I wasn't going to take his creepy BS laying down.

"Mark, what you're asking me is *none* of your fucking business. What did you really come here to talk about?" I was seething. The vodka gave me liquid courage, even if it fed the fire braising my stomach.

"I wanna know why you've fallen in with a really bad crowd, girl. What kind of man would I be to let his little cousin hang with thugs and terrorists? It's one thing to bring shame on the family. Quite another if you end up behind bars for ten years with some serious fucking felonies under your belt."

"You know about the Devils." I gripped the sides of my chair, trying to keep still. I wasn't sure which urge was worse – jumping up and running away, or raking my nails across his stupid fucking face.

The green eyes weren't familiar and comforting anymore. They were monstrous.

"Of course. That's why I'm here. Did you really think I came to Bumfuck, Montana just to reminisce about old times?" He turned his nose up. "I'm a very busy man."

"Busybody asshole, you mean," I muttered.

"Careful!" Mark held up a finger, his face wrinkling in a sneer. "I'm not the one making fat stacks with killers. And before you try to deny it, Emma, let me assure you the ATF has everything. Your business partners are like a plague creeping West. That piddly salary they pay you is nothing compared to the fifty million the club rakes in running drugs and guns up to Canada. You ought to ask for a raise."

I rolled my eyes. He'd showed his hand, and it didn't scare me. Not when he was just spouting crap with no teeth.

The bite will come, I thought. I just didn't know how.

My mind was reeling. The venom coursing through my veins stirred red hot anger. Was this what he wanted? Blind rage to make me screw up and let something juicy slip?

"Yeah, asshole?" I tried to say it calmly. "If you're so sure about them, then why don't you have the whole club in jail already?"

"We need some hard evidence. The men you work for are very good at covering their tracks. Plenty of contacts and corruption in the local police means they can kill, deal, and sew terror without paying for it. How else do you think they've gotten away with the insane body count they've racked up?"

I gritted my teeth. "You don't understand. They've never killed an innocent person to my knowledge. Only thugs who deserve it."

I thought about Maverick's old lady June, and Saffron too. Any of those girls would've spat in my cousin's face if they didn't gouge out his eyes first. The MC saved their lives.

They've proven themselves to me too, despite my early doubts and the souring with Tank. Before, I was pissed digesting his words, but now I was getting irate.

Jerking up, I knocked the tall glass to the floor. It fell with a loud thud, nearly shattering on the spot. Mark got up, walked over, and picked it up, studying the gaping crack in the side.

"Hm. Butterfingers." He raised his eyebrows, turning it over in his hands before he sat it on the banister just an inch from my hand. "Who knew you'd grow up to be such a clumsy, stupid bitch?"

I gasped. He kept coming, and I stepped back, running out of space after a few more steps. He must've seen me balling up a fist. He was cornering me, forcing me against the wooden enclosure around my porch.

I didn't care who the hell he was: cousin, ATF Special Agent, asshole! The way he moved his hand in his jacket, pushing the fabric aside, on the other hand...

My eyes landed on the gun in the holster near his hip. He tapped it with his pointer finger, deliberate and dangerous. Fear joined the anger bristling in my blood.

"Don't make me call for backup or do something really fucking crazy, cuz. I don't want anybody here getting hurt. That's the point of all this. I'm trying to help you help your stupid self."

"Help me what? What do you want?"

"Your cooperation." His face was like stone, frigid and merciless. "I could've taken this shit into my own hands and raided their clubhouse while you were there. Could've hauled you off to prison and blocked Aunt Mavis' calls while she screamed at me to bail your ass out. But that would've been the hard way. I'm offering you a chance to keep yourself out of this, and your momma too. All in exchange for getting me what I need to nail the Devils to the wall."

"I'm not doing shit for you! Even if I wanted to, do you think these guys will beat down my door to spill their guts about all the dirty things they've done? It's a brotherhood, cousin. What they say stays with them, and nobody else. If you weren't so fucking stupid and judgmental, you'd know that. You'd know they're brothers…"

He nodded briskly. "Stupid, huh? Yeah, I must be quite a retard to have your whole history in my file. That transaction report about your big bad loans? Just the beginning. I'm going to get that evidence one way or another, cuz. If you don't help me out, then one of those fuckers will slip up or kill somebody out in the open before they can bury the evidence. It's just a matter of time."

My breaths were coming slower, shallower, ragged. Despite the cool, crisp autumn air, I couldn't get enough oxygen with him so close, smothering everything. I reached out, no longer thinking about the gun, and pushed against his chest as hard as I could.

"Get the fuck away from me!"

Surprised, he stumbled backward. When he steadied himself, he started to laugh. Jesus, was this really the same boy who used to giggle while me and my other cousins played hide and seek? What the hell happened?

"Just keep fucking with me, Emma. I'll make sure you exchange those baby blue scrubs for some bright orange.

You know the women's prisons out here are horseshit. Nothing but junkies and girls who chopped off their hubbies dicks after taking one too many busted lips. Hope you're staying single. Because by the time you come out, chewed up and fucked, no sane man'll ever want anything to do with you."

I shook my head. If only a nod or a few tears would open up a hole and make him disappear. I pinched my eyes closed and saw scarlet red. When I opened them again, he was closer, looming over me, one hand on the banister next to me.

"I'll give you tonight to do some real hard thinking. We'll see if you can make a smart choice for once in your shitty life. If I have to put you behind bars with your nasty fucking bosses, I will, and I'll tell Aunt Mavis exactly why well before the trial. Think it over."

I couldn't help it. I broke down and started to cry. There was nothing worse – *nothing* – than imagining my mother's heartbreak when she found out I was working for a motorcycle gang. I was supposed to be the *good* daughter, the well educated nurse who'd gone to college and came out a pro, not reduced to working retail or stripping like my sister Katie.

Wherever the hell she was. Mom sent her packing when she found out sis was doing drugs and working at the old Grizzlies' strip club, the Dirty Diamond. I was grateful she was gone. At least asshole Mark went after me to poach bikers, and not my little sis.

"Think hard, Emma," he said again, gradually moving away. "Give me a call when you've made up your mind. Oh, and don't get any bright ideas about tipping off your friends. The penalties for interfering with a federal investigation on a domestic terror group are brutal, I'm told. Hope you wisen up and help me serve some justice."

He pulled a business card out of his wallet and stuck it in a crack on the old banister. Then he began to go, walking toward his car in the distant shadows.

"I don't care what you want, asshole!" I yelled after him. "Don't come near me again. I'll come to you."

Would I? He'd made his threats perfectly clear.

One thing was certain: any man who showed up to torment family was capable of anything.

I stood on the porch, waiting for him to go. I was so focused on watching him get into his car I didn't see the huge shadow stepping out until it was too late.

Tank was the worst person in the world I could've seen just then, and the bastard also picked the worst possible time. My heart thumped against my ribs and I went off, trying to escape him with a warning, sick to death at all my nightmares rampaging onto my doorstep.

When that didn't work, I beamed hot death and laid into him. I told him all the sick, fucked up, poisonous things I'd wanted to say since I found out he was fucking a whore. I was absolutely done being torn up and abused by other assholes.

Tank, the club, cousin Mark…

The last one had his claws in me from the very start. He didn't wait to lay in, using me without any disguises.

Damned if I was going to let anybody else shred me on my way to disgrace or prison or God only knew what. I turned around, and told the asshole squeezing my arm exactly what would happen. I seized the one thing I could control and let him have it, forecasting the whole miserable future, the one that would never, ever include him.

I am not your girlfriend. I'm not your co-worker. I'm not even your friend. And I'll sure as hell never be your old lady.

The words echoed in my head long after he gave me that look like I'd just shot him in the chest.

Good. Now he understood what he did to me, exactly why I never wanted to see his stupid cheating face around here again.

He took off, leaving me alone. I crashed to the ground, slumping with my hands on my face. My practical side wondered if I was going to have a stroke.

Outside, his motorcycle blasted to life, tearing through the darkness like a thundering wraith.

"Fuck!"

I was alone. So totally screwed and alone, facing a doomsday decision that meant the end of the life I knew no matter where it lead.

Play along. Play stupid. Play him.

The words were rolling around in my head when I cracked my eyes open. I couldn't have slept more than two hours the whole night, and now I had a full shift ahead at the hospital.

I was sore, every muscle ringing with pain. None of it worse than the heartache Tank's visit left behind.

Shaking, I reached for my phone near the bed. The water bottle was next. I stared at my phone while I pumped cool nourishment into my system, fighting the hangover pounding in my temples. My stomach growled.

Burning. Empty. Pissed off.

I ran for the bathroom. Every nurse knows that nausea when it hits with no return. Jamming my fingers down my throat, I leaned over the toilet and let loose, spilling bile.

I let go of everything and collapsed when it was over. Strange that becoming emptier made me feel better.

My stomach had a couple minutes to rest, and then I sipped more water. Nothing about the shit to come was going to be easy.

Just like this hangover, I had to force the pain out faster, anything to get it over with. There was no point in prolonging the inevitable. I wasn't a tattle by nature, and I wasn't going to become one now.

I couldn't rat out the club, but I couldn't let Mark come down like a soulless avalanche. I reached for the phone, squeezing the card he'd given me in my free hand as I punched in the number. It went straight to voicemail.

"Mark? It's Emma. You're a bastard…but I'll do it. I'll try to get you whatever you need. But I want proof you're granting full immunity." I paused and swallowed bitterness. "And I need you to take your shit after we're done and get the hell out. Call me. I'll be working six to three today."

There. Done.

I'd bought myself a world of pain, but I'd bought myself some time too. There was practically no chance anyone was going to come out of this unscathed.

As long as I had that chance, however miniscule, I was going to take it. The club had treated me well. Whatever the government thought, they weren't just violent outlaws and killers. The Devils were the only thing between this town and far worse demons.

I'd give the man his damned evidence. Just not the kind that would lead him anywhere besides chasing his own tail.

A couple days later, I was called to the clubhouse. Mark met me as I got off my shift at the hospital and helped wire listening devices. One went under my belt, and another was in the purse, tiny black things that were supposed to send their recordings straight to his server.

I barely said anything. Wasn't sure what was worse: the horrible deception I was about to lay on the club, or having his filthy hands all over me.

When he was done, I drove in.

Saffron sat at her bar, an old rag wrapped tight around her hand. Blaze was next to her. Mixed anger and relief flashed in his eyes as I approached.

"Here she is!" he said, taking a few steps to meet me. "Christ, woman. What the fuck took you so long? She's hurt!"

"Sorry. Lead nurse held me over a few minutes too long." I stepped past him, in no mood for his attitude. "Come on, Saffron. Let's get you into the infirmary."

Her face was tight with pain. At first, I figured it wasn't going to be anything major. When I sat her down on the stainless steel table and unwrapped her hand, blood gushed down her palm, seeping out of a nasty cut straight across her whole hand.

"Holy shit! What happened?"

"Late fucking night. The boys were having fun and drinks. Guess I had one too many last night too. When I got in, the place was a mess. Some asshole left his pint glass higher than I could reach on the storage shelves. I tried to get up there and grab it with an empty box. The damned thing broke. I slipped, hit the shelf underneath it, and now I've got glass splinters embedded in the hand with my ring!" She looked down, wiggling her fingers slowly.

When Saffron saw the blood smeared on her gold engagement ring, her face wrinkled. "Shit! That's a bad omen if I've ever seen one!"

"Calm down." I pulled up the stool next to her, antiseptic and gauze in hand. "We'll clean you up. The ring should be fine. There's no need to get superstitious here. You know Blaze isn't going anywhere."

"Easy for you to say, miss smarty-pants! Things've been too quiet around here lately. I've got a really bad feeling about the boys going off and patching over the other club. Blaze says it'll be okay, but the danger is all in what he's not saying. I've been here long enough to read between the lines. Yeah, yeah, club business. I know. I – ouuuch!"

She doubled over dramatically as I splashed the wound and rubbed alcohol around it. The pain savaged her before she could say anything incriminating to the stupid bugs hooked to me.

If anything would distract her, it was this.

Took my full attention to hold her hand open, watching the clean wound. She was a borderline case for stitches. I chewed my lip.

"Holy fucking shit, girl! Why couldn't you *warn* me first? Brings back bad memories of that night with the Grizzlies. I don't think the cigar burns hurt half as much as having you pour that crap on this cut."

"No?" I raised an eyebrow, trying to keep her focused on benign things. "Hands have some of the most sensitive skin on the body. Fortunately for you, this'll be over quick."

I decided against stitches. Instead, I carefully finished wiping the cut and shook her wrist until she relaxed, allowing me to wind clean gauze around it.

Saffron held up her newly bandaged hand and wrinkled her nose. "Still hurts like hell. Don't I get any cool drugs out of the deal?"

"You sure do." I walked over to the bin where we kept the medicine stockpile.

Picking up a bottle, I tossed it to her. Saffron fumbled, cursing as the bottle stopped rolling around in her lap. The bum hand made it a lot more challenging than it sounds.

She looked at me, brow furrowed. "You know, Em, your bedside manner's in the toilet lately. What's up? Is it whatever the hell's going on with you and Tank?"

I shook my head. No way was I getting into this here and now. Not when I needed to capture something mundane on tape to keep my dickhead cousin off my neck for another day.

"Just busy. That's all." I kept my words short and sweet. "Overtired and overstressed between this place and work."

"You can't BS me, now, nurse." Saffron laughed. "I'd be an idiot if I hadn't sharpened my ears after all the crap I've been through this last year. Tell me straight. What's wrong? It's got to be him."

My lips twitched. I suddenly had the overwhelming urge to break down and spill everything: Tank's betrayal, the tension at the hospital, the asshole blackmailing me who just so happened to share my DNA and a direct line to mom, who'd never stop seeing me as less than an angel until the bitter end.

"Here's your Tylenol. Prescription strength. Should take the edge off nicely, Saffron." I paused. "Oh, you don't want to be drinking with this stuff. But I think you already know that. You had your fill during burn recovery."

"You don't have to tell me twice. I'm not doing a lot of that anyway with the wedding coming up. My stupid brother put me off benders too." Her lips twitched bitterly.

She'd barely heard from her vanished sibling since the showdown with the rogue Grizzlies. Saffron was still upset about him taking off and going back to the club that had brought so much carnage to the Devils and many more.

Her good hand jerked out, caught mine, and pulled hard as she stood up. "I can't drink. But you can. Let's go to the bar."

"But I still have –"

"All kinds of crap you can do perfectly well with something sexy purring in your system. The brothers aren't going on any runs today. I'm pretty sure nobody's going to come home with a scraped knee or a bullet in the leg. Come on. You need something to soothe that bad juju."

I swallowed the lump in my throat, looking down nervously at the recorder clipped to my belt. I was the only one who knew it was there, but the damned thing was listening, capturing every juicy little detail for Mark's ears later.

I couldn't fight. Saffron sat me down and moved surprisingly quick for a girl who'd just sliced her hand open. I wagged my finger at her as she pushed my favorite tall beer across the counter.

"Go easy on that hand. Blaze should have the prospects covering for you the rest of today."

"Already done, Em." She leaned across the counter, a bright, worried sheen in her eyes. "I'm not working right now. I'm talking to a friend."

I almost choked on my citrus sweet brew. Shit, the woman knew how to pull on the old heartstrings. No joke.

"Tell me what's going on. I've tried to coax the truth out of Tank before but the big dummy keeps his mouth shut way too well. What did he *do?*"

Crap! I definitely didn't want the recorder to hear this. I scraped my glass loudly on the counter and swiveled my chair, tucking my shirt a little tighter, anything to put an extra layer between my voice and the bug. Probably wouldn't work, but at least it would make me feel better.

"He cheated." Saffron's eyebrows went up. "He fucked me over when I thought he was finally coming around. Turns out he's just like the others here. I don't know why I thought different. Tank's no different than Stinger, Smokey, Stone, and all the rest, drinking and whoring his life away."

I shuddered. The pain was really starting to put the squeeze on my heart. Shaking my head, I reached for her good hand when she offered it. Saffron squeezed my fingers tight.

"You gotta be shitting me, girl. Are you *sure* that's what happened? I'm here all the time and I've never seen Tank drooling over any woman except you."

Damn. That made it even worse. He'd done it in private, away from me and the old ladies and even his own brothers.

Despicable bastard, I thought. *How could I have ever been so delusional? How could I have thought I loved you?*

"He told me so himself. It was right after your mom's funeral, before all the other crap came down." I was pissed, sick to tears, but I managed to keep my words vague for the mic. "He said he fucked that slutty blonde who's here full time. Marianne."

Her name tasted like ash on my tongue. God, if I could've just banished her from my head forever, I would've done it. And Tank's filthy ass too. Imagining them together knotted my intestines like nothing else.

"That slut!" Saffron showed her teeth. "She sleeps around a lot, yeah. Kind of her job. I thought she was one of the better ones. Always seemed to keep to herself when the boys aren't coming to her. It took me a long time to stop eyeballing the bitch around Blaze after he claimed me, but I never saw her make a move on him. Not once."

There's a lot that goes on here even old ladies don't know, I thought.

Her words weren't any consolation. I gulped the beer, pouring it down my throat until the carbonation hurt, desperate to blast away the panic, hate, and shame clawing at my chest.

"Hasn't he talked to you?" Saffron straightened up, wincing as she put pressure on her bandaged hand. "I mean, he's here at the bar a lot, drinking all alone. Fucking sad sack. He's been like that ever since the fight at the –"

"Let's not talk about that." I wasn't sure which was harder: blinking back tears or being constantly paranoid one of us would slip up and give Mark what he needed.

Saffron blinked. "You're right. It's ancient history now. What I want to know is what you plan to do about this."

"Do?" My turn to blink like a fool.

What could I possibly do about him, or any of this? I wasn't going to say it, but I wanted to.

If only I could've ripped off the mic and told Saffron how fucked I really was. Not to mention how damned stupid. Any sane woman would've thrown a cheating man to the wolves, and her wounded heart with him.

Not me. Tank's dagger hurt, and it was still there too, far more than the dangerous family betrayal Mark sprang on me.

"Yeah. Aren't you going to talk to him? Give him a big damned piece of your mind?"

My heart sank. I remembered our last conversation earlier that week, right after he caught me following the fight with Mark. I'd told him exactly where to go.

"I already did. The idiot came to my house a few days ago. Don't know why he followed me home in the first place. It was a really bad time...family stuff I don't want to talk about. I laid into him and told him to stay the hell away. I let him know I wanted nothing to do with him ever again."

I clanked my glass. God, I needed a refill.

Saffron pursed her lips. "Hm. Something doesn't add up. All Tank ever talked about was keeping you safe. He told me so while I was getting my last tat for Blaze, and that was *after* he supposedly did the dirty deed with the slut."

"I don't know." I shrugged.

"No, neither do I. I'm not going to let this go, Em. Don't get it myself. I'm going to find out exactly what the hell's going on around here…"

Saffron turned, exited the bar, and took off down the hall.

"Wait! Where are you going?" I called after her, but she wasn't stopping.

Shit. I hadn't even gotten that refill before she started to move.

I stared glumly around the bar, wondering why the place was so damned empty today. The door to the garages was wide open, as it usually was. I got up and walked over slowly, leaving the bar's low classic rock thumping in the background.

When I was closer, I heard voices. Unmistakably male.

Carefully, I peeked outside. Several guys stood in a small group around their bikes, a big crate in the middle. Blaze, Tank, Moose, and Roller were all there, along with a man I didn't recognize.

"Well, let's see it, Bolt," Blaze said. "I'd really like to know why Throttle's telling us to be so fucking careful with this shipment."

The skinny stranger who had to be Bolt kneeled, crowbar in hand, grunting as he pried open the lid. I gasped when I saw what was inside. So did everybody else – and it took a lot to surprise men in this club.

Shaking, my hand tore at my belt, desperate to switch the damned thing off. Mark told me to leave it on at all times, but I could make excuses later. I had to if I didn't want to rat everybody else out.

The pile of bazookas was so incriminating it would've gotten every Devil rounded up coast to coast.

"Fucking-A! Christ!" Blaze circled the arsenal, prowling around it like a wolf.

Tank looked on coldly. Moose laughed and shook his head. Roller ran a tense hand through his spiky crew cut, eyes ready to pop out of his strong young head, plucking at his lip ring.

"Un-be-fucking-lievable!" Blaze sputtered again. "What the fuck's going on in Dakota? I was cool running autos and ammunition and all the usual stuff...didn't think we were getting into the business of transporting shit to shoot down fighter jets!"

"It's for armored columns, boss." Tank looked up. "That's the official function, anyway. Anti-tank units souped up after the Cold War. Uncle Sam's got way too many of these in stockpile and nobody to dance with, unless the Russians or Chinese lose their damned minds. It's not real useful in the brush fire wars. Terrorists don't have tanks."

"Real shitty timing too, Prez. We've got that thing with the Rams tomorrow." Moose shifted, heavy on his feet. I could practically feel the stress building hot acid in his gut.

"Tell me about it! I don't need any reminders, asshole." Blaze circled tighter, angrier, beaming hatred at the weapons piled on the ground.

"It'll be all right. I just need two of your guys to keep the truck safe. Throttle couldn't spare anybody for escort duty. That's why he's asking for direct escort from our Montana bros for this shipment," Bolt said, standing up and putting the lid down. "Those are the units. All stacked up in one pretty box, instruction manuals and everything."

"What about the fireworks?" Tank said.

"We're letting those chill in the truck," Bolt said. "The less moving missiles around when they don't need to move, the better. We just gotta take it to port in Tacoma like usual. Got a freighter waiting for us from Malaysia. They'll take it from there, and pay up too."

"Damn. We're turning into a real international business. Didn't see that coming." Moose smiled and looked up at Tank.

The giant who ripped my heart out just glared, silently shaking his head. If he had any wild opinions about it, he was keeping them to himself.

"Well, fuck," Blaze growled. "This is something I ought to call Throttle about myself and find out what the hell he's doing, but we don't have time for that. If the Rams get pissy or – hell – the Grizzlies catch wind of what's moving through their territory, all our asses will be in a whole heap of trouble. Truce or no truce." He turned to Bolt and took several steps forward, looming over him. "I want this shit gone tonight. Drive the graveyard shift if you have to. You asked for two guys? I'll give you three."

He pointed. "Roller. Go get Smokey and Stone. This is a damned good chance for those boys to earn their patches."

"Holy shit. Me, Prez?" Roller tapped his cut in disbelief. "You know I don't have any combat experience like our brother here…"

Tank stared glumly. Blaze walked up to Roller and slapped his shoulder. "No, bro, don't pussy out on this. Tank's got more important shit to do with the rest of us tomorrow. Come on, Roller. I'm trusting your ass."

"Emma!" Saffron tapped me on the shoulder.

I nearly went through the ceiling. Spinning around to face her, I came face-to-face with Marianne, the whore who'd crashed my world apart, everything I'd wanted with Tank. My hands wrestled near my pockets, struggling to flip the recorder back on.

If I was going to throw my asshole cousin a bone, then it was better he got a bunch of filthy personal shit than anything that might incriminate the club.

Saffron had her good hand on the bitch's arm like she was hauling around a bratty girl. The blonde slut was in her robe, an annoyed look clouding her face. She didn't look half as pretty without her makeup.

"I brought this bitch over so you can hear it from the horse's mouth." Saffron jerked at her arm. "Go ahead! Tell her what you just told me."

Snarling, Marianne twisted her hand, tearing away from Saffron's grip. "Fuck you, bitch! I'm not under your damned control and I don't owe anyone anything. First you wake me up and haul my ass out here like I'm some kinda criminal. Now you want me to talk to this stupid nurse?"

Saffron wasn't taking her shit. I jumped out of the way just in time as Blaze's old lady plowed into the slut and pushed her to the wall.

"Fuck! Bitch! I'm gonna fuck you up!" Marianne clawed, trying to get momentum. She thrashed at Saffron's arms and caught her hand.

I watched her overpainted fingernails slide across the bandage. Saffron shrieked, mad rage building in her eyes as she went for the whore's hair with her good hand. She pulled so hard the bitch kicked, and they both went to the ground.

"Jesus fucking Christ!" Moose burst through the door. The other guys were right behind him.

When Blaze saw me looking on aghast at the two women rolling and hissing on the ground, he ran. "Fucking shit! Stop, baby. Get off that fucking whore!"

Blaze dragged her back while Moose went for Marianne. Pulling them apart was just as bad as separating two wild animals determined to claw each other to tatters.

Behind them, Tank, Bolt, and Roller watched, ready to step in. Funny, in its own twisted way, to see all these badasses lined up to keep a few crazy girls from bringing the whole clubhouse down.

"This slut started it!" Saffron growled. "Takes a pretty stupid fucking slut to attack an old lady."

"Bitch!" Marianne spat. I got caught in the mist and wiped my face, wondering how many nasty germs were crawling over me, even with her constant screenings. "You're the one who dragged me out of bed! All over some shit that's none of your goddamned business."

"Shut up!" Blaze roared. He turned to Saffron, a tenderness behind his fury. "What the hell's she talking about, baby? Is she telling the truth?"

"I don't owe you shit. What went down with *him* is our secret. Not yours and not this damned quack's!" Marianne pointed to Tank. Her eyes darted to Saffron, Blaze, me.

"You'd better start talking, lady." Moose reached up and jerked on her hair. "Tell us what the fuck's happening here. Don't forget this is our fucking clubhouse, and you just clawed up a brother's old lady. You got no fucking right to *anything*."

Blaze nodded. "He's right. Don't let all the fucking you do in that room go to your head, bitch. You're nothing, here for my boys' pleasure. That's it. Any girl who's been claimed will *always* mean more than your overstretched pussy."

My eyes went to Tank. His huge chest was rising and falling in big waves behind his cut. The bastard was nervous about something.

Fuck it. I had to get to the bottom of this.

Before anyone could jump and hold me back, I stomped forward, looking straight through Marianne as I reached up and slapped her across the face. Hard.

The whore's jaw dropped. Her whole face twitched, rage and sadness dashed with cold shock.

"Spit it out, you bitch. We don't have all day."

Roller's hands were on my shoulders before I knew it. He pulled firmly until I took a step back.

I let out a heavy sigh, cheeks on fire.

Mark was going to have a field day with this. Whatever. I'd kept my word, and the only drama he was going to get would be useless to the Feds.

"Okay!" Marianne shrieked at last, slowing her next breaths as Moose gave her hair another warning tug. "Okay, okay, okay…you want the fucking honest-to-God truth?"

She looked up. All the brothers were watching as she stared me down, clearing her throat like it was full of mud. Tank's eyes were fixed on her, tight like they were about to explode.

"Tank and I never did shit. The only time he came to me was for a massage after his workouts. He never saw me naked once except when I was next to Stinger, napping in between lays. One day, this giant bastard comes –"

Blaze interrupted, raising a finger. "Watch your fucking tongue. You talk like that about a brother again, and your ass is gone."

She sniffed. "He comes in with a stack of bills when everybody's moping around. He still had his cane. He told me we'd been fucking all day, ordered me to lie to anybody who asked. He paid me to bullshit." Marianne shrugged. "Easy money, so I took it. Not half as fun as it really would've been riding his cock, though."

I closed my eyes, a big vein twitching in my temple. When they popped open, I wanted to throw myself at her, claw the bitch to pieces for doing this and fucking with Saffron's cut. But deep down inside, I knew the whore didn't deserve it.

The only fucker who deserved hell for his stupid, stupid mistake was staring right at me. I jerked, broke Roller's hold, and ran. I heard his boots pounding the floor, coming to catch me, but Blaze yelled first.

"Let her go!" He growled. "Man, fuck this sideshow. I'd call Marianne a worthless bitch for what she's done, but I wonder if maybe you deserve it more, Tank."

Tank. No. No, no, no...

My legs hurt, overwhelmed with the crazy emotions surging through me. I was almost to my car when I heard his voice.

"Emma! Fucking wait! Let me explain this shit..."

I threw myself in and left my seat belt off. I had to get going, had to get away from all this before I lost my mind. By some strange miracle, my hands jabbed the key into the ignition in one jerk, and I floored it. If the gate wasn't open for the truck with the weapons, I would've crashed right through it, tearing away as fast as I could.

So, that was it. The asshole lied to me. He *had* betrayed me – just not the way I thought. And now my stupid brain was trying to decide if this was better or worse than having his dick inside that nasty fucking bitch.

I never understood how I got my car home without running straight off the road or plowing into another car. My eyes were so teared up I couldn't see the mountains, the only things that never changed in this screwed up, brutal world.

When I got home, the first thing I did was fling open my purse and switch the damned bug off. I'd left it in the infirmary the whole time, so that one didn't pick up anything except my conversation with Saffron.

My phone had been ringing off the hook. Half a dozen missed messages from Saffron. One from Blaze's burner phone.

I slammed it on the counter. I'd leave a message for Saffron later about caring for her hand, but that was it. Slumping against the wall, my hands went for my belt, trying to work off the stupidly tight clasp to get the recorder off.

I was so distracted I didn't hear the motorcycle roar in until it was right on top of me.

Damn! What now?

Muttering and shaking my head, I stomped to the door, wondering if Blaze and Saffron had followed after all. If they had, I was determined to tell them both to lay the hell off. Let me have my space. Right now, the club was aiming all its drama in my direction. Saffron's injury was minor enough to count me out.

Sure, I signed up to treat everything and stay on call. But I never agreed to having my heart torn out on a daily basis and hearing different stories from an asshole crush and a biker skank.

The locks clicked open and I yanked the door open. There was no mistaking Tank's huge shape for anyone in the early autumn darkness.

"Can I come in? We need to fucking talk, babe." He had one hand on the door.

Something told me if I said no, he'd tear the flimsy screen right off and climb in anyway. Fury beat thick in my heart, reverberating to the furthest corners of my body. God, why was it always such a shock to see him?

I couldn't remember a time when I'd ever looked at Tank and felt anything less than agonizing pain or giddy hope. He was a living, breathing, tattooed drug. Like any other drug, he was bad for me, even when he felt amazing. And despite my best efforts, he just kept finding his way home, no matter how we tried to keep our space.

I shrugged. "Fine."

His intense mask slipped. Surprise glowed in his eyes, but he wasn't wasting any time. The door jerked open and he stepped in.

I didn't retreat. There was no fighting this anymore, no brakes on this crazy fucking train slamming straight into my life, wrecking what little I had left. My fists were shaking at my sides as I forced myself to look at him.

Look, damn you. Really, really look.

"What happened back there was fucked up," he said, coming closer. "You were never supposed to know. I should've known better than to trust a filthy whore."

"Oh, you mean you know how it feels to have somebody feed you bullshit?"

Anger flashed on his huge, handsome face, and then boiled back, leaving sad acceptance. "Never meant to hurt you, Em. You gotta know that's the last goddamned thing in the world I'd ever want. You were supposed to keep away from me, forget my ass, live your life without getting shredded by my violence and hurt…"

Wow. How was it possible for a man to talk like he was so damned concerned and be so oblivious simultaneously?

I shook my head. "You don't get it, do you, Tank? I was *ready* for you. Ready for the stupid club too and your place there, despite the things about it that scared the hell out of me. I can face my fears. You're the one who can't."

Oh, that pissed him off. He stepped forward, his huge body driving me several clumsy steps backward, and then against the wall. But Tank kept coming, only stopping when he hovered over me, the six foot plus giant he was.

"If any man called me a coward in the line of duty, I'd knock his fucking teeth out." He paused, nostrils flaring, snorting a sharp breath. Then we locked eyes. "Just between you and me, you're goddamned right. Don't know why I can't just let go, walk away, make us both forget about all this shit for good. With you, babe, I'm a fucking chump *and* a coward. I can't stand thinking about you getting hurt, but I can't stay the fuck away either. I don't even know what the fuck's going through my splitting, bleeding skull anymore, not since you put your fire there and made it burn through bone."

He raised his arms and slapped his fists gently on the wall. It was like a gigantic, frustrated lion standing over me. Except this lion was the most beautiful creature I'd ever seen. I had to think hard just to keep breathing.

Big mistake. Whenever I sucked in a breath, my lungs were filled with him, that divine mix of spice, sweat, and engine oil that always swirled around him.

"Truth is, I'm confused as hell. Not just because I'm scared of some asshole throwing you on his bike and keeping you ransom – or doing something worse like what those fucking jackals did to Saffron. I'm scared shitless you'll take over every atom in my body. It'll all be yours, babe, and I won't be able to do a goddamned thing. If you're on my mind like this right now, then what the hell would it be like if you were mine?"

Hot energy seethed inside me. I was shaking, overheated, losing myself in the churning blood surging through every capillary. Every glance his way sent lava pumping through my veins and fire in my panties. My heart beat so ragged with want and hate and need I thought it was going to breakdown right there and leave me collapsing in his massive tattooed arms.

Not the worst way to go. Or was it?

He was conflict incarnate. So frustrating and so damned irresistible at once, everything I wanted and everything I should've had the good sense to avoid.

What kind of woman does this? How could I possibly want anything to do with him after he'd lied to me? But how could I ever let him go when hot, wet, and desperate didn't begin to describe what blew up inside me every fucking time I was in his presence?

I felt like I was losing my mind. Tank was frustrated too, his huge chest rising and falling just inches away from me. Neither of us had the words for the harsh lightning building between us.

Energy came, hot and swift, magnetic and mad. It did the talking, all pheromones and blood, especially when it zipped up my thighs and stopped, pulsing in my center.

"Look at me, babe. You understand what I'm trying to tell you?"

His arm slid down, hand open. He gently laid it on my head and reached his fingers out, tracing my jawline, stopping on my chin.

Don't look. Don't look. Don't look!

The mantra was worthless. When Tank lifted my head, I dove into his eyes, surrendering to their honey hued tides.

"I'm trying to tell you how fucking sorry I am for everything I've done. I was too damned stupid to realize *I* was the only threat you had all along, the only bastard hurting you. I'm the one who wasted all this time, constantly trying to push you away, blasting my fucked up brain with Jack 'til I hoped I wouldn't wake up the next day with your ghost in my skull..."

I shivered, fighting back tears. He wasn't lying. Everything he did hurt like hell, but then *he* suffered too. God, how he'd suffered, a good man turned into a cold, lifeless drunk all because we were apart.

"Let me tell you something else," he continued, his voice a firm whisper. "Everything I fucked up, I'm gonna set right. I promise, babe, and I'm swearing now like I've never sworn on anything in my whole damned life. I can't have your beautiful body dancing in my head twenty-four seven anymore, knowing I can never reach out, touch you, fuck you."

My eyes went wide. I knew how bad he wanted it – both of us – but now he'd said it. For the first time, he'd admitted how much he wanted his hard slab of a body pressed up against mine, a hot boulder crashing over me, driving deep.

The fever in my veins went from smoldering to inferno. I pushed my tongue against the roof of my mouth and tried not to pant, too stupid with desire for words.

Jesus, did I ever have a single prayer? The way lust instantly decimated my anger screamed *no*, and now I was falling into him, lost in his words, his power, his delicious musk.

"I never fucked a whore and I ever will again. How could I drop down to that after tasting your lips? It's like going back to crude fucking moonshine after sipping smooth Kentucky booze. You hear me, babe? You understand what I'm saying?" He sucked in a deep breath, curling his hand behind my neck. "Don't tell me no. You do that, you better get Blaze on the line. Somebody's gonna have to haul my ass away in a straight jacket, wrapped up like a fucking mummy, if you tell me all these little love bites are never gonna lead to the whole damned feast."

His hand went down, tracing my spine, rubbing the soft fabric of my shirt. Heat darted beneath my skin, spreading everywhere he touched.

Mindless. Consuming. Wild.

Insatiable.

I pulled forward, leaning into him. The energy between us was wrapped around my neck like a leash, and I couldn't resist his sexy gravity a second longer.

Tank was ready. So was I.

His lips crashed into mine. As soon as they did, the fire shot to my head, only to hit the ceiling and go racing back down again. I didn't know it was possible to feel so damned wet and hot at once until his tongue plunged into my mouth.

He kissed me deep, twining his tongue with mine, and then veering back to brush past my lips again and again and again. He was *already* fucking me, mouth to mouth, dirty and delightful.

I turned into aching mush in his hands. Tank caught me as I started to slip, moaning into his mouth. The little noises only seemed to feed him. Soon, he was pouring his hot breath into me, fanning the flames in my depths.

His body crashed forward, pinning me to the wall. Both his hands caught my ass and squeezed. When he had his feel, he grunted, satisfied but still so needy.

My hips rolled against his. His nasty, nasty tongue wasn't enough. The new shock hit him and he broke the two minute kiss, sucking in sorely needed air.

"Fuck! No more teases, babe. This cat and mouse shit's gone on way too fucking long. I'm gonna show you something you'll never forget. I'm gonna fuck you senseless, Em. Every inch. Every damned nerve. Every rosy, pink little tip of your skin's gonna sing for me."

He fell to his knees, hitting the wooden floor with a loud bang. I gasped as he hugged my legs and pulled me tight, throwing my hands on his shoulders for support.

"I'm claiming you now, babe. Long overdue, so fucking long. Need to mark my place right between your thighs. And when I stake what's mine, there's no going back. I don't give a shit if we still have issues. We'll work them out, hot and wet and sticky. Flesh speaks louder and truer than any words ever will."

I spun back against the wall as he reached around. His strong hands began tugging on my pants, faster and swifter than any man I'd been with before. Tank obviously knew his way around, or else his confidence put to shame all the boys I'd bedded before.

Right here, right now, this was a *man*.

For one terrifying second, I feared he'd brush the stupid wire still clipped to my belt. If he found it, I was a whole different kind of fucked.

But no, he skimmed past, missing it. His thumb popped my clasp and my zipper went down. He grabbed both sides of my hips and pulled, unwrapping me, baring me to him.

Sweet, cool autumn air kissed my legs as my pants fell. I moved to step out of them, trying to get out of the hot mess and into the cool, before he bathed me in fire all over again.

"Fuck, babe. Don't move a muscle. You're so fucking wet…" One hand went between my thighs and spread, cupping my mound through the thin soaked fabric. "Stay still. We don't need to go anywhere 'til I deal with this sweet fucking pussy…"

"Tank, no, I need to –"

He wasn't taking anymore denials. No ifs, no ands, no buts.

Growling, he jerked my panties down in one swift pull by the sopping wet gusset, leaving me exposed, naked and shamefully dripping.

Finally, I was beginning to understand what it meant to be *claimed*.

Tank's face pushed deep, straight between my legs. His stubble ranked my thighs on his way up, kissing and licking and ravishing my skin. My legs started to shake. Little whimpers escaped my mouth.

Men were supposed to be the ones who had to worry about coming too quickly, dammit. But here I was, terrified I was going to go to pieces the instant his mouth landed on my clit.

Good thing it wasn't a long wait.

My thighs convulsed, locking around his head as he pushed his tongue in, diving for the slick, wet center. His tongue snaked across my folds, teasing at first. Each lick against my velvet heat got faster, stronger, harder.

Oh, God. My fingers tensed on his huge shoulders. He seemed to like the sharp sting of my nails through his leather cut, moving his head from side to side, deeper into my pulsing core.

The fire was rising up in great waves now. A few more strokes, and there would be no containing it.

Damn him for being so right.

All the pain, all the heartache, all the longing died in this orgasm, this reset. My whole body tensed up and my lungs pumped, desperate to funnel precious air into my trembling body. I was melting down on his face.

My greedy hips shifted, pumping my pussy against his lips, preparing for the way he'd finally fuck me. I couldn't imagine his cock if his tongue was this good, all talent and strength in one handsome bundle, the same as the rest of him.

I didn't dare look down until the fiery end. Just before my eyes rolled back, I pushed one hand through his short spiky hair, feeling him growl against my clit. One touch on my nub and his tongue spread out.

Thick. Demanding. Just like the heat pouring out his eyes.

Come, babe. Let me wring your fucking body out and fill it up with pleasure. Let go.

I didn't hear the words. I felt them, rippling through my flesh, all his commands. I jerked and doubled over as the fire turned hot, wrapping around me and squeezing tight.

When I came, I saw stars, and then white hot nothing. Peaceful, and so fucking perfect.

My brain shut down and wouldn't feel anything else except the ecstasy flooding me. Tank's hot tongue never let up, not for a single second, thrashing more licks around my clit as I gushed and convulsed.

I was a whimpering, lost mess. All the pent up juju came flooding out, electrifying every muscle, banishing all the bad things that went down before.

I was still shaking and groaning lightly when he pulled away. Cool air snapped against the firestorm he'd left on my skin, except for the places where his lips gingerly stamped my skin, working their way up.

He held me, making sure I could stand on my own two feet. When he was on his, I wrapped my arms around him, throwing my face against his broad chest.

"Tank," I whispered.

Nothing else. All I needed was him and that sharp one syllable word.

"Fuck, babe. Love the way you stick to my lips." He flattened one hand on the small of my back and jerked me forward, lifting my legs out of my fallen clothes as he pulled me up into his arms. "*Now,* it's time to leave that shit behind. We're going upstairs."

"Mmmm!" I grabbed for his neck, loving the way he cradled me like I was weightless.

The raging fire he'd dashed only a minute ago was back, beating louder than ever in my blood. My inner whore surfaced, the bad girl I'd always wanted to be. I dug my fingernails into his neck, craning for another kiss.

Tank and I locked tongues as he carried me up, straight to my room. It wasn't much. The club's recent cash infusion hadn't changed my spartan life much at all yet with so much going to the loans.

But it was plenty fine for what was going to happen next. I let my legs hang, gently bobbing my feet, brushing his side.

Halfway up the stairs, he broke his kiss and stopped. "Damn, babe. You kiss me again like that, and I'm gonna take you right here on the stairs, sixty degrees high and balls deep."

I licked my lips and resisted the wicked temptation to do what he asked. Tank doubled the last few steps, heading straight for my room. Inside, he kicked the door shut with one foot.

Spinning, I slipped from his grasp and padded on the floor. He swooped in, pressing me up against the wall next to my dresser, smothering me in another breathless kiss.

My hands reached for his chest, finally savoring those muscles I'd wanted for so long. Moving my hands, I swept his cut aside. His broad shoulders jerked, helping it drop to the floor, and now there was nothing hiding him except the tight gray shirt underneath.

My nails tensed against his rock hard abs, perfectly poised. I chewed his bottom lip, felt him grunt fire in my mouth. Tank pulled away, but I wouldn't let go, holding his lips with my teeth until his strong neck broke the kiss.

"So fucking hot. You wanna play rough, Em? Didn't know you were that kinda girl." He reached behind my head and fisted my hair, giving it a swift jerk.

Tension throttled my veins. It wasn't just desire anymore, it was total *need*. I needed him to take me hard. *Rough* just like he said.

Slowly, I raked my nails along his chest, dragging them up as we kissed. Tank pushed me against the wall and took a step back, never taking his eyes off mine. His hands grabbed the edges of his shirt and pulled. He rolled it off his head, and I was face-to-face with the devil incarnate, all the menacing ink I'd seen while he was sick.

Except this was different. This time, the Prairie Devil's intense grin matched the fire in his eyes, the *promise* that I wasn't walking away before I turned to ash.

He leaned in, reaching for my hair, jerking my face to his chest. "Go ahead. Show me what you can do with that sweet tongue, babe. I know there's a sexy fucking knockout hiding behind that shy little nurse. Let her play."

"I'll try." My face reddened.

His words snapped me back to the insane reality of what was happening here. With my old hookups in college, I never got crazy into it, never felt driven to perform like I did now.

I wanted to please Tank as bad as I needed him to work me over. Shaking off the reluctance, I wrapped my arms tight, pulling against his hand as he guided my face to his chest.

God, he tasted as good as he smelled, as sweet as his lips. I kissed my way down his chest, planting one peck right on the Devil's black mouth. Then I went lower, lower, tonguing the crevices between his hard abs with my tongue.

I let my hands wander. One went lower, straight to the junction of his huge thighs. If his chest and arms were like stone, they didn't have a damned thing on his cock. My fingers squeezed, rolling back up it, slow and intense.

He sucked sharp air. "Fuck! Let's go, babe. Down and dirty, all the fucking way…you can squeeze it harder than that."

His fingers twined with my loose blonde locks. One more gentle push and I dropped to my knees, fingering the clasp on his jeans. Tank undid his belt while I worked off the rest, holding my breath as I waited to see that cock with my own greedy eyes.

We both pulled on his pants and boxers. It popped out with a smart snap, and next thing I knew I was looking at the biggest, meanest erection I'd ever seen in my entire life.

Of course, *big* was nothing but a crappy understatement when it came to him. If his most tender part didn't match the rest of him, it would've been a sin. Thankfully, God wasn't cruel.

The biggest surprise was at the tip. I gasped when I saw the little silver bead glistening on his swollen head. Tank rubbed his hands through my hair and grinned.

"What's the matter, babe? You never seen a pierced dick before?"

I answered him by sucking my lip.

Mind. Blown.

This whole crazy adventure had just flipped up another notch. My pussy pulsed, tensing between my legs when I imagined what it would feel like against my bare wet silk.

No delays. We'll never find out if we don't get that thing as hard as it can go.

I reached forward and rubbed him, hungry to explore every inch.

The heat in his eyes peaked as I leaned forward, nuzzling his thigh with one cheek. My hand went around his monstrous shaft and rolled up it. It seemed like it took forever to reach the tip. I clenched my fingers tighter as I went, fisting his girth, loving the molten heat pulsing against my fingers.

Holy shit.

The fever in my blood quickened. I vaguely wondered how I'd ever fit him inside me, but damned if I wasn't going to try. He'd be a *very* snug fit, and the bead was just the icing on top.

I stroked him up and down, finding my rhythm, waiting until he closed his eyes and rocked back a little before I took the next step. When he wasn't expecting it, I shifted and placed his cock at the tip of my mouth, giving it a small peck before I opened wide.

"Oh, babe. That's it." His fingers pulled at my hair. "Right. Fucking. There."

Yes, sir, I thought, sucking harder.

My tongue swirled around his fat head, discovering his taste, his shape, his fire. I went as deep as I could. It was an accomplishment just to draw in a few inches of his heavy cock.

His balls puckered in my hand as I bobbed up and down. My tongue flicked his surface, focusing on the metal bead, swirling it around and around. His fluid trickled into my mouth, oily lubrication, an omen of the torrent that was sure to come when he did.

I moaned louder, never taking my lips off his cock. He seemed to enjoy the extra vibration, stiffening when I let my tongue, voice, and fingers all work in unison.

His balls were boiling, getting hotter beneath my palm. I squeezed them a little harder, losing myself in his taste and scent and my own thick, wet cream.

"Fuck! Okay!" He jerked on the blonde reins in his hand, pulling me off him. "Hell of a warm up, babe, but I want the whole fucking mile. It'd be a goddamned shame to blow my load down your throat when I haven't had that pussy. Let's go."

He grabbed my wrist and picked me up. More kissing, more of his hands all over me. I leaned into him, rubbing my bare hips against his cock, brushing my slick folds over it. Each time I moved, we both jerked, shocked by the anticipation of being so damned close to being joined, fucking like animals in rut.

He ripped off my top and bra in a flash, pushing me down sideways on the bed. His huge bulk completely covered me. His hands grabbed at my breasts, pinning me down, helpless and wide open for more of those sultry deep kisses.

My nipples throbbed between his fingertips. He alternated between rough and gentle, shifting for a better angle, pinching one bud while he rolled the other in a mad circle with his tongue.

Was torture the right word for something so amazing?

I wasn't sure. All I knew was that I couldn't take much more than a solid minute. I needed him inside me, and I needed it *now.*

I rubbed my smooth legs on his, brushing up their hairy, muscular trunks, trying to make him feel the insatiable need inside me. It must've worked because he jerked up, eyes all dark except for the blaze in the center.

"Fucking hell…baby girl…" His voice was low, as if it was hard to speak through his lust. "Hope you're fucking ready for this dick because there's no stopping it. Here it comes, babe. Here comes our first fuck, and neither one of us are ever gonna forget it."

He wasn't screwing around. He was screwing *me,* and the conviction in his voice was the same as when he swore his new loyalty, before we'd torn off our clothes.

The blood in my head turned thick and hot and strong as whiskey. It buzzed until I nearly blacked out, shivering in awe when I felt his swollen cock against my folds. It lingered there for a second. Just rubbing, working, teasing my clit.

Then Tank raised his massive body up and pushed. His cock angled down, found my entrance, and slid in, filling me to completion in a white hot second.

"Oh!" I grunted, eyes wide, trying to stop tensing up so I could relax and take every wonderful inch.

He wasn't waiting. He kept pushing, deep as he could go, breath pouring ragged from his lips.

"Christ, Em. You're so fucking wet! Tightest pink glory I've ever felt in my whole damned life. Hold on, babe. Grab onto something. This fucking train's going off its rails and there's no stopping it."

He lifted himself up and thrust back again, ramming his thickness deep, stretching my tender flesh. My legs pinched tight around him. My vision blurred and I think I screamed.

Tank moved like the world's biggest and baddest tattooed piston between my legs, grunting each time he spiked down, throwing all his energy into his hips. I didn't notice the bead on his cock during the first few strokes. But when I did, it turned every nerve to instant fire.

Oh, oh, oh.

Fuck, fuck, fuck!

My clit throbbed and sang. All the blood in my body pooled below the waist, charging me up like a battery about to explode. The insane friction in all the places he touched was too much, too hot, too perfect.

I reared up and convulsed, throwing my hands around his neck, digging in for dear life. My pussy clenched harder than ever, sucking at his hardness, shooting straight to heaven each time that nasty little bead tapped my soft wall.

I must've scratched the hell out of him, but he didn't miss a beat. Tank just kept coming, baring his teeth as he fucked, faster and harder than before. There was no stopping him, not even while my orgasm turned me into a quaking, rasping, uncontrollable slut.

I was just coming down from it when he pulled out. His big hands folded on my hips and picked me up, flipping me around.

"On your hands and knees, babe." He reached for my wrists and spread my hands on the old headboard. "You're gonna need all the leverage you can get when I bust inside you. I'm fucking coming soon and I'm not pulling out."

With one hand, he spread my legs apart, grabbed both my shoulders, and pushed back in. The bed shook like an earthquake as he fucked the living hell out of me. My breasts flopped wild underneath me, shaking as much as my knees. I clawed at the headboard for support, trying to remember to breathe.

The level headed nurse in my head wagged her finger. I shouldn't have been taking him without a condom, even if I was on birth control. But it was too damned good to stop. I punched the nurse out cold and let him take me, leading me into the tsunami of pleasure rushing at me from behind.

I felt like a virgin again. No man had ever taken me like this, down on all fours, ramming himself into me like an animal. And Tank was a savage fucking beast, digging his thick fingers into my ass, slapping it with his pubic bone each time he dove deep.

I slipped and fell down face first on the pillow. Just in time because all my muscles were winding up, ready to take flight, hurling me off the cliff.

I threw my legs around his, squeezing with all my might, and ripped loose. I came, screaming at first and then freezing in electric silence, blazing past a hundred degrees as he kept pumping.

"Oh, fuck! Don't you stop coming, Em. I'm filling this sweet little cunt up *now*."

I blinked through the ecstasy, and then my eyes snapped open, rolling in their sockets. His cock swelled, bigger than before, pulsing against my cervix. He held it there, growling as he emptied his balls, firing jet after jet of hot seething come up into me.

Now, it was my turn to grunt and thrash like an animal. My half-spent orgasm started all over again, hips bucking at his cock. Tank cursed and hollered, losing his mind as my greedy pussy milked him.

Fuck!

It was the last word I heard from him before I faded. The buzz in my head ignited like a sun, burning up everything, knocking out all my senses except the unstoppable tingle between my legs. The pleasure came in sharp rhythmic bursts, my sex pulsing with his, a vessel locked together to take his steaming essence.

His loud, ragged groan brought me back to life. He slipped out of me and left his seed to spill, shaking the bed as he moved around.

Tank crashed down on his back. It sent a ripple through my little bed, tossing me high. I landed on my chest, savoring the sweet moist heat on his chest. All his manly sweat mingled with the spice and motor oil that was always there. Just past his skin, the entire room smelled like sex, and I had a feeling it was only going to get heavier.

"Rest up, babe. The night's young. I'll tell everybody in the club to walk on eggshells tomorrow so there's no extra shit waiting for you." He smiled, touching his big hard forehead to mine.

"Huh? What do you mean?"

"Nobody's getting hurt and dragging you over for work. In case you didn't know, I haven't had a good fuck for months, and you're the only damned woman who's been on my mind morning, noon, and night. By the time we're finished, neither one of us is gonna be able to walk."

I laughed. Tank moved in for another kiss. One lead to another, and soon his magnificent cock was stiffening against my thigh. He rubbed it against my leg, wrapping one hand on my ass.

His palm came down on my skin, clasping me tight. I jerked, flapped against his erection, and looked at him in shock.

Did he really just...spank me?

"Spread those pretty legs when I say. You understand claiming you means we're fucking on demand, right?" Before I could answer, he smothered my lips in another heavy kiss. "When I'm not with my brothers, I'm gonna be right between your legs, Em. Can't even look at you without my balls giving me shit. I'll take you out, yeah, anywhere you want. Just as long my dick ends up right where it belongs, right in this tight fucking pussy that belongs to me."

He cupped my mound and squeezed.

Insane. I should've told him I didn't want to be controlled. But as soon as his skin was against mine, his lips engulfing everything, I melted, surrendering to the big oak who dominated my whole mad world.

VII: Gone to Hell (Tank)

My phone growled on the floor sometime at the ass crack of dawn.

I woke up in a stupor. One glance of Emma's perfect ass reminded me where I was, and what happened too.

Not like I could fucking forget for anything. Even if my brain did, my dick remembered, savoring the feel of her sweet pussy wrapped around all ten inches. The phone rumbled again, somewhere in my discarded jeans.

"Fuck," I muttered softly. Tried hard not to wake her up as I shuffled around the dark room, snatching at my clothes on the floor.

Blaze was on the line. The Prez told me to get my ass back to the clubhouse ASAP. Our patch over with the Rams had him more on edge than usual. He sounded pissed, demanding I drag myself in earlier than usual to check all the gear one more time before we headed over to meet them.

I threw on my clothes, stuffed the phone in my pocket, and eyed Emma sadly. Leaving so soon was the last fucking thing I wanted, but orders were orders. Brothers were family.

The club was my whole life. It was one helluva night, but I still had a long road to figure out how I was gonna weave her into this insane existence seamlessly. Safely too.

Sorry, babe. I've gotta get this shit over with, I thought, taking one last good long look.

No longer. Staring too much would've made my cock rage. Going into a situation like what was ahead, I didn't need any distractions.

A quick run out the door and I was on my bike, roaring down the road. When I got to the clubhouse and parked, Blaze was already outside with Stinger, waiting for me.

"Where the fuck were you?" Blaze growled, coming toward me as I climbed off my Harley. "I saw you going after her. You didn't back here all night. Dammit, Tank, if you hurt that poor girl again I'll –"

"We had a long talk. Everything between us is cool. Call her yourself if you don't believe me, boss." Fuck. Blaze could be a real asshole sometimes, and I had to muster my strength to keep it respectful. "Just give it a few hours. She's sleeping."

I looked over his shoulder. Stinger was right behind the Prez, wearing his huge shitty grin. He winked, laughed, and grabbed us both by the shoulders.

"Come on, brothers. Tank knows what he's doing. Glad you were finally able to fuck some sense into her." He turned to Blaze. "Don't we have more important things to do than yammer about Tank's latest conquest, Prez?"

Blaze looked intense, angry as hell for several long seconds. Then his face wrinkled up and he burst out laughing, beating a heavy hand against my back.

"Your business is your biz, you magnificent bastard. Stinger's right. If Em's cool, then so are we. I just want to get this shit with the Rams done. Let's get to work."

The sun was barely over the mountains as the club rode in a column. I was third in line, right behind Blaze and Stinger. The rest of the boys followed behind me in a truck, a full compliment except for Roller and the prospects who'd gone West.

Moose drove the pickup. Told him to bring it along in case we found anything in their nest worth hauling out.

Blaze briefed us on the situation again, and I made sure we were all locked and loaded going in. The Pagan Rams had their clubhouse about an hour West on I-90, up near the Idaho panhandle, the wild edge of Devils' territory.

My phone vibrated in my jeans. Had a bad feeling it was Em, probably pissed and wondering why I'd disappeared without a trace. Lady Luck spat in my face with the timing of all this.

The best fucking night I'd ever had threatened to turn to shit at sunup. Whatever, there would be time to make her understand later, after we reined in the Rams and had one less thing on the club's radar.

Blaze slowed down and turned onto the service road as we neared our destination. Adrenaline rumbled in my veins, same as it always did before combat.

Whatever happened today, or however fucked up things were later, nothing was gonna take that night away from me. I wouldn't let it. I had her, marked her, filled her to completion.

Completion? Not quite. My cock wanted more.

I must've fucked her at least five times through half the night, and I was still hard each time I thought about her. I thought the hardest part was behind me, wanting her, but this was something else. Em was a damn addiction.

Fuck, would I ever get enough of that woman, or was she just gonna stay planted in my skull 'til the day I died?

"Okay, boys. Look alive!" Blaze yelled behind him. We rode between the tall trees now, down an unpaved road leading through the land owned by the Rams.

The bastards were smart. They kept things tucked back, preferring to hide the old way, before the bigger MCs decided they were better off in the open, posing as legit hobby groups and businesses. These assholes hid on wild land like bandits, leaving nothing to mark their place before the dilapidated cabin except for a sign with their symbol and a rusted flap of metal that read NO TRESPASSING.

Their sign was a grinning ram's skull, horns pointed at an unnatural angle, sharper than any damned sheep I'd seen. A bigger version was lit up in neon over their clubhouse entrance, hanging on an old porch. Their place looked like an old mountain tavern converted for more serious business than catering to summer tourists.

We all stopped and cut our engines. Reb and Moose stepped off their bikes, hanging around for backup while Blaze and Stinger went forward. They slowed after a few steps, giving me a chance to catch up.

"Nobody home. Or maybe the fucks are all asleep. Guess they've been on good terms with the Grizzlies so long it's made 'em lazy." Blaze stepped forward, approaching their front door, waving to Stinger and I. "Come on. Surprise inspection. Leave the white gloves in your saddlebags."

Stinger smiled, but I was more serious. All my instincts said something was fucked up here.

We stood next to Blaze as he pounded on the door. Another minute passed, and nobody answered. He grabbed the knob and twisted it.

It popped open, screeching on its old hinges. The place smelled like shit inside. Old tobacco mingling with stale beer, old burgers, and who the hell knew what else. Stinger winced, rubbing his nose.

"Hey!" Blaze cupped his hands over his mouth and bellowed. "Where the fuck are you guys? We've got a meeting today."

Around the corner, a voice moaned. Loud and female. Then it happened again, and a man added his rough cry to the mix. Somebody in here was screwing.

"You gotta be jerking my dick. Assholes are too busy fucking to answer their own door?" Blaze reached near his hip, fingering the nine millimeter he kept there. "Stay focused. Might be dealing with some goddamned junkies."

"I don't like this, boss," I said.

"We gotta do what we gotta do. Let's go meet their asses if they're too damned busy with pussy to say hello."

He went forward, stomping toward the dark hallway around the corner. Beer bottles and crumbs were all over the place. More on the bar up against the wall, complete with dirty dishes adding their stinking residue to the mess.

Fuck. This shit looked like a Grizzlies' den. Guess living balls deep in bear territory too long had given them the same bad habits. I wondered what other dirty secrets were hidden in this fucking cave.

Stinger and I rushed after Blaze. We caught up and found him stopped a few steps down the hall, pointing.

A skinny man's pale ass bobbed in the air. His jeans were twisted around his ankles, and he had a woman face down on a crappy mattress. The Pagan Ram's patch stretched tight on his back each time he thrust, creating more of those soft, shaky moans.

Blaze looked like he was about to explode. He swung forward, taking wide steps up to the dude in mid-fuck. No surprise, the Prez didn't take well to being ignored. The boss rarely repeated himself too, and never with assholes who gave him no reason to.

One swift jerk threw his hand on the man's shoulder and knocked him off the woman. The Ram tumbled up against the wall.

Surprised the shit out of me how fast he hit the old wood. Blaze had given him a solid throw, but he hadn't tossed him *that* hard. It was like he was hurling a skeleton.

"God damn! What the fuck?" The stranger looked up with a sunken face, gray beard bobbing angrily. "Who're you assholes, and what the fuck are you doing in our clubhouse?"

The whore was just as skinny, and apparently just as whacked out of her head. She didn't move a muscle to cover herself up or even close her legs. Just rolled over and looked at us dumbly, as if we were a man train, and I was next in line to fuck her.

"Cover this bitch up!" Blaze growled, grabbing the man by his cut. His eyes flashed to the man's chest. "VP? You gotta be shitting me."

"Yeah. I'm Socket." He cleared his throat, taking a good long look at our colors. "Suppose that makes you the new boys in town, the Prairie Dogs or whatever. You looking for Block?"

Blaze's jaw twitched. He was one twist of the dagger away from cutting this fucker open for insulting our club.

"Yeah. Bring his ass out here right now, and then step aside so we can have a look through this clubhouse. Only gonna give you one chance. Hope the rooms back there aren't as fucked up and filthy as the rest of this place. I don't know what the hell the Grizzlies let you get away with while they played sugar daddy. But God knows I'm gonna find out."

Socket pursed his lips. He scrambled to his feet, fumbling to pull up his pants. Stinger turned away in disgust at his flaccid cock.

"Whatever. I'll go get the Prez," he said.

The man wandered down the hall and pushed open one of the doors further down. Damned thing was just as loud as the one leading into this place.

The Rams, like their shrieking hinges, were a fucked up machine that hadn't been oiled for decades. I was still getting a creepy ass vibe, but I wondered how the fuck these dudes were ever dangerous. They'd clearly let themselves go since the edgy shit kicking days Moose told us about in Sturgis.

We stepped back into the bar area, waiting for the Prez.

"Helluva way to greet the new patch, boss," I said, trying to diffuse the tension.

"Yeah. I gave these assholes two weeks' notice too." Blaze shook his head. "Fuck me. I'm starting to think this was a bad idea. Should've disbanded 'em. None of these motherfuckers are wearing our colors 'til they clean up their act. Throttle would have my ass nailed to the cross if I patched them in looking like this…let alone wasting our time and money protecting a buncha scrappy fucking crooks."

He wasn't bullshitting. I remembered an old story back in North Dakota about Voodoo. Some dipshit had snitched on the mother charter in the eighties after being caught skimming profits from the club. The rat wound up naked, nailed to a Saint Andrew's Cross, and dumped off in the badlands.

Throttle was another hardass, just like his old man, Voodoo. Nobody wanted to piss him off, especially Blaze, even if it would take a colossal fuckup or outright betrayal to spill a brother's blood.

"Here they come," Stinger said.

We listened. Several heavy boots clomped toward us. Four dingy looking guys total, three new ones plus Socket. Nobody in their group could've been a day under fifty, and a couple dudes looked quite a bit older.

"You Block?" Blaze narrowed his eyes at the biggest one with the most patches on his cut.

The old man in the middle stopped, face like a mask. His hair was long, dark black streaked generously with gray. An uneven smile twisted his wrinkled face, and he extended a hand.

"Yeah. At your service, man. President of the Pagan Rams."

"Prez?" Blaze ignored the handshake, looked down and sniffed. "Gotta say, I've never seen anybody so fucking unworthy to wear that patch – and I've tangled with *a lot* of Grizzlies."

The Rams all blinked in surprise. Block bared his teeth, turning his open hand into a fist instead. "That so? I get it, Blaze. You Devils assholes think you're tough shit. You chased the big bad bears up over the mountains and now you think everybody ought to do things your way – including bow down and suck your cocks."

"No, I think they're *going* to do it my fucking way!" Blaze jerked forward, getting right in his face. "No sucking or fucking needed. No negotiation either!"

The Rams' hands went in their pockets. Stinger and I ran forward, throwing ourselves against the three dudes before they could move. The asshole named Socket blasted his nasty fucking breath right in my face when I slapped his ribs.

One guy got his switchblade free in the commotion and pushed it out, brandishing it near Blaze's face. I was fucking faster.

Had my gun out and pressed to his temple in a heartbeat. The fuck was so surprised he stumbled and dropped his weapon. The knife clattered to the floor.

Blaze lunged. Grabbing Block by the throat, he carried the bastard to the bar and slammed him down. The other Rams struggled against us, but didn't put up the fight I expected.

Pathetic. Was this the way clubs got when they were all old and toothless? Why hadn't these fucks recruited new blood to keep their asses spry?

"What the fuck is this?" Block spat. "We had a truce, a patch over. I didn't give you assholes the right to take over my fucking clubhouse!"

"My territory, my fucking rules. You'll do what I say. No questions asked. You still want to wear this patch and have our protection? Or do you want us to shut down your joke of an MC instead? Cause if you're not up to snuff, Prez, you're intruders in *our* fucking territory."

Blaze grinned. "Doesn't look like it would take much to kick your asses West with the bears."

Stinger and I laughed. I kept my gun on the two guys. They both eyed me like I snatched cold beer out of their hands.

"Fuck you." Block grunted and went limp. His physical submission was enough.

Shrugging, Blaze backed up, letting Block stand. The Rams' leader wiped his faded cut, coughing as he fought for breath.

"You boys got five minutes to screw your heads on and take this deal, tell us you're gonna cooperate completely, or I'm calling the rest of my brothers in to clean this shithole up in the name of the Prairie Devils MC. Here's exactly what's gonna happen if you want to keep your cuts: you shut your mouths, settle down, and let us have a good look around. Promise to clean up your fucking act. You'll get your stamp of Satan's approval and go on your merry way."

Block clenched his fists, shaking with rage. "What's the difference? Sounds like we're somebody else's bitches whatever we do."

"Better a bitch than no club at all, yeah? You don't like it, fine. We'll rip those fucking cuts off your backs and burn the damned things. Probably do the fucking things a favor by killing a few fleas."

Block shifted his weight. He folded his fat arms. He didn't like it, but it looked like he'd accepted the inevitable, readying himself to suck it up and suffer through it.

Slowly, he raised his arm. "Okay. We'll let you have a look. But nothing leaves this clubhouse without our approval, right?"

"Depends on what we find," Blaze grunted.

Had a feeling he was wondering what that meant we'd find here. We waited several seconds for Block to mouth back, but his lips stayed shut. Maybe the wily fuck had more sense than I thought.

"One more thing," I said, stepping forward. "Gonna need you boys to empty out your pockets. Stinger and me'll be patting you down."

Disgust poured off the four Rams as they let their belts fall to the floor and started turning their pockets inside out. Stinger checked Block and Reaper, while I did the same for the other two, Socket and Gutter. I collected a couple more switchblades and a big silver magnum off the floor. With the gun in hand, I paused, turning the fucker over.

Hadn't seen one like this since Afghanistan. This hardass dude named Cole had one just like it. He treated the fucking thing just like his baby, even when it was useless against Taliban guerrillas. The man was like a berserker with that damned thing in his hands, charging to hell while mortar shells rained down around us.

I was lost in my head wondering whatever happened to that crazy dark eyed sonofabitch when Blaze grabbed the radio on his belt. Reb and Moose came through the door a minute later, heavy firepower in their hands. Block took one look at their shotguns and snorted.

"You really think we're gonna try anything?" He sneered. "Come on, guys!"

"Safety first, Prez." Blaze laughed. "We do shit by the book and we're not about to stop anytime soon. Moose, Reb, watch these sorry fucks while we have a looksie down that rank smelling hall."

Blaze, Stinger, and me were on our way. The Prez wasn't kidding about the stench. At first, I thought it was just the beat up old mattress where we caught Socket fucking that scrawny slut. Fuck no. The whole place stank bad, like someone or something was living in a hole.

Old war memories punched me in the face – especially the nose – a second time. Dead, rotting flesh was a smell I'd never forget without a lobotomy.

Blaze was about to push open the first door when I reached for his shoulder.

"That's no ordinary stink, boss. Hold up. You've smelled that shit before, same as me…"

Stinger and Blaze both raised their eyebrows at the same time. Blaze's hand fell off the knob and his face tightened. He knew damned well what it was.

"Fuck me. If these idiots have got a rotting corpse holed up in there, I swear I'm gonna –"

He never finished his sentence. Blaze's handgun came out and his anger took over. One kick and the old door ripped its top hinge, spinning uncontrollably against the wall. The putrid odor slammed into all three of us, stronger than before.

The stink made me cough, despite being ready for it. Hell, I would've been surprised if there *wasn't* a ripe stiff laying up on the old bed, a cheap blue sheet draped over it. The dead body didn't shock and awe.

What put my senses on red fucking alert was the loud sniffle in the other corner, sharing the room with the stiff.

I moved in first, Blaze and Stinger rushing for the body. Had my handgun locked between my fingers, pointed at the deep dark chasm in the wall. The fucking thing looked deeper than a walk-in closet, and darker too.

"Get your ass out here now!" I roared, ready to shoot. "You've got five seconds to show yourself, and the countdown's already started."

Stinger and Blaze turned to face the same hole I did. Their hands were on their weapons, ready to lay into whoever the fuck emerged from the blackness.

My heart jumped into my throat when the skinny young woman hobbled into the light. Her long striped shirt was almost as greasy and stained as the filthy sheet covering the corpse, and her pale white legs were scratched to hell. Nothing but panties below, barely covered by the grimy rainbow top.

"Holy fucking shit." Stinger's jaw practically slammed into the floor.

"What's wrong? Are you hurt?" Dead silence after Stinger's question. The girl's lips barely moved. She looked pretty fucking bad. "Talk to me, girl!"

I lowered my gun as he hauled ass, catching her just before she began to fall. Blaze's keys jingled. He pushed something small and heavy into my hand.

"LED light. See what the fuck else is back there." He shook his head. "Christ. Bad enough we've got a body back here to deal with. Now here's little miss Dracula too. Soon as I find out who the fuck died here, I'm gonna slaughter those Rams."

I stepped into the closet as Blaze walked to the body and tore off the sheet. Stinger clasped the strange girl tight. She couldn't have been much older than twenty, and had the vacant eyes of somebody who'd seen too damned much, eyes too sick to even sob all over the VP's cut.

Light in hand, I went in. The creepy ass closet wasn't really as deep as I thought. The hole in the wall had a big cardboard box in the back and a worn plastic shelf full of dirty bowls and cups. The box stank like piss, so strong my nostrils burned.

I held my breath, throwing the light up and down, making a full three-sixty to see if there was anything interesting holed up in the darkness. Nothing materialized.

When I came out, Stinger leaned against the wall, running his fingers through the girl's dirty hair, trying to comfort her. He looked up and had serious shit stirring in his eyes.

"Get her out of here. Don't know how Blaze wants to handle this shit, but there's no sense in letting her stew a second longer in this cesspool."

"Thanks, brother." Stinger turned back to the girl, slapping me on the shoulder as he helped her out into the hall. "It's okay, baby. Whatever the fuck they've done to you, we're gonna make it all right. That's a fucking promise…"

"Prez?" I joined him next to the bed. The sheet was pulled back, and a big square faced man was staring up at the ceiling, a gross film over his eyes.

"You know who this fucker is?" Blaze asked. I shook my head. "That's Mickey James. Biggest gun runner on the whole West coast. Can't count the times I drank with this bastard back in Iowa and Dakota when he came by the clubhouses for business. Maverick and me hauled shipments for this dude in the Nomads on Voodoo's orders. Escort duty. Now, he's in the middle of fucking nowhere, dead as a doornail."

"Helluva mystery." I was stumped. Seriously.

Blaze was chewing his emotions. When he met my eyes, his were sharp, dark, full of future blood. I could tell there was only one decision sparking in his brain: whether to take the body now and execute every last Ram in this shitty place, no questions asked, or if we were gonna give these assholes one chance to explain themselves.

Without a word, Blaze turned sharp, moving down the hall. I was right behind him. I'd never been a superstitious man. Still, this place's atmosphere would've sent the willies up a gravedigger's spine, and I sure as shit wasn't hanging out with a dead body while we had bigger sheep to gut.

Last night seemed like a distant dream. I would've given my left nut to be back in bed with Emma, leaving the stiffs, assholes, and fucked up girls a million miles away.

Just me, her, a bottle of Jack, and a whole lot of fucking. Heaven.

"Well? Did you boys find whatever the fuck you were looking for?" Block looked up from his seat at the bar.

Blaze didn't say shit. I was two steps behind him as he closed on the Rams' Prez. The other geezers jumped on their feet as the boss' gun came out. There was a gnarly crack like wood splitting as his pistol whipped Block's jaw.

The asshole spat several bloody mouthfuls, grunting as pain throttled his skull. Several old teeth rattled on the floor. One was still spinning as it came to a stop against my boot.

"You asshole! Why didn't you fucking tell us you had a torn up bitch and a dead body back there?" Snarling, Blaze pressed the barrel to Block's temple, his hand shaking furiously. "You think we're all as drugged out and stupid as you? You think we wouldn't find it?"

No answer. Moose and Reb kept their shotguns trained on the other three. I was ready to pounce either way if anybody tried something stupid.

"Answer me!" Blaze's howl echoed through the empty clubhouse.

Outside, a feminine wail answered, and then Stinger's voice, trying to be soothing.

Fuck. Things are going from stupid straight to hell. Somebody's gonna get their skull split, I thought, adrenaline humming in my veins. *Don't give a shit as long as that somebody isn't wearing our patch.*

"We wanted you to find them," Block said finally, using one wrist to wipe blood off his mouth. "Had a feeling you'd know what to do. You've already shown you're younger...healthy...able to handle shit like this."

Blaze's rampage simmered down one notch. He pulled the gun back, until it was no longer digging into the man's temple, but he never took it off him.

"What the hell are you talking about?"

"Happened the night before last. Mickey stopped by. Hadn't seen that fuck for years, not since he had us store some shit for the Grizzlies to pickup." Block paused, swallowing more blood so he could speak. "Heh. He'd be amazed to know you're all upset about his dead ass. Thing is, we're not the only ones who've had our asses turned upside down and hung up to dry since you Devils claimed this state."

Blaze narrowed his eyes. Everybody else shifted uncomfortably. Red and Moose were just a pube away from pulling the trigger if the Rams at the other end so much as flinched.

"Go on," Blaze growled. "Nobody's done shit for Mickey in this club since Voodoo met his maker."

"Yeah. Well, business has been tough along all the usual routes with all the fighting going on between you and the bears. Mickey showed up half-drunk two days ago.

Soon as the fuck had a couple more beers in him, he let loose, telling us all about how pissed he was that the Devils were hauling their own shit, too busy to take his loads to the coast anymore. Wasn't real happy about your deals with the competition either. The Russians take the shit you hand off all over the fucking world. Mickey's client list was looking mighty dry because they're handing your shit out to warlords like free vodka. He was pissed at you, pissed at business, so he offered us a deal..."

The tension lighting up Blaze's face was thick as mud. Finally, he lowered his gun.

I wasn't sure what to think. Block had definitely gotten the boss' ear. If it was a fucking story, then the bastard was a damned good liar.

"He was gonna reach out to the Grizzlies. See if we'd do runs under your noses across the Idaho panhandle and pass his shit off to them in Washington or Oregon. Guess he thought the bears needed to beef up their defenses and their war with the cartels in SoCal would turn 'em into good buyers." Block looked up, eyes like steel, holding Blaze's gaze. "Of course, we refused. Didn't want to go behind your backs, taking your cut of the profit"

"Fine. Why the fuck is he dead?" Blaze snorted.

"Desperate motherfuckers do stupid things. When we told him we weren't interested, he started swinging his fists." Block pointed to the heavier guy with gray hair and glasses. "Reaper here knocked his ass out with a bottle. He was still breathing. Figured we'd throw him in the back to cool his heels. When we found him the next day, he wasn't breathing. Must've hit him harder than we thought and killed him in his sleep. Honest. Asshole doesn't have a scratch on him. Must've had a bad ticker or something. Look him over yourselves."

Blaze turned to us. "Bring the body out here."

Moose nodded. He passed his shotgun to me while him and Reb got moving. I cradled the deadly weapon in my hands, eyes focused on the Rams we had against the wall, waiting for one little jab to pull the trigger.

Something didn't smell right. And it wasn't just the filthy fucking smells in here. Too bad I couldn't put my finger on it, or I would've warned him, would've pulled the Prez aside and told him these fuckers were bullshitting us.

The Block who was talking now didn't seem like the one earlier. Felt like a rat playing helpless old man. My fingers tightened on the gun, wishing the fucks would give me one good reason to pull the trigger.

All my nerves were hopping like caged up monkeys sensing a storm. Same fucking feeling I used to get on patrol outside Kandahar, right before mortars started falling from the mountains, trying to blow my squad to hell and back.

Five minutes later, they laid Mickey's body out on an empty table. Blaze and I checked him from head to toe. The fucker's story checked out, much as I didn't want it to. There wasn't a sign of foul play on him. Just a little dark bruising on the head, right where Reaper said he cracked the glass against his skull.

"Well?" Blaze looked at me, twirling his gun in his hand.

"Looks like these assholes might be telling the truth. *Maybe.*" The words came out rough, right through my clenched teeth.

"Anything you see here that says they aren't?"

"No. Nothing on this body, anyway. Gotta wonder why the hell they had the girl living in the closet like an animal. She was there long enough to eat some meals and piss in the box."

Good fucking question. Blaze turned his gun at Block again. "You heard Tank. Who the fuck is she? That's one part of your story that I'm not buying."

Block smiled. His lips were still bloody. He stood, hands spread out carefully. That harmless old man act just went double.

"I couldn't tell you. Only one who can is *her*. She rode in with Mickey, some whore or something, who the fuck knows. Girl seemed woozy when she came in. She started screaming like a banshee when Reaper whacked his ass out. She laid on the floor and wouldn't get up. We put her in there after a fight. Even when we found him dead and tried to take her out, she wouldn't move."

"You're telling me the four of you assholes couldn't drag a skinny little girl somewhere safer?"

Block shrugged. "She spit and clawed like a wild animal when we came close. Wouldn't let us anywhere near her. And fuck, what were we supposed to do? Bring her somewhere she could rat and scream, and drag the Devils in too?"

Blaze's face curdled. The asshole had a bitter point.

"Yeah? And what about her pants? Where the fuck are they?" Our Prez looked like he was about to explode, a wild animal on the hunt for one tiny crack in Block's story, same as me.

Reaper cleared his throat in front of me. I clenched the shotgun tighter, watching carefully as he reached for the shirt collar underneath his cut. He pulled on it hard.

Deep, ugly scratches lined his neck. "We left her alone after she did *this* the first time we tried to move her. Bitch almost nicked my fucking jugular. Tore her khakis to hell in the struggle, so she went without."

Blaze's temples bulged, working his jaw. He was torn, same as everybody else. I could see it on my brothers' faces. Moose and Reb just as eager to finish these fuckers as I was. But if they truly weren't bullshitting us...

Fuck. Club charter said we didn't kill in cold blood. Wasn't so much the ethics as the fact that it was a bad idea sure to invite trouble. More stiffs meant more investigations, and way more unexpected consequences.

"Okay," Blaze said at last. "We're taking the body and the girl. We'll see if this story checks out."

"They're yours. We were fucking waiting to see what you'd want to do. You can have his body and the girl...maybe bring her back when you're finished? We'll keep her in good faith. She's this club's problem, not yours. You're free to take our property per the agreement, but she's not anybody's old lady or even a slut. She still belongs to us." Block made a doubtful face, forcing out his words. Then he looked up, fixing his eyes on Blaze. "You see? We're cooperating. We're earning your protection, brother."

It was Blaze's turn to feel venom in his blood. "Yeah, well, you fucks have got a lot of talking and a lot of cleaning to do before we go there. And don't you dare call me brother, asshole. Until we decide what to do with your asses, consider yourselves under lock down. Nobody leaves this fucking clubhouse for so much as a beer run 'til we're satisfied you're gonna keep those colors."

"All right. And the girl? You'll bring her back?" Desperation rang in Block's voice.

"Don't tell me you're really that fucking stupid?" I stepped forward, steam in my veins. "Why the hell would we ever bring her here when you had her living like a dog? Maybe the Grizzlies let you fuckers keep women chained up like strays. That's not the way things roll in this club, is it, Prez?" I looked at Blaze.

He nodded, dagger eyes all on Block. The rival Prez stared at us with killer eyes. My muscles flexed instinctively, ready to rumble if he stepped an inch out of line. Finally, he looked down, letting out a long sigh.

"She's only coming back when we're good and ready, and my boys will be with her. You're not having her alone to yourselves again. Don't even fucking ask."

"Okay. I'm cool with that." The dark note in Block's voice said otherwise. "We're all cool, friends. We can iron out the fine print later. Right now, we're good…"

"We'd better be. Because if you're not, we'll be dumping off four more bodies with Mickey in the Montana wilderness."

Blaze signaled. I picked up their weapons, everything Stinger and I collected in a bag, never lowering my gun 'til we were out the door. I slammed the door behind me, rattling their shitty old structure.

Before I started my bike, I peeked at my phone.

Fuck. Three new voice mails. All from Em.

It was bad enough we had to undo all the hell the fucking Rams had raised, especially taking a long trip out of our way to drop off Mickey's corpse where nobody would find him. Now, with the stray we'd picked up, Emma was gonna be at the clubhouse for sure, and she'd be laying into my ass for disappearing without a kiss goodbye.

I watched her come into the infirmary. We'd just gotten out of church where we debriefed the Rams situation when my girl showed up. Blaze decided the best thing to do was see if the mystery girl's story contradicted Block's.

I was in there with her for the exam, same as Blaze and Stinger. The VP wouldn't step away for a goddamned second, even when Blaze ordered her to take a shower. He stood outside, towel ready, following her around like he was already bound and whipped.

Who better than me to recognize a crazy crush when I saw one? And who better to suffer when Emma came in, shot me a fiery look, and then wouldn't meet my eyes again the whole time she looked the chick over.

I sat in the corner, listening as she talked.

"Alice. That's what she told me her name is," Stinger said. "She was in worse shape when we got her to the clubhouse. Had to slow down on my bike a few times to make sure she kept her hands around my waist on the mountain curves."

"Hmmm..." Emma shined the bright light into her eyes. "Pupils are normal. No sign of brain damage. What is it you want to know?"

"What the fuck really happened the night she showed up at the Rams' clubhouse. She says she doesn't remember a damned thing," Blaze said, pacing the room. "Is it possible she's fucked up her head, nurse? Or is she fucking us instead?"

Stinger shot the Prez a dirty look. I stood, ready to get between them if I had to. Alice looked up, rubbing her eyes after Emma finally stopped the light.

"I...I told you already. I don't remember anything. Nothing but my name...hiding in the closet...those men. Jesus, I hated them. I just can't remember why." She chewed her lip, scared as a cornered kitten.

"It's not unheard of, Blaze," Emma said. "I'm not seeing any obvious physical damage here. But that doesn't mean she's lying. The brain can short circuit if it's been through a terrible trauma. I'm no psychologist, but there are tons of cases where the brain suppresses something terrible to keep its sanity. You don't know why she was with the dead man, this…?"

"Mickey." I walked up, answering her question, forcing her to look at me.

Blaze slumped back against the wall, pounding his fist on the brick. "Fuck. No, we don't. Maybe she was his slut or his old lady like Block claimed. Who the fuck knows."

"I don't think she's that kinda girl, Prez," Stinger said firmly. "She's not a club slut. I can spot those bitches from a mile away, and this isn't one."

"Yeah, yeah, you're right about that." Blaze chuffed, humor and frustration building in his throat. "Whatever, bro. Just get her the fuck outta here and find the girl a room."

We waited for Stinger and the girl to leave. When the door was closed, Blaze looked around, first at me and then Emma.

"We're not done, Em. I'm gonna keep you doing regular checks on this chick 'til she tells us something useful." Blaze stepped past us and stopped at the door. "Look…the tension's so fucking thick between you two I can cut it with a knife. I don't know what the hell's about to go down, but I can guarantee it's a fucking storm. That means I need everybody focused, all hands on deck."

I nodded. Blaze's eyes pierced me. I held my ground as he pointed a finger.

"Get a room, goliath. Fuck her, fight her, I don't care. You two star crossed lovers do whatever the fuck it is you need to do to fix the shit between you. We've got no time for distractions." Blaze spun, stepped out the door, and slammed it closed.

I took a good long look at Emma. I started to walk, working my way around the table. Barely reached her in time before she was doubled over with laughter, bright and bubbly and totally unexpected after the dark fucking morning.

"What! What the fuck's so damned funny, Em?"

"His face..." She gripped the table's metal edge to regain her balance. When she took a good look at me, more sharp laughter came pouring out.

Like a fucking idiot, I started laughing too. How the hell could I do anything but join in? It was crazy and senseless, yeah, but damned if I could resist that sweet sound coming out of her, everything I loved floating like a kite in those precious chirps.

I threw my arms around her waist, hoisted her up, and made her laugh harder when her feet left the ground.

"Stop it!" Emma beat on my biceps. "Stop, Tank. I'm supposed to be pissed...you left me."

"Babe, I don't give a shit. You can hate my guts 'til you set yourself on fire, just as long as something makes you happy and I get to hear that laugh."

No mercy for her. Emma was still laughing and fighting me when I got her against the wall. One kiss and she became pure blonde honey, flowing against my lips, hot and potent, making me crave her more with every kiss.

I locked my lips on hers a little tighter whenever she tried to speak. My whole body pinned her on the wall, locking her tight, making her listen damned good to my apology. All written in flesh.

I'm sorry, babe, I thought, accenting my lips on hers.

I'm sorry I ran this morning. I'm sorry club business dragged me away from your perfect ass. I'm sorry I'm gonna make up for it by fucking you 'til you can't remember your own name, much less what happened a few hours ago...

My cock strained against my zipper like a wild animal. He wanted her bad – no, *needed* her. Took all my will to stop before I ripped off her bottoms and pushed between her legs, fucking right here in a room that was supposed to stay sterile for some very serious shit.

Snarling, I broke my kiss. Emma fell, touched the ground with her feet, and sucked in precious oxygen.

"Tank...you can't leave me like that again. You didn't even call and you ignored my messages." Darkness prickled at her eyes, fighting with bright desire.

"Real sorry about that, babe. It was my fault. Forgot all about what was coming last night, when all my attention was here..." I reached out, cupped one breast, and squeezed 'til I heard her breath going ragged.

"Never expected Blaze wanted to start so damned early. We had to suit up and go ASAP, dealing with another club." I paused. "I'd say more, but it's –"

"Yeah, I know," she sighed, rolling her eyes. "Club business. And I'm getting close to being one more old lady strung around on a ride going wherever you damned well please, right?"

"Old lady?" I slid one arm around her waist and jerked her tight, cradling her against my chest. "Is that what you want? You want me to claim you in front of this whole fucking club?"

All the hot desire and frustration on her face wilted. Now, she was all red, lips quivering like she'd just let me in on the biggest secret in the world.

"Don't you worry for a single second, babe. That's gonna fucking happen, and soon. You're off limits. You're mine. I don't give a shit how many times I fuck up or how much club business gets in the way. There's no stopping us." I brushed my head against hers, leaning in, laying her little forehead against mine. "You understand me? Pretty soon every brother from here to Minnesota's gonna know you belong to Tank, and nobody else. You want a ride, babe? Then come the fuck on."

I yanked her hand. At first, she struggled against me, trying to tug her little fingers free, begging me to "wait!"

I ignored every fucking whimper. Had to. If I ignored those, then soon she'd be giving me the kinda sweeter pleas I craved, sighing and screaming like a banshee as I reminded her there was no stopping this, no stopping *us*. And there was sure as fuck no stopping this dick.

Soon, we were the club's garage. Her resistance sparked all over again when she saw me pulling her toward my bike. I stopped, turned, and grabbed her.

"Tank! My car is here! I need to –"

"You can beat on my back all you want, babe. Need you to get used to this machine if you're gonna be my old lady. Let me help you on and get you ready. You're coming one way or another, and I want those fingers wrapped around me tight all the way."

Moose was drinking, tuning up his bike over by the wall. He looked up when he heard all the commotion. The older brother waved to me just as Emma started to relax, letting me hook the helmet on her head.

"Take her home, caveman!" Moose growled. "Looks like you've just found your mate after a lotta searching in the jungle."

Brother, you got no damn idea, I thought with a grin.

Emma flushed bright red. She was beside herself at his jeering. Amazing how the girl had spent so much time around the club but hadn't gotten used to all our coarse ways.

"Yeah. I've found her." I wasn't looking at him when I said it. I was staring right at Emma, trying to send the lightning rolling through me out my eyes and into hers.

I climbed on the bike, threw my own helmet on, and fixed her hands snug around my abs. Fuck, she was perfect there. I started to get giddy as a kid on his first Harley, knowing it was gonna be the best fucking ride of my life.

Why the hell did it take so long to get here? Why the fuck did I ever think she was gonna end up anywhere else? Why did I spend two fucking seasons trying to fight this glory?

"Keep this place tight and clean, Moose," I yelled. "Make sure nobody gets a bloody nose. We won't be back here tonight unless it's a real emergency."

"See you in the morning," he chuckled knowingly, taking another long pull from his beer as we drove out.

Emma was shaking like a leaf. She gasped each time the engine roared a little louder, digging her fingernails into my muscles. I took the street roads slow, steady, intentionally making the long way to her neighborhood.

"Relax, baby girl. Let your body get used to it. You're not gonna fall off while you've got me to hold onto. Promise."

It took a few more miles for it to sink in. Finally, she listened, straightening up as her trust grew. Her hands relaxed a little on my waist.

Oh, yeah. That was goddamned nice. Feeling her caressing my skin rather than digging into it like a frightened cat was a big improvement. She had a long way to go before we'd be taking joy rides together in the rain on my bike, but this was an awesome start.

I was about to turn down the home stretch to her neighborhood when she gave me a gentle scratch and leaned her lips to my ear. "Keep going, Tank. This is kind of fun."

Fuck me if I didn't grin like a total idiot. I turned off at the last second and headed for the city limits, away toward the mountains. She tightened up a little bit again when we started up those high, windy ass roads. The steady speed I held taught her pretty fast that it wasn't any different than going slow, and up here the cool autumn air was sweet as chilled wine.

I took a long loop for the next twenty minutes, turning around at one of the old logging camps up in the hills. On the way down, she gushed in my ear, awing at the sunset's beauty and the icy wind in her hair.

Shit, before long we were gonna need proper jackets as winter came rolling in. But today, the glacial edge made having her pressed up against me on my bike extra perfect, an icy-hot contrast I wanted to feel all over.

I'd never say it out loud, but this girl made me tingle like a fucking kid. She gave me a childish excitement with a man's deep needs, and right now both those forces were stirring up my blood, making me kick my ride into higher gear to get home sooner.

A few streets down, Emma clasped me tighter again, working her wicked fingertips a few inches lower than my belt. Dangerously low. I hunched up straight, rock hard, trying to make my impatient dick wait a few more minutes to get her home.

Soon as we were in the driveway, I killed the ignition and jumped off. Had her up in my arms so I could kiss her in record time, tearing off her helmet to make room for my lips. They were impatient sons of bitches, refusing to wait another second to taste her heat, her need, the raw sex dripping off her.

"I thought I'd still be pissed," she said in between kisses. "You proved me wrong, Tank. Looks like you really know how to make up for a crappy morning after all."

"Riding smooths over everything. I've always treated that shit like God's own therapy, babe." I kissed her again, holding her tight, inching us toward the front door. "It's not just the Harley's purr that makes things right."

"Oh?" She asked, pushing her key in to unlock the door.

I waited 'til we were inside to finish. "Yeah. What's really gonna make it all better is you all over me, naked and gorgeous as the day you were born, riding this fucking cock 'til I growl as loud as my bike. That's real medicine, nurse. And I'm gonna need a lotta it, right in my burning blood. Stat."

I reached for the bulge I'd carried in my jeans all the way home to Missoula and squeezed. Emma's eyes went down and she gasped, then curled her lips in a smile, flush with anticipation.

Kicking the door shut behind me, I grabbed her. We were up the stairs so fucking fast I barely felt them crashing beneath my boots. Up there, I flattened her to the wall, tearing at her clothes.

It all came off in fistfuls. Sweater, blouse, bra, stopping one hot second to tweak those pink perky nipples. Then I undid her belt, shaking off her jeans, pinching her panties on both sides and ripping them down her legs.

Fuck, she felt incredible against me. My hand went low as we kissed, feeling for that tight warm pussy I needed like oxygen. Her cunt was so slick and hot my fingers sent rough heat through the rest of me when I pushed them into her softness, feeling her depths, thinking about the way my cock would be in there soon.

Emma moaned, arching her back, pushing those squeezable tits into my chest. She scratched at my neck, then her nails slipped lower, edging my cut.

"One second," I grunted, surprised I could still form any words with heavy lust sitting on my shoulders like a drunken drummer, beating on my skull.

I tore off my clothes. Emma backed up, enjoying the show. When my boots were off and I shed my jeans, I let the cool air dance on my naked skin for a second, savoring the anticipation.

Okay, there. I'd done all the fucking savoring I was gonna do without being balls deep inside her. No more delays, no more teases.

Just raw, hard fucking.

And Emma was as ready as me. Somehow, the little minx slipped onto the bed while I stood there like a fool. She sat up, gold hair sitting in sexy curls on her shoulders, tits out and legs spread. One hand toyed with her clit, spreading that molten precious pussy for me.

"Oh…oh, fuck." My cock pulsed.

It jerked me forward like a goddamned magnet. I got between her legs and pushed her down, down, taking her underneath me, right where she belonged.

"Tank!" My name melted into a hiss as I grabbed her breasts, squeezing them like a Viking who wanted to test out his brand new conquest.

My cock sat right between her sweet wet lips, ready to stretch her, fill her in one thrust. Fuck, it was hard to hold back, hard to even focus on her rosy nips peaking in my hands and mouth.

I kissed her deep, rolling my cock up and down, marinating myself in the only cream I wanted on my skin for the rest of my days. Hot, slick, inviting as all hell...

I pulled back to bite my own tongue as I changed angles. Her eyes wavered as she stared up at me, breasts rising and falling with her heavy, wanton breaths. She almost mirrored me, adding her own feminine twist, sucking her bottom lip against her teeth to chew away the insatiable tension.

"You're so fucking sexy, babe. You don't even know...love the way you keep that look all fired up just for me." I cupped her chin in one hand and titled it up, readying another kiss.

"It's all yours. *Take it.*" Emma's words ended in a throaty purr, her legs winding around me, sleek heat pushing on my calves.

Fuck, fuck, fuck!

I couldn't take a second more of this torment. I plunged in, burying myself in her steaming, delectable little cunt, going all the way 'til my balls rested plush on her ass. Soon as I started to fuck, she bucked back.

We found our tempo fast, and she followed me as the frenzy rose. I kissed her and slapped her flesh with mine, our skin turning sticky as summer heat.

Outside, autumn was taking Missoula by the balls. But in here, it was the Fourth of Fucking July.

I raked her deep, filling her for all I was worth. And still, I wanted to go *deeper,* straight to her soul, the only place I could get when edging her womb wasn't enough. I grabbed her legs.

Emma had the full plump figure I enjoyed, but being a nurse kept her healthy and limber too. I threw her legs over my shoulders as she moaned with delight. I took her deeper, deeper, driving straight down, scraping my trimmed hair on her clit.

The friction pushed her off into the ether. Soon as I saw her clawing at the sheets and winding up like a spring, I smiled. I kicked my hips into higher gear, fast as they could go, sending her over the edge and clenching my ass so I'd hold back.

I had a lot more to give her, and I wasn't gonna bust my first load yet. I fucked her savage, straight through her screaming, clawing, sweat soaked climax, beating the hell out of her rickety bed each time I dominated her little puss, loving how it greedily sucked at my cock when she came.

The bead in my cock rubbed perfect. Must've hit her g-spot a hundred times, turning her body into a hot slick rod for pure pleasure.

I grinned through the heat. Every girl who'd ever had my dick inside them loved that fucking thing, but seeing Em come on it was a special kinda magic.

Come, babe, come. And keep on fucking coming. You're never more beautiful than when you're wrapped around me, losing your pretty head on my skin.

You work enough miracles for me and this club. Let me work one for you.

Gonna keep your brain switched off bullshit, tuned to feeling me inside you, and nothing else. Gonna make you crave this fucking dick 'til you need it so bad you'll never doubt us again, never doubt the way I'm gonna be in you my whole life, especially when you're in this bed wearing nothing but an old lady's cut.

Fuck! Imagining her in leather like mine with PROPERTY OF TANK on her back almost made my balls spit fire. Blaze gave Saffron one just like it with his brand. Only problem was Emma's mom had created the damned thing. I hoped like hell her mom wouldn't raise shit over her bedding a biker.

No, fuck bedding. *Loving* one, loving me with the same kinda crazy electric heat I felt when I loved her.

I pulled her off me just as she started to pant and open her eyes, coming off her high. I rolled, flattening myself on the bed, pulling her up onto me.

"Let's go for another ride, babe. Hop on and jerk this dick off with that hot ass silk between your legs. Don't stop 'til you're overflowing with my come."

Emma blushed. She was getting better each time we fucked, but the girl had a long way to go to catch up with my dirty talk. No problem. We had a long life ahead to work it out, and more fucks penciled in than I could even count.

Having her up above me, riding dirty and wet, was so hot I wondered if the bed was gonna burst into flames. One thing was for sure: something was about to blow inside me, a little closer to a full on meltdown each time she bounced her ass in my hands.

I pulled her along, loving the red blush on her face. She got hotter, redder, wilder with every stroke. At first she it was slow and coy, like sinking into a hot spring. But once my girl got going, she let the fire shooting up her clit carry her away, bucking and grinding and panting as her orgasm closed in.

Her tits were flopping, ornaments screaming sex above my face. I reached up and squeezed, growling as her pussy convulsed around me. She threw her head back, hips swinging, desperate to capture every inch my cock had for her in its piston strokes.

Fuck! I gave it up.

My cock tensed to steel as I jerked inside her. My hands were on her ass again, holding her tight, fusing her hips to mine. Blew my load so fucking hard it rattled every bone in my body.

We came together. Two roman candles going off as one, coming our brains out in every twitch. My heartbeat grew to a roar in my own damned ears, the same steady pulse I had heaving my seed up into her.

Fuck, it was perfection incarnate. The tempo made me think about lots of things: gunfire, rain, fire oscillating, crackling wood splitting in its hearth.

"Tank...Jesus..." Her soft murmurs brought me back to reality.

I looked up, feeling my cock soften just slightly in the hot, sticky mess I'd left inside her. There was no pulling out. Not this time.

I reached up, caught one side of her pretty blonde locks and pulled. She was still trying to speak when I smothered her mouth with mine, shoving my tongue in her mouth. I'd let my tongue do the talking while I got hard again. I'd let it do the fucking too.

When I promised I was gonna fuck her senseless, I *meant* it. With her naked beauty draped all over me, there was no damned way I was getting up 'til we were both so spent we couldn't move.

After a few deep kisses, Emma understood.

We kissed and kissed 'til I was hard enough to thrust. Then I flipped her over on her back and joined my cock to her again. It was the second of many fucks that night, each one meant to show her that she was *mine*, dammit, and I was never, ever gonna let her go.

It was my turn to wake up alone and confused, karma being a fucking bitch after leaving Em this morning.

My eyes burned like hell. My stomach growled. It was still dark. Couldn't have been asleep more than a few hours after the way I laid into her. Last thing I remembered was Emma collapsing in my arms, gently dozing to sleep with her cheek on my chest.

What the fuck? Where is she?

I sat up, thinking maybe she'd gone to use the bathroom. I rubbed my hand across the faint outline on the bed next to me. Still warm.

My ears pricked up like a wolf tracking prey. Didn't know why, but something put me on edge. Somewhere in this house, something was fucked up.

I stood, reaching for my jeans and boots. I threw my pants on and started lacing up the boots while I strained to hear.

Damn. I would've settled for anything except this dead dark quiet. Running water, footsteps, voices…

Voices.

I couldn't make them out with total certainty 'til I poked my head outside the room. No, it wasn't my imagination. Downstairs, she was talking to somebody, and some asshole was talking back.

It wasn't a happy conversation. I knew the angry, scared, frustrated pitch entering a woman's voice better than she knew it herself. I'd seen too many girls hurt over the years in this life not to recognize it.

Fuck. I'd forgotten to throw my nine millimeter back on after our run in with the Rams. Damned thing was at the clubhouse, sitting in my locker.

I reached into one pocket for the hunting knife I hid inside. Had to creep like a fucking cat on the steps to avoid making them scream beneath my weight. The old stairs groaned a few times, but it wasn't shrill, not enough to tip off whatever fucknut was down there twisting my girl's panties.

Prowling closer, I cupped one hand to my ear and listened.

"No – no! I don't care how bad you need this, Mark. You shouldn't be doing this. And you sure as *fuck* shouldn't be pounding on my door at four o'clock in the morning!" Emma was irate.

I pressed my back to the wall next to her kitchen, listening close, evaluating the situation. Who the fuck was Mark?

"Really, cuz? You're telling me you don't like being inconvenienced? Good, bitch! Imagine how I feel listening to those fucking recordings and finding out you turned them off at all the best parts! You helped those vicious freaks, *helped them* cover up their crimes." Something slammed down on the counter.

Had to be the asshole's hand slapping silestone. While his back was turned, I peeked around the corner. Neither of them saw me. I recognized the tall, wiry bastard who'd been on her porch before. Same dick who'd given me that nasty fucking look as he climbed into his car.

Everything coming out of his mouth was confusing as hell. My brain didn't understand, but my fists knew better. They wanted me to reach in, grab that fuck by the throat, and stuff him in the sixty gallon garbage can in the garage.

Shit, if he got any closer, laid a single finger on her, I wouldn't be in here fucking off. I wouldn't be able to resist throwing the asshole through the nearest window...

"Well, cousin? What do you have to say for yourself?" He held his hand up, pushing it close to her face. "No, that's okay, don't answer me. You answer the AT-fucking-F. I don't care if you're family, Emma. You're interfering with a federal investigation right now, and you better have a damned good reason for tampering with my data."

"You're right, Mark! I am!" Her whole body jumped as she screamed. Emma's robe flapped open on top, and she pulled it back together, turning away from him and snarling. "I don't care who you are or what I've done. You have no right to barge in here like this. Show me a warrant or get the fuck out of my house! I'm done. It was a mistake to act like I ever wanted to cooperate."

"Warrant?" He slapped the counter again and started to laugh. A high, whiny sound perfectly suited to a bitch like him.

"Cuz, I'll do you one better. It's all right here. My authority begins and ends with this badge." He held up a leather holder and let it fall open. "You see that, Emma? Special Agent. I don't need a fucking judge to bring down a bunch of terrorists from out East shitting up this state! And I sure as hell don't need it to demand answers when you're stonewalling me, you ungrateful little *cunt.*"

I pinched my eyes shut. Fuck, my fists were shaking now. So hungry, so hot, so ready to beat that fucker senseless. I wouldn't bother dropping him off in the garbage and kicking the can down the goddamned driveway.

This asshole was talking about my club. He'd just threatened Emma *and* my brothers. We'd reached ninety-nine percent certainty he wasn't leaving this house alive. Now, I just had to figure out how I'd send him to meet Satan, as soon as he gave me a few more morsels of why.

I had to find out how deep the shit was facing my club.

"I see it, *asshole*," Emma growled back with equal piss and vinegar, matching his nasty fucking tone.

Her hands moved. She jumped back as the asshole blinked dumbly. She snatched away his badge and held it up.

"Oh my God!" Her jaw dropped, sheer terror lining her face. "You...you lied to me. What the hell is going on? This is expired."

Mark stood there like the dipshit he was for several long seconds. Then he took a long step forward, cornering her against the little table near the wall.

"Give that back," he said coldly.

Emma laughed, amused and enraged simultaneously. "Did you really think I wouldn't notice? You idiot! The corner's clipped! I know what that means with passports. I did study abroad in college. If they cut the corner to make civilian IDs invalid, I'm going to bet that applies to ATF badges too. You're not an active agent at all, are you, Mark?"

He stopped in front of her, shaking his head. He wasn't just a sinister man standing before her anymore. This was a fucking time bomb.

"Give. It. Back."

"No." Emma looked up, tears in her eyes, shaking her head. "No, Mark. I'm going to keep this fucking thing and show it to some real cops. How much you want to bet you're a mad dog on the loose? I'm sure they'll be happy to find out they've got a rogue agent on their hands. What did you do to get drummed out of the force, anyway?"

Mark lost it. I was rushing toward him before he broke Emma's neck, but not fast enough. Her eyes bulged as he picked her up by the throat.

She dropped the badge and slammed it against the wall, kicking and flailing against him, trying to break his horrid grasp.

"Bitch!" he roared, ready to throw her against the stove or refrigerator.

"Motherfucker!" My scream deafened everything as I rammed my shoulder into his as hard as I fucking could.

Something snapped as he whirled, dropping Emma and bouncing back and forth in her narrow kitchen. Spice jars crashing on metal and tile. A stack of oranges went tumbling to the floor, and I crushed more than a few under my boots in my rush to grab that asshole before he could do anything else.

"Tank! No!" Emma tried to scream with all her might when she saw the killer instinct in my limbs, but he'd hurt her throat.

He *hurt* her throat. Damaged her. Wrecked her sweet fucking voice.

The asshole bounded off the stove and was drawing his gun when I plowed into him again. The fuck fired, up above my head. The bullet went right through the ceiling.

It was the last sound that motherfucker ever heard.

I tackled him to the floor, cracking his damned skull on the table as we went flying. I didn't need my gun or knife for this shit. I put my fists on his fucking face again and again, landing more blows when I felt it. The bastard's hot, thick blood on my skin was like a matador flashing bright red to a bull.

I kept going as Emma screamed hoarsely behind me, busting his teeth, obliterating what was left of his eyes. The warmth was starting to leave his worthless carcass forever when I finally stopped.

Holy fuck. Emma was sobbing behind me. All I wanted to do was reach out and comfort her, tell her it was all gonna be okay.

But there was blood, so much blood, all over my fucking hands. I'd killed so many fucks over the years with knives and bullets. None of those jobs threw this much red gore all over me, like I'd wandered out of the goddamned slaughterhouse.

Before I could move a muscle, the front door in front of me collapsed. Three chubby cops came storming in, guns drawn, every one of them pointed at my head.

"Freeze! Put your hands in the air where I can see them! Right now!"

The whole world went white.

I reached high above my head and barely felt the cop struggling as he tried to fit the handcuffs around my huge wrists. I saw nothing. Nothing but white and black and red 'til they turned me around, leading me away like the drugged up bull I'd become.

"Tank…" Emma was still flattened against the wall on the other side of the room.

The tears in her eyes made them glow like lightning. Her whole face contorted, ripped apart by pain, staring at me as long as she could before the sobs clamped her eyelids shut.

"Let's go! Move it!" The cop barked, poking me in the ribs to nudge me around.

I followed.

Crunched up in the tiny squad car, I finally figured it out. The sick jokester who ran the universe gave us this time together so I could do my fucking job one more time. I'd protected her, and I'd protected my club.

Now, my ass was heading behind bars, and I'd be damned lucky if I ever saw Emma or my brothers again without being stuck in an orange jumpsuit behind plenty of glass.

VIII: Torn Apart (Emma)

A dream became a nightmare. It was all so surreal, and I couldn't believe the whirlwind that started as soon as Tank was in custody.

Two long days at the police station, Missoula cops and men from the ATF grilling me, asking me everything I knew about Mark and the Prairie Devils MC. The shifty lawyer the club sent told me there was nobody after the club except my dead rogue cousin. I didn't have to answer anything they asked about my involvement with the Devils, so I didn't.

I gave them nothing more than what everybody across the Midwest already heard: the Prairie Devils MC was a group of motorcycle enthusiasts with an eye for business. Their parties were legendary, their charity work put them in lots of folks' good graces, and they were a better support network for all the vets in their ranks than the Feds.

Nothing more to it.

Nothing. If only it were that fucking simple.

At least they couldn't charge me with anything. I had the marks on my neck to prove Mark attacked first. It was amazing what a few seconds of a man's fingers digging into the tender flesh on my neck could do.

I thought the interrogations at the police station were the worst of it. But that was before Blaze.

As soon as I was at the clubhouse, I was in his office, down on my knees. The pointed questions kept coming over and over, offering certain death if I answered wrong, or just couldn't convince him I was telling the truth.

"Did you rat out the club?"

The third time he asked, hovering over me, angry muscle about to explode, I collapsed. I was a stupid, sobbing, screwed up mess.

"Never! I didn't give my cousin a damned thing. Everything he fit me with, I turned off when I was here. It was just one time...and he got shit. Nothing incriminating. Nothing important. I swear, Blaze." I looked up, trying to see his devilish face through all the tears. "I swear on my mother's life – on *Tank's!* – nobody got anything about your MC. I couldn't let them. I couldn't wreck the Devils after spending so much time here. Please, I swear..."

When I looked up again, he was gone. The door closed, rattling on its hinges. He was pissed, but he'd accepted I was telling the truth.

I only realized it later because none of the brothers came to make me disappear. At the bar, Saffron tried to console me. I didn't tell her about Blaze's harsh interrogation. He'd been a demon, but he was doing his job as club President.

I tried to drown my sorrows in booze. She offered me my favorite beer, but I refused it for whiskey. Ugh. How the hell did everybody around here drink this stuff constantly?

Dark brown bitter venom bit deep. Tasting it made me cry more because I thought about Tank. It was what he'd sucked down during good times and bad – especially when things between us were *really* fucking bad.

Us. When I thought about how they'd locked him up and left him to rot, I knew there'd never be an us again. Nothing more than two desperate faces pressed to prison glass, if I was lucky.

I'd lost him.

Even in death, asshole Mark had taken him away, destroyed the happy moment we had, the start of what was supposed to be our everything, our eternity. I didn't feel bad about my dead cousin.

I hoped he was rotting and burning and suffering wherever he went.

He caused all this by running off the rails and blackmailing me when he wasn't even a real agent. The men at the police station confirmed he'd been discharged from the bureau over six months ago for breaking lawful procedures on a cartel drug case.

Tank sacrificed himself to protect me. That big, crazy, hardheaded man had killed for me. And being locked up to pay for what he'd done, to pay for *me,* was surely worse than death. Every man in this MC gladly preferred death to going behind bars. Prison was worse, a place where they'd know they were never drinking or fucking or riding again.

Imagining Tank alone in some dingy cell made me bawl so loud Saffron had to lead me to his old room, before I split every brothers' eardrums open and flooded this clubhouse with my grief.

"It's him, isn't it?" Linda laid a gentle hand on my shoulder, the first real contact we'd had that was more than professional since Tank got her off my ass.

One more thing he'd done for me. Keeping her and the admin off my ass. Harsh, but effective.

There was no use in hiding it. I nodded, staring sadly into my cup of green tea. I was in the break room, alone and sulking before she came in.

"I read all about in the papers. What your cousin did, the way he mopped the floor with that guy…" Linda paused. "Frankly, the bastard deserved it."

I looked up, daggers in my eyes, thinking she meant Tank.

"I'm talking about your asshole cousin."

What? I wondered if I heard her right.

I was floored. Foul language and bloodlust wasn't the head RN I knew. Where did that stuffy granny go? The woman who withdrew her hand and circled the table to sit across from me was somebody totally different.

"I was harsh earlier, Emma, and I'm sorry. I want you to know I'm here to help. Not because you're part of my team – because I'm your friend."

I shook my head. The whole damned world kept going topsy-turvy and batshit insane.

"Why, Linda? You're the one who tried to warn me about all this after they —"

"I know." She held up a hand. "I wouldn't take the job you're doing off the books. I was mad they even offered it. But I don't blame you for doing what you need to. You've got a motive way more important than money now. This whole thing reminds me so much of Red..."

She closed her eyes, rubbing them behind her glasses. I sat up straight. She'd never breathed a word about anyone named Red before. Sounded like a road name.

"My daughter and her kids are all I have left of him," she said with a sigh. "It was before I married Hugh. That sweet man has given me so much. Only man in the world who'd pick up a single mother in nursing school and keep on giving long after the nuptials. But the one thing he didn't do was everything Red offered...and he never *killed* for me."

Cool lightning crept up my spine. I realized Linda was giving me her confession, reaching out to me the same way Saffron had as a biker's old lady.

"I was his. He was mine. It was the late seventies. The whole world was changing. I was a different girl then. Came from a broken home and started whoring around the Grizzlies club near Wallace just to get the hell out of Idaho. I never expected to fall in love.

"Red was everything. The only thing bigger than that man's tattooed muscles and his beard was his heart. He gave me his brand and a baby girl before things went to shit. God, being his old lady meant the world to me." She shook her head. "One day, a bad deal went down. I was managing a little tourist shop just along the state border. Didn't make much serving beers and selling bison blankets. But it was the perfect place to hide our loot, everything we were saving for a house and Betsy's college.

"Like any man with a Harley, Red wasn't perfect, though he'll always be in my heart. When he drank, he talked a lot. Sometimes too much. The Grizzlies were bringing in more riff raff, about the time when old man Stomp retired and left the club to his VP, Fang. Some junkie asshole who came over from one of the little MCs they'd gobbled up around Coeur d'Alene heard about our cash.

"Red laughed too much after losing a couple thousand during a drunken poker game with his brothers. This asshole figured out there was more where that came from.

"I didn't see him coming. Neither did my little girl. The bastard broke in when I was closing up the shop. Ripped my baby girl out of her seat and put a gun to her head…"

Linda closed her eyes. Her face was tight, and she had to fight to hold in the tears.

Jesus, so did I. I'd only heard of Red a couple minutes ago, but he already made me think about Tank. My heart was breaking right alongside hers, a memory so intense and vivid I could see it as she told the story like it just happened yesterday.

"I managed to get him away from Bets and walked him to the stockpile we kept in a safe out back. Red showed up just in time to pick us up. He figured out fast something was fucked up. I watched him creep up behind the man while the weasel was distracted, hunting knife in his hand.

"Red was fast. Efficient. Unfortunately, so was he." She sighed. "The jackass spun as soon as Red grabbed his head and put that knife in his throat. Somehow, he got a clean shot off before he bled out. The bullet went through my old man's heart. I held him as he died, felt the very second his soul gave out and his heart stopped pumping blood in my hands. I tried like hell to seal his wound, knowing it wouldn't do any good. I tried and watched him die."

I lost it there. Tears started pouring out my hot red eyes. I grabbed Linda's hand in both of mine and squeezed as hard as I could.

God, how many times had Tank's blood been on my hands? If things had gone down differently with Mark, it would've happened again, maybe for the last time.

Bad as this was, he was in prison. He wasn't dead. And as long as he drew a single breath, I wasn't giving up.

When I visited him in jail yesterday, he'd tried to show me the door. I ran from that glass, trying to forget his heavy chains and orange jumpsuit, trying to scratch away the horrible words that kept rolling around and around in my head.

You wanna talk about regrets? Only one I got is breaking your heart. But if that's what it takes to keep you safe, then

I'm game. One day, everything'll make sense, and I'll be nothing but a distant fucking memory.

Get the hell out and go live enough for both of us.

No, Tank. I wouldn't do it, no matter how many times he ordered me to with evil words. Didn't he see it?

Without him, there was no living. Without him, I was hollow, dead, ruined.

"Em, I left that lifestyle after Red. Losing him hurt too damned much. I tried to forget about it until the Devils showed up and started raising hell in town. At first, I wrote them off just like the filthy Grizzlies. The bears are a gross shadow of what they were when Red was alive..." She wiped her eyes with her free hand, trying to calm down. "I wrote you off too. Thought you were a fucking idiot for taking their money. I tried to scare you straight with that stunt about the medical supplies all those months ago..."

I nodded. Finally, I understood. "Oh, Linda. It's okay. I wish I'd known. If you'd told me about Red before..."

I stopped. *I would've done things differently* was at the tip of my tongue, but it would've been a lie.

No. Hell no. If I'd known about Red, the only thing different would've been rushing to Tank's side sooner, loving him more than any woman should.

I wouldn't have let him tell me no, the same way I won't hear it now.

"I was wrong, Emma," she continued. "I've been coming around to admitting it for weeks. Red's been on my mind a lot, and I've been seeing his ghost twenty-four-seven since I heard about what happened with you and John."

"Tank," I said. "His road name's Tank. I don't care what they call him when he's locked up. Tank, John, whatever...I'm a total helpless fool for him. And I'm going to keep loving him the same way you loved Red."

She nodded, solemn and approving. "You do that. Don't let him push you away! Don't let a few prison bars come between you two either. If Red had gone to jail, I would've been right there waiting. Just between you and me, as wonderful as Hugh's been for me since my young days, I'd give *anything* on this entire screwed up planet just for another hour with that man."

Linda was looking right through me. It was like she could see him standing behind me, a phantom in the flesh, the man she'd loved and suffered for and kept loving long after he was dust.

"I won't do anything different," I said, feeling my heartbeat filling my ears. "I can't! Thanks, Linda. You just got a ton of crap off my mind. I'm finally awake."

She patted my hand. "Same here. And don't forget – if there's anything I can do to help – call me. I don't care if it's three o'clock in the morning. Call me, Emma. Best way I can honor Red's memory is making sure you ride off with your man, no matter how wrong it seems or how many laws you have to break."

She got up and left the room. Probably needed more tissue after spilling her soul, and I didn't blame her.

You're wrong, Tank, I thought with a grimace. *I'm not going to let you change your mind again. Somehow, someway, I'm going to dig my heart out and push it into your cell if I have to.*

You saved me. Now, I'm going to do the same.

My dead fucking cousin and the law won't kill this love.

"Well? What is it?" I was in the infirmary getting frustrated as hell. It was the second time I'd asked Stinger the question, and he was dancing around his issue like a bashful teen.

I was looking forward to an evening at home catching up on sleep after a long shift at the hospital and hearing Linda's sad story. But that wouldn't do when my burner phone rang and Stinger needed to see me.

He shot me a severe look. Far too serious for the strong jaw that normally carried his huge smile. "Think I need an STD test, nurse. Need to make sure our fucking whores haven't passed on anything lately."

I raised an eyebrow. "They were both clean when I checked them last week. A little longer ago than that, actually, thanks to all the crap flying around here. Why? Is there something you want me to know about?"

Stinger covered his mouth, clearing his throat. "Uh, it's my left nut. My testicle. Sorry. Thing's been sore and itching like hell this past week, ever since we returned from our biz with the Rams. Thought it was jock itch at first or just some discomfort from riding. But it's not going away…"

"All right. I can check on that for you. I'm a professional, Stinger. There's nothing to be ashamed of."

"Right, right. You're right about the bullshit going down too. With everything coming down lately, Blaze is knocking heads to make sure we're all focused, staying in perfect shape. He wants you to grill Alice again next week..."

"Here." I pushed a small plastic bottle into his hand. "Fill that up next time you're in the bathroom and bring it to me."

He nodded. "We're working on Tank's thing too. It's all Blaze is thinking about when there isn't some other distraction with Throttle out East or checking up on the Rams. We're lucky he was here with us to pay those fucks a visit. We might've never gotten her out safely without his help."

My eyebrow quirked again. "Is that what this is all about, VP? Our forgetful guest? Are you thinking about letting Marianne and Sangria have a rest while you go after her instead?"

Stinger's face tightened. "Fuck no. Shit, Emma, can't a dude worry about his sac? I'm not like Blaze and Tank. I'm not the settling type. She's club business. I'm just looking after her."

I suppressed a snort. How many times had I heard that in this clubhouse? Well, really only once since Blaze and Saffron were the lone couple who'd truly found their happily ever after. Maverick and June were only around to catch tiny hints of their passion.

But *when* Tank came home, we were going to find our happy ending. I wouldn't have it any other way.

"Right," I said, holding in the sarcasm. "I'll have your test results out quick. Also need an updated history of any sexual contacts."

He laughed. "Baby, I'll get you everything you need. I love talking dirty."

I grabbed the clipboard behind me and shoved it to his chest. Stinger looked surprised, spinning it around until it was upright.

"What's this?" He asked.

"Write down anything you feel I should know about. I know we're winging it here, Stinger, but I'm still keeping proper medical records like any other clinic. There's only one man I want to hear dirty talk from, and he isn't you."

His big toothy grin melted. Just then, a heavy fist pounded on the door.

Blaze didn't wait for an answer before he popped the door. "You guys done in here, or what?"

"Yeah, Prez. I was just leaving." Stinger shoved the plastic bottle into his pocket and pinched the clipboard under his arm, scuttling out the door. Probably hoping Blaze wouldn't notice and give him any shit.

For a second, I thought the President was going to razz him rough. But he let Stinger go without a comment, turning to me instead, his face deadly serious.

"I came down hard on your ass because I needed to, Em. You understand that? Had to protect my club. This MC has always had a zero tolerance policy for rats. Main reason we're still around and not swept up in some fucking RICO sting."

I nodded. He'd been a real bastard during the interrogation, but I really did understand. I wasn't going to let my ego get in the way.

"Good. Listen, all the brothers got church tomorrow, and we're gonna make a decision about something that's got a good chance of getting Tank home."

"Really?" My breath hitched and I leaned forward. Totally desperate and giddy, yeah, but I didn't care.

"Don't get too excited. It all hinges on whether or not the Feds will take a fucking deal. And even then, they might not let him come home right away. It'll be a reduced sentence. The man's facing murder. That's heavy shit, something the club lawyers and bribes can't wave away like magic. And remember, this is only on the table if every brother in this club agrees to give up our collateral, which is gonna raise some uncomfortable fucking questions by itself."

"I understand." I leaned on the wall. "Anything you can do, Blaze, I'll appreciate. He was protecting me as much as he was the Devils."

"You don't need to tell me, woman. Now it's our turn to bail his ass out, and I'm gonna do everything I can. Hold tight. Be ready to drop by when your phone rings. I'll send my old lady to pick you up."

He turned and started to storm away. I chewed my lip, barely yelling after him before he was out the door.

"Hey!" I yelled. Blaze turned, one hand on the door. "Things haven't been so bleak around here since Saffron's mom died and you chased down those rogue Grizzlies. I was just wondering...how're the wedding plans coming?"

"We're still on track," he growled happily. "Nothing in this world's gonna keep me from making it all official with my girl. Can't imagine getting married without my biggest bro right at my side. You too, Em. Wedding won't be the same if you're not there with his ass in Reno next Spring."

"I know," I said gently, looking down at the ground.

"Keep hoping, and keep after him too. I heard how that stubborn bastard tried to turn you away when you visited a couple days ago." Blaze snorted. "I don't give two shits how many times he goes back and forth. I know a bro when he's head over boots in love with a chick. Whatever the fuck he says, don't listen. Tank *loves* your ass, Em, and he'll never stop 'til he's done breathing."

The door slammed loudly, leaving me alone with my tears. Somehow, this situation was *worse* than worrying about crazy rivals from other clubs storming in and hurting us.

Armed men were scary, but at least I could fight them, and so could the brothers. Freeing Tank was all in the hands of bureaucrats, badges, and suits, strange machinations behind the scenes I barely understood.

I couldn't help him. Not directly.

All I could do was keep on loving him, and I'd do it until my heart melted to mush.

My phone jerked in my pocket while I was wiping down my hands at the hospital. An elderly woman coughed all over me in a fit so bad she'd clawed at my hand, tearing my gloves.

Flu season was coming, and getting sick was the last thing I needed. I followed all the hospital's dull guidelines about disease control to grim perfection.

"Shit!" The phone's vibration took me by surprise. I rinsed my hands off and quickly dried them on the sterile towel before I reached for it.

VOTE WENT MY WAY. ALL YEAS. SAFFRON'S COMING TO PICK UR ASS UP NOW.

Soon as I read Blaze's text, I ran to Linda. She pulled in another girl to cover my shift as soon as she realized it was about Tank. Half an hour later, I was riding in a newer black hatchback with Saffron, a lovely step up from the crappy car she'd had when she met Blaze.

We rolled into the Missoula PD's parking lot. The tension was building, so claustrophobic I swore my ribs were going to crack if my heart thumped any harder.

"You'll be okay, Em." Saffron saw my hand shaking and reached for it. "So will Tank. I used to worry like a nervous wreck every time Blaze went on some dangerous run. The fear's all gone since that night they tortured me and I almost lost everything. I trust Blaze. He didn't let me die. He won't let Tank rot behind bars either."

I nodded, struggling to regain control. Thank God I didn't break down right there. I couldn't stop thinking about all the awful ways this whole thing could go wrong.

Still, I didn't dare tell Saffron about Linda and Red. That story was for my ears only, a bittersweet reminder of everything I'd lose if the boys couldn't cut a deal to bring my man home.

I took the steps into the police station one at a time. Once we were inside, Saffron sat in the waiting room. An officer called my name and led me to a dingy looking meeting room behind a thick door.

Blaze and two bulldog faced men in suits were waiting for me inside.

They introduced themselves as Jones and Smith, both clean cut, pale faced, and nearly identical. The red and green ties were the only obvious difference. Jones was the District Attorney, and Smith said he was with the ATF.

"Miss Galena, if anything happens here today, please understand we'll need your full testimony for the record." Jones tapped the fancy recorder laid out on the table between us. "Normally we wouldn't involve you this early on, but our guest here insisted."

Damn right, the little nod Blaze gave them said.

"Mister Sturm –" Smith started before Blaze cut him off.

"It's Blaze to everybody. You can put whatever name you'd like on the official records. I'm making this deal on behalf of my brother and the whole club. I'm not just speaking for myself here. I'm a rep, same as you two Feds are for your alphabet soup agencies."

Smith smiled uneasily. "Understood. Well then, *Blaze*, would you like to elaborate on your preliminary offer?"

"How about the body of Mickey James, biggest asshole weapon's smuggler on the West Coast?"

Both their expressions tightened. I knew a man's poker face when I saw one, and right now I was looking at two on these Feds.

"You're confident James is dead?" Jones asked.

"Certain. We buried the motherfucker ourselves." Blaze laughed as the men's eyes got an uneasy glimmer. "It's not what you're thinking. We didn't kill him. Found him with some new friends of ours, and they were persuaded to let us haul his body away."

"Hm. James would've been a whole lot more valuable to us alive. A verified death would close his file, sure, but not many others. Homeland Security will probably take the body with mixed feelings at best." Jones looked to his partner. "What do you think, Smith? I'd like to recommend an early parole for John Richmond under these circumstances. Five years. Maybe three if James' body leads to tying up any loose ends."

Blaze slammed his fists on the table. "That's fucking bullshit! I ought to drop off Mickey's bones after they've been gnawed up by worms. They'd be in better shape than my bro after three years in your shitty prison."

My heart clenched when they said *three years*. Jesus, and that was just a tiny improvement over five. Half a fucking decade.

It might as well have been an eternity. I looked at Blaze, feeling like I had a bomb sitting next to me, a very dangerous one in a place swarming with cops and agents.

By some miracle, I was keeping my cool better than him. I wondered if he was about to go ballastic and get us all arrested.

"We'll take custody of the remains with full immunity for your club, of course." Smith was trying to be reassuring. "Normally, the ATF is obligated to bring in other departments when there's any violent crime. This time, we're willing to cut you a deal with no further investigation into the Prairie Devils Motorcycle Club at this time, plus –"

Smith trailed off when he saw Blaze flexing his arms, shaking his fists. Jones' eyes were on the Satan's Scythe patch on his cut, a constant reminder to anybody who understood the club's symbols that this wasn't a game.

"All right." Blaze said, a little more calmly. "Let's talk about a counter-offer."

Jones looked up. "What do you have in mind?"

"I'll do your damned investigation for you," Blaze said, lifting a finger and wagging it in their faces. "Only if you let Tank out next week. We'll post full bail. Give him two weeks to work with me. I need him. He's my…safety expert, and a damned good detective too. If we can't turn up anything juicier about Mickey's trade, then he'll go right back to jail and wait out his three years. No bullshit."

The two men looked skeptical.

"That's highly unorthodox, Blaze. Not only are you asking us to look away from an investigation that may promote more criminal activity, but we'd have to trust your man will surrender himself if you don't provide suitable evidence."

"Tank won't fight it. He'll do anything for this club, and damned near anything for the girl here next to me." Blaze narrowed his eyes. "It's me you've got to worry about. I'd rather see myself end up behind bars before a bro who was doing what's right, cracking skulls in self-defense. You know, everything your fucked up system ought to prevent from happening in the first place. I'll tell you this: I got better control over my club than you ATF assholes have over your own fucking agency. Emma's cousin wouldn't have pissed on everybody and gotten his ass killed if you'd kept the reins."

Smith cleared his throat and shifted uncomfortably. Inside, I was smiling, shaking my head. I wondered how any woman ever ended up with these weak, clinical professionals when there were badasses in the world like Tank and Blaze.

"You boys want to find out what Mickey's been up to or not? Obviously, you've been jerking your dicks in that direction for years with nothing to show for it. Your methods don't work. Mine will. Just give me a chance to flex and let my brother out."

Jones stretched in his chair, taking a minute to breathe, rubbing his face. He looked tired. Finally, he leaned forward again, hands folded.

"The DA's office is willing to entertain this on a controlled basis. First, you'll report in on your progress and let us know the location of John Richmond at all times."

Smith looked at the other man sourly. Then he nodded, slow and certain. "We'll give it a chance. I'll have to call in a few favors back home, but my guys should choke it down. Lord knows the case has been cold for years. Understand your club is going to tread as gently as possible. No violence. No smuggling. And absolutely no tampering with a Federal investigation on your part."

Blaze locked eyes with the man for several long seconds before he extended his hand. "You've got yourselves a deal. Now, let Emma tell you her side of this shit again so we can get Tank home."

All eyes were on me. I couldn't look at anybody except Blaze. The small bright stars in his eyes told me he heard my thanks loud and clear without even saying it.

He'd just given me back my giant, muscular, heavily tattooed world. Or at least a *chance* at keeping Tank, making him understand I wasn't going to walk away from this no matter what.

If I wasn't sitting next to two government drones who were about to grill me for the thousandth time, I would've threw my arms around Blaze and gushed out my gratitude like a stupid schoolgirl.

It took two days to process him. Linda gave me the entire day off for Tank's release on Friday.

The brothers were all planning a big bash with girls, loud rock, and tons of free flowing whiskey. One explosive party before they hit the road the next day, trying to turn up whatever they could find to secure Tank's freedom. I wasn't sure how I was going to survive the countdown to Tank's homecoming – if it could be called that.

Really, release day was either a welcome home or a send off to prison.

I could tell Blaze was on edge when he called me to the clubhouse on Thursday. When I got there, he was waiting in his office with Stinger and the pale dark haired girl. Alice looked up at me with the same confused, vacant eyes she always had.

"Need you to try to get something useful out of her, Em," Blaze said. "The Rams are riding our asses. They can smell the shit that's about to come down with Tank and the Feds. The assholes spotted our prospects when I sent them out to move Mickey's corpse to a safer place. The fucks have been laying off the meth and booze long enough to do more spying than I gave 'em credit for. Bigger balls too since they're giving us shit about the girl."

"Fuck the Rams," Stinger snarled, an unusual break in his normally chill demeanor. "If those bastards want her brought back to their ratty little clubhouse, they'll have to come here and take her."

"Christ, Sting." Blaze turned to him and shook his head. "Get some fucking pussy that's used to taking dick and stop worrying. Like I said in church, she's not goin' anywhere. She's too valuable."

He looked back to me. "I still need to know who the fuck she is and what she was doing living like a dog in their storage room. Help me figure it out, Em."

My adrenaline surged. I didn't understand what the hell he wanted me to do. I wasn't a psychologist, much less an interrogator. I'd examined the girl three times, always checking for brain damage or something that would explain the amnesia.

It wasn't her body that was keeping her mouth shut. It was her mind.

Still, I couldn't just sweep his concerns aside. He'd given me so much with this deal, and Tank's future freedom depended on turning up *something* about the dead man the law could sink its teeth into.

"I'll do my best," I said, forcing confidence into my voice.

"Good,. I'll leave you three to deal with this. Roller and the prospects are coming home this evening from a run. I gotta go." Blaze turned smartly and dashed out the door, leaving it to slam shut behind him.

Now, it was just me, Stinger, and Alice. The girl sat there like a zombie the whole time. I'd never seen anyone so disinterested in herself while a bunch of strangers squawked about her fate right in front of her.

"Go easy," Stinger said sternly. "She's still plenty shook up from living the way she did. Those motherfuckers had her holed up like a monkey."

I studied her carefully. Stinger had his reasons for wanting to keep this gentle, but my brain screamed at me to do the complete opposite.

True, I was no psychologist. But there was something more than the vacant, depressed dull sheen in this girl's eyes every time she looked at me, something she wanted to say. I wasn't buying her total amnesia.

I crouched down at face level, eyeball to eyeball, gripping the chair behind her shoulders. "Alice, I need you to tell me anything you remember – *anything* at all – about the man named Mickey James and what you were doing at the Pagan Rams' clubhouse."

She stared at me for a second. Then her eyes quickly shifted away. "We've been through this before…I'm lucky to remember my own name. Nothing else. I was sick. I woke up in the closet. I was scared to come out when I saw the dead body so I stayed there, cowering every time they brought me meals. I don't remember anyone named Mickey."

Stinger was leaning back on Blaze's desk behind me. He broke forward with a snort, pacing the floor around us.

"Don't understand what the fuck Blaze expects you to do. Alice doesn't know shit. Whatever the hell happened with the Rams, it was bad enough to make her forget, just like you said."

"No," I said, never taking my eyes off her. "She can't give us the big picture. But she might remember some details. There's got to be somebody home in there."

Finally, the girl looked up, more than a little fury dancing in her eyes. "Stop talking about me like that. I didn't ask to be here. I don't understand why you and these bikers are keeping me here."

"Easy, baby." Stinger put his hand on her shoulder. "We're just trying to help a friend, and help you too."

She rolled her shoulders. I took a few steps backward as she thrashed, throwing him off her. Stinger looked hurt, and then angry.

The sugar wasn't working. Time for the spice. Tank's face was all that was on my mind as I circled her, closer and closer. I reached out and grabbed her raven black ponytail, tilting her head with a twist, forcing her to look at me.

"Emma, what the fuck?" Stinger's hands were on me in an instant.

"You guys are too scared to get tough with a girl unless she's being a real bitch. I get it, you don't rough up girls. Thing is, I'm not bound by your club charter. This bitch is hiding something, Sting, and I want to know what."

"Let go! Stop hurting her!" he growled, digging his fingers into my shoulders.

It hurt, but it wasn't a fraction of the force he would've used on a man. I knew the VP wouldn't hurt a woman unless she was threatening their life or fucking over the club.

"Oh, please." I twisted her ponytail, harsher this time. Alice whimpered. "She's had worse. If she'd tell us what, then I wouldn't have to keep doing this."

I pulled harder. Alice jerked, but her struggle only made her hair pinch tighter in my fist. Behind me, Stinger shifted his hands, ready to pick me up and carry me away if he could just get my death grip off her.

"Dammit, Em, I'm fucking warning you."

One more pull. Harder! Wicked determination stormed through my blood.

I yanked. Alice came completely out of her chair, grunting in pain and falling. She hit the floor. Soon as I lost my grip, Stinger whipped me up off my feet and rushed to the nearest wall, pinning me down.

"Everybody's losing their fucking mind around here!" he roared. "Look, nurse, I know you're upset as all hell about Tank's situation. That's still no excuse for you to treat this poor girl like a piece of fucking –"

"Okay! I'll…I'll talk." Alice's voice cracked as she stumbled to her feet. "You people are nuts."

Stinger's grip on me instantly relaxed. He turned around, face lined with surprise.

"I'm going to tell you everything I remember," she said, staring with hateful eyes. "After that, I want to forget about all this crap. I want you to let me go. If you keep holding me here, you're no better than the Rams. I can't be a prisoner to a bunch of bikers!"

Stinger stepped up, his eyes hard and dark. "I'll check with Blaze. You're right, Alice. Long as we're certain you're safe, there's no reason to keep you here."

Ignoring him, Alice looked at me, my signal to come closer again. She stepped away from Stinger and sat in the chair, ready for confession.

"I'm not faking my bad memory. I don't remember any man named Mickey James or even what happened in that clubhouse. I don't remember shit about my old life. All I know is how I got there…"

"Go on. Please," I added as an afterthought.

"I was riding with a big man across the plains. Had to be Wyoming or some other place rugged and windy. He didn't talk much. He was…familiar. Had a strong silent way about him, but I'm sure he wasn't a lover. Maybe an Uncle or something. The drive was intense. We were under a lot of pressure. He drove a huge truck, and it was filled to capacity. So full the cargo nearly stretched into the cabin. He kept telling me not to worry, that we'd have a way to unload all this crap as soon as we got to Montana.

"It was some kind of deal. The cargo looked like crates, weapon boxes, bombs…stuff you'd see in a war zone or a movie. I only remember seeing it once or twice when he opened it at night, whenever we pulled over to sleep."

Stinger's eyes lit up. So did mine.

"Did you guys see a truck when you visited their clubhouse?" I asked him.

"Fuck no. That shit had to have gone somewhere if it was really the kinda shipment she's talking about. Fuck, I have to tell Blaze. If we can find this damned thing or make the Rams cough up what they did with it…"

He didn't finish before he rushed out the door. I was smiling, filling in the blanks. If the brothers found this stupid truck with its illegal cargo, then Tank had a good chance of keeping his freedom.

Alice got up and started walking to the door. I stepped up before she reached it, grabbing her shoulder.

"What! Why can't anybody here just leave me alone?" She snarled, trying to twist away.

"Stop being such an ungrateful bitch. I get it, Alice. I really do." I took my hand away and she turned around to face me. "You're pissed off, confused, and you've got no clue what's going to happen next. What you don't understand is these guys are the good ones. If they hadn't paid a visit to the Rams, you'd still be there. Probably somewhere worse."

She cocked her head, wondering what I meant.

"You think they were just going to leave you cooped up in that room? They would've had to deal with Mickey's body at some point. MCs are very good at making things disappear, even sloppy ones like the Rams. What would they have done with you? Do you have any idea how big a favor Stinger and Blaze did bringing you here? They saved your fucking life."

Vivid red flooded her cheeks. I wasn't sure if it was genuine shame or just more misguided anger.

"You're not my big sister," she said coldly. "I'm not a biker's whore like all the girls here. I don't care what Stinger's done. He's just another man who acts like he's helping. Really, he only cares because he wants to get between my legs…he wants to fuck me and throw me away."

Damn. Why couldn't she see how wrong she was? The temptation to reach for her hair again and make her head spin was becoming irresistible. Maybe I should've gone lower to find the stick shoved deep in her ass.

I was a nurse, after all.

"Maybe keeping yourself cooped up here with these deadly, crazy bastards is for you, Emma. It's not for me. Soon as somebody gives me the okay, I'm gone, and I won't look back." She sighed, bright anger and frustration leaving her body. "I can't remember who I am or what I'm supposed to be. All I can do is start a new life, get my shit together, and figure things out. None of that involves you, Stinger, or anything remotely attached to the Prairie Devils MC."

Alice turned. This time, I let her go, watching her skinny legs bobbing like a cat's.

She deserved a choice. I couldn't fault her for that.

Processing her crap in my head made me think about everything I'd done to lead me here. I thought about Linda's tragic end with Red, and how all this crazy shit screamed I was meant to be here, in this club, in with Tank.

I'd gone too far, too deep, to go anywhere else and live a different life. And once he was free and clear, I'd never imagine another life again.

I wanted to be his old lady like nothing else, and I was going to be. Even if I had to suffer.

The next day, it was a full convoy riding to the prison. I went with Blaze and Saffron in the truck. They towed Tank's bike behind them, and I couldn't wait to be on it again, pressed up against his back while we drove home to the bash at the clubhouse.

I waited nervously by the prison gate. At two o'clock, the buzzer rang, and three men came out of the guard shack.

The two guards escorting him looked like children next to a giant. The man in the middle was *my* giant. God, he looked magnificent.

He was back in his jeans and cut, sporting full colors. All the brothers began to holler as soon as they saw him. Moose and his old lady, Connie, kicked up the most noise. Saffron reached for my hand and gave it a quick squeeze.

"This is it, Em. The moment you've been waiting for."

Tank's eyes didn't go anywhere else as soon as he saw me. They locked on tight, stormy and strong as ever. Potent emotions surged, drilled deep, and then exploded like a bomb.

When he was through the gate, I ran the last few feet over the rugged pavement. He opened his arms right before I crashed against his chest.

I seriously wondered if I'd feel his embrace, or if he'd push me away, determined to shut me out forever. But no, they closed across my back, and then closed tighter. He pulled me off my feet and threw his lips against mine.

The guys went nuts, and so did the two old ladies. Crazy didn't begin to describe the shock tearing through me.

The fire, the fear, the giddy excitement just having him against me again…it was all here, roiled to perfection in the embrace where I belonged.

I broke the kiss, loving the way his rough taste lingered on my lips. "I was afraid you meant what you said behind the glass…"

"I did when I said it, Em. I was pissed off and determined to make sure you lived the good life. Couldn't think about anything else after I fucked up and did what I did. I killed that asshole, and I wanted to kill this too, anything to keep you away from me so you wouldn't waste your life on a caged animal." He gave me a small smile. "But a man's got shit to do in the tank except think. I thought hard. I figured it out. I'm done fighting – don't care how fucked up or bleak things get. Babe, I couldn't give your sweet ass up and push you away if I tried. There's only one thing worth changing here: I got to get my damned head screwed on straight and stop jerking you around every time something goes to shit."

I blinked. Then I burst into a great big grin, amazed he'd finally come to his senses. I was moving in for another kiss before he stopped me.

"Hold up. Need you to understand I'm not home free. If I can't help Blaze and the boys track down some shit to feed the Feds, then I'm gonna go right back in. Won't see you again for at least three years."

Every time I thought about it was like a punch in the stomach. But I kept my gaze fused with his, lost in the beautiful moment nothing would ruin. I nodded.

"And if that happens, I'll be waiting. I'll come see you every single time they let me. I'll be right *here*, Tank, ready to be your old lady, ready to be claimed."

"Then let's not waste another second. Whatever the fuck happens when my two weeks is up, I'm not gonna squander another day just calling you my lover. You're more, babe. So much fucking more." He grabbed my wrists and tugged me forward, toward where the guys were waiting.

Blaze came up and slapped him on the back. "Goddamn, it's good to see you breathing this cool mountain air again. Come on, bro. We're gonna forget this fucking bullshit for one night and blow off some steam at the clubhouse. We can get to work on keeping you out of this shithole permanently tomorrow."

"Just a second, Prez. Before we go home, I got something I need to say."

Blaze's eyes narrowed. He looked to me, then to Tank. A slow, knowing smile spread across his face.

"Greedy bastard. You just can't wait another second, can you?" Blaze laughed.

Before me or Tank could say anything, he clapped his hands loudly and walked toward the gaggle of bikes and cars pulled up to the prison road. Blaze waved his hands, reaching out, encouraging all the brothers and their girls to approach.

"Get over here! Move your asses. Tank's got a speech to make before we hit the clubhouse and break into that Jack."

It was strange to be the center of attention for this gruff looking crowd. Everybody was silent as they stared, all hard biker eyes and several glances from old ladies that weren't much softer. Saffron was practically beaming, biting her lip, silently pulling for me.

This is it. Sweet, sweet anticipation.

I looked at Tank. Suddenly, he whirled me around, throwing me against the huge slab of his chest. His strong shoulder bobbed against my ear as he spoke, rock hard muscle dancing to his words.

"Brothers and friends, you've all been damned good to me this year, sticking by my side whenever I was torn up on my ass or locked up here in the slammer. You know this club is my home and you're all family. That said, the girl I'm holding here and now has turned into even more, a special kinda family that cuts just as deep as the blood in this MC and the patch."

The women suppressed their giddy laughter. There were a few snorts, brothers waiting with baited breath.

"As of today, Emma Galena is *off fucking limits,*" he growled. "She's mine, all mine, and only mine. You'll all be reminded soon enough, every goddamned day when she's wearing my brand. We don't have a fucking clue what's gonna go down the next couple weeks…"

I looked out to the crowd. All the gazes were so intense. Saffron and Connie's eyes had gone soft, happy, dreamy. Blaze's gaze was hard as ever, one hand tight around his old lady's waist. He nodded as Tank continued.

"Maybe I'll be right back here behind bars in a couple weeks. Maybe I won't. Whatever happens with me and the Feds doesn't got shit on what's going on with my old lady. She's mine no matter where the hell I am. Dead, imprisoned, or alive." His chest rolled higher as he took in a big breath, hot and angry as hell. "You take good fucking care of her if I disappear. No bullshit. If I find out any man is circling her – brother or not – I'll dig my way out of this prison and split his fucking skull myself.

"Em and I have wasted too much fucking time to let anything else stand in the way. Right here, this day, I'm not wasting a precious second more. I'm taking this girl to the clubhouse, slamming the door to my room, and showing her what being claimed like this really means. We'll see you all for drinks in a few."

Tank jerked me up. I squeaked in surprise. Now, I was in his arms, being cradled like a kitten.

Heat waves kept pulsing through my body. I was flushed blood red from hearing him pour his heart out in front of an audience, but it was nothing compared to the lightning zipping through my veins, the sheer need to feel him do everything he promised.

Brothers laughed, jeered, and clapped as he started forward. Blaze reached out and gave him another slap as he passed, carrying me like a caveman, a warrior, a badass.

I saw a brief flash of Stinger, smiling a grin that put even Saffron's silly, happy smile to shame.

The empty spot next to him was telling. Alice was nowhere to be seen. I hoped Tank wasn't the only one who'd come to his senses soon.

A couple minutes later, I was on the back of his bike, holding on tight as the convoy got its drivers saddled up and took off. We rode in the biker column. No formation ranked by officers this time because Blaze and a Moose had their trucks.

I rubbed his rock hard belly a little after every mile. Being on the bike this time wasn't half as unnerving as the first. The cold was starting to bite, but being pressed up flat against him felt so good. I lost myself in his warmth and the engine's steady, peaceful rumble.

God, a solid week behind bars hadn't done anything to erase his scent. I leaned on him and inhaled deep. This man didn't need expensive cologne to smell good.

It was all him, an intoxicating blend of musk and leather, pure strength surrounding my brain through my nostrils. Tank groaned several times at the stop lines closer to the clubhouse. Once, my hand brushed a little too low beneath his belt, grazing the ridge between his legs.

Steel lined his enormous length, thick and ready and so fucking hot. I had a mischievous feeling hobnobbing with the brothers and their old ladies was going to wait a good long while. Same as the drinks.

Who the hell needed to load up on beer and Jack when everything I needed was at my fingertips? Tank was a huge, sexy, tattooed addiction I'd be enjoying for the rest of my life.

We were the first ones inside. Tank helped me off his bike and we headed down the hall, straight to his room. He mentioned how he couldn't wait to get his own place after this latest shit storm was through.

"You've got a place at my house," I said, lacing my fingers tighter through his.

He looked at me and grinned, shaking his head. "No, babe. You're gonna unload that piece of shit rental and move somewhere nicer with me one day. Don't think any of us are real interested in eating on that fucking kitchen table ever again after what went down there…let alone doing anything else there."

I smiled at the wicked suggestion. And I needed to cling to that thought too, had to focus on the future instead of reliving that terrible night where he beat my asshole cousin to death on the tile floor.

The brothers were streaming into the bar, boisterous and full of dirty jokes. Their sounds formed a distant, happy clamor as we pushed our way inside his little room. He'd cleaned up good since our dark time apart.

The place still stank faintly of whiskey, but all the empty bottles were gone, leaving a spartan chamber that was all ours. Nothing but a dresser and a bed that was way too small to get in the way of us. Small or not, it would do.

I flashed him a coy smile and started to walk forward. I couldn't wait for him to see what I had on underneath my clothes, brand new lingerie I'd picked out the night before and thrown on this morning.

Before I could take another step toward the bed, Tank jerked back on my hand. I turned. We shared another fiery gaze for several long seconds before he threw his arms around me and twisted, spinning us across the room.

I bumped against the door, gasping for badly needed air. God, just having him this close, this intense, smothered everything except the fire pulsing in my blood. The way he was looking at me threatened all my breath, dark tiger eyes set in a man's face.

"There's three parts to claiming an old lady," Tank said. "One's a warning and a flash of fists, letting every asshole in the whole damned world know they're going to get fucked up if they get an inch too close to what's mine. Two, I get my brand on your beautiful ass. You're gonna look great wearing my patch and my ink on your skin, Em. Fuck, I'll put it there myself. Tomorrow. No more wasted days. Every one with you has got my whole fucking world from now on."

I looked up slowly, trying not to melt underneath his gaze. "What's number three?"

"I hold you to the wall and fuck your brains out 'til you can't stop screaming, babe. I'm gonna make sure everybody hears your moans over all the rock and dirty jokes behind these walls. I want every man in spitting distance to know your ass is mine forever, and only one dick in the world knows how to work that sweet pussy right. You're gonna lose your voice screaming my name over and over and over, making up for all the time we've wasted without you wrapped around every horny inch of me."

Holy, holy shit. I was breathless, embarrassed, and yes, red as the sun. Not to mention totally, phenomenally turned on.

He wanted his brothers to hear us? Brothers, old ladies, whores? *Crap!*

I scratched at his neck, mouthing his name weakly, trying to change his mind. I wasn't ready to put on a show, though it seemed kinda hot in my heart's naughtiest spot.

"Tank, I –"

No dice. As soon as he leaned in and licked up the nook of my neck, it was all over. I rocked back against the door frame, moaning as he tugged at my shirt and slid his smooth tongue over my skin. Then I gasped, louder, when his other hand circled down, cupping my ass for a possessive squeeze.

Before Tank, I was never ravished. I never thought I'd give myself up and totally surrender to a man, following him into filthy, devilish things good girls didn't do.

I never thought I'd become another Emma, reshaped by his wicked mind and non-stop fire. Never thought I'd lose my sanity in his sin, every tattooed granite inch of what he offered.

But there I was, kissing him back as he pillaged my body, crushing my breasts flat against his chest and pinning me to the door. The wood bobbed gently in its frame each time I arched back, and there was a lot of that after his hand slipped into my jeans, skipping my panties. He found my wetness and shoved two fingers in, circling my soaked heat, claiming what was *his.*

"Oh, fuck. You've missed this shit as much as me, haven't you, babe?"

A low, deep moan was my only response. His thumb brushed my clit and my whole body jerked. My lips popped open, a rictus of pure pleasure, solidifying in a rosy ring as his pressure circled my nub.

"It's only been about a week," I teased.

Tank reached one hand to my jeans and pulled. My open belt slapped my thighs as they fell to my ankles.

"Far too fucking long. From now on, we're fucking every week, every damned night if that's what it takes to remind you where you belong."

He didn't need to say it. *Underneath him,* I thought, shuddering as he swirled his fingers inside me, heavier than before.

His strokes were coming faster, shallower, matching the circles around my clit. Everything he did was amazing, but I really needed him inside me. If he wanted to throw me against this door and make me scream, then I had to have his dick.

I reached to his bulge and squeezed. Jesus, he was hard, ready to bust right though his fly.

One pinch was all it took. Tank's face was dead serious as he stared at me. I flicked my tongue against my lips, licking them like the filthy wildcat in heat I'd become.

Tank ripped at my shirt. I was surprised nothing was shredded as it went flying off my head, same as my jeans. He only stopped for a second to admire the new lingerie I had underneath it.

His wolf whistle reverberated in my ears. "Fuck, baby girl. Did you plaster that pretty lace on just to beg me to fuck you harder? 'Cause that's what it's telling me to do. Hard, relentless, no holding back...shit. I don't wanna break you."

His hips rolled forward. Removing his hand, the big bulge in his jeans brushed my wet panties, already soaked from the heat steaming between us.

Tank pulled me away from the door, tight against his chest, driving his tongue against mine again and again.

My moans were coming in waves now. Hot, erratic, flaming with desire. I opened my eyes wide and stood on my toes, tilting my head against his.

"*Please.* I need you."

Next thing I heard was his belt buckle clanking as it went off. His pants dropped and he kicked them off, same as his boots. The cut and shirt fell last, and then his hands were on me again, jerking my panties down my legs.

He squeezed my breasts through the bra as he got behind me. His thick cock rubbed up and down, nestling between my ass cheeks, full and ready.

"I'll take that plump little ass someday, babe. Right now, I'm gonna remind your pussy what it needs. Bite down and put your hands against the door. I don't care if you rattle that fucking thing off its hinges. We're fucking right now, and we're not stopping 'til my nuts are dry and your clit can't hum another beat."

In one thrust, he was inside me. Tank rutted deep, pulling out before he swung forward again. My hips jerked against his. His hands tightened on my breasts, holding me in place, snug against him for the savage, delirious intimacy we craved.

He filled, stretching my tender flesh as he pounded.

Harder, deeper, faster.

My pussy lost control after just a few more thrusts.

Maybe I was responding to the fear I'd have to wait years to feel this again. Or maybe I was just that wanton, that stupidly horny, addicted to his flesh.

Whatever. I came, and that was all that mattered, flattening my palms against the door as every muscle in my body seized up.

"Tank! John!" I said his real name, desperate to fuck and feel every part of the man inside me.

Tank pinched my breasts hard when he heard it. One popped out of its cup and fell into his hand, the tender nipple catching between his rough fingers.

He growled in my ear as I started to scream. "We both know what I'm called. Don't give a shit what name you choose, just as long as you're feeling it, fire in your pussy so hot you can't groan another word."

Oh! Oh! Oh, shit! My brain sank into an orgasmic coma.

I came hard, sucking his dick deep inside me, begging for his come. He reached up, fisted my hair, and pressed me tighter to the door, sealing the space beneath us.

I was halfway through coming when I heard several loud male voices outside. Two brothers were heading for the bathroom on the other side of the hall. When they heard me coming, they stopped, listening as I moaned and whimpered in his hands while my pussy gushed all over him.

"Shit, Stone. You hear the kinda benefits a man gets when he earns the patch?" Smokey laughed, so close I swore his face was only a couple inches from the door.

"All the more reason to hurry it the fuck up. I hope they vote us in soon. This club's gonna need extra guys on hand if things go to hell."

"Let's not talk about that. Come on. Let the big guy have the homecoming he deserves. The man's been through enough for both of us. The brothers are gonna shit when they see what we just pulled in from the garage..."

A door creaked open and the voices disappeared. Tank had only slowed his strokes, and he picked up again when they were gone, railing into me with shallower, faster thrusts while my sex recharged for another release.

"You hear that, babe?" he whispered, pulling on my hair. "There are men who'd kill for what we've got. This is fucking special, and we'll keep fucking 'til we never, ever forget it."

I moaned as his cock hammered deeper. His free hand went around my stomach, jerked me to him, and toyed with my clit while his hip sped up. Soon, I was bucking back against him, my sex drunk brain trying to remember his words.

Special was too weak a word. This was a once-in-a-lifetime kind of love. Tonight, things were perfect, beautifully tuned to the want and need and love conquering every inch of us. Maybe tomorrow would be different, but tonight was ours, just Tank and I fused together.

His breaths were falling against my neck a minute later, heavy as dragon's smoke. I was on the edge when he jerked, muscles coiling up behind me, the rattle in his throat exploding while his fingers pinched my clit.

He smashed into me one more time and held it. I gasped as he swelled, exploding a second later. Jet after jet of his fiery come hurled up into me, brilliant as shooting stars, the deepest gift his flesh could give.

The heat – God! The unbearable, unstoppable heat!

It pulsed through my whole body, curling in my fingers and toes and flashing up to my head, swarming me in pulsing bliss. My cunt bored down on him and clenched tight, milking him with all its might, making me come apart as my orgasm wrapped its rough hand around my throat and refused to let go.

We were a hot, sweaty, sticky mess by the time the fire simmered lower. He pulled out, leaving a long rope of seed trickling down my thigh. I reached down and rubbed it, moaning when I sensed his heat.

His arm went around my belly and twirled me around to face him. More kisses came, deeper and hotter than before, savoring the moment.

"Fuck, babe. I'm never gonna stop loving this. Don't give a shit if I'm so damned wrinkled someday I can't see my own ink. Long as I'm up against you, feeling that heart beat through your skin, I've got everything I need. All the fucking love that matters."

Finally, it was my heart's turn to throb. For the strong, silent type, Tank really had a way with words when he got passionate. I smiled like a glowing prom date into his next kiss.

"I love you too," I whispered, my voice shaking a little as I said it.

Tank's face was serious again, but his eyes were smiling. He jerked me up across his shoulder and let our clothes pile together. We were heading for the bed, and I knew it was going to shriek a lot louder than the old door by the time we were done with it.

Too bad. With this beautiful man, anywhere was good. I didn't care if he screwed me in the dirt as long as my limbs were twined with his, taking him deep inside me.

We fucked hard and long for the next couple hours. It felt like half the night had passed by the time we were finished, sweaty and exhausted. Damn, I needed a shower before we showed up at the party.

Tank got up first and threw on his pants. "Gonna go get us some water, babe. Prison water's shit, and I'm thirsty. Plus my throat feels like a fucking wasp crawled down it after all that hard work."

I laughed. If it was work, then it was the best labor anybody could imagine.

He had a point. The sex took a lot out of me, leaving me more drained than before after days of worry. It was good just to have him home. I was peaceful, and I started to doze, thinking about getting up later and joining everybody for drinks. Beer sounded like heaven after love and sex.

I screamed when I heard the crash. It sounded like a bunch of glasses had tipped and shattered at once, so loud it shook the door. Tank was roaring my name before he was in the room.

The door burst open just as I sat up, heart racing.

Shit! I knew this was too perfect.

"Emma! Come quick, babe. Need you right now." He threw the door open and ran over to me, jerking me up on my feet, pushing clothes into my hands.

"What is it? What's wrong?"

"It's Moose. He's having some kinda fucking heart attack or something. You gotta help him."

I barely had time to throw on my stuff in the rush to get out there. The night was flipped, everything darkening by the minute. Unfortunately, I had an ugly feeling we were about to spend it a hundred and eighty degrees away from the sex and love I imagined, plunged into the blackness that seemed to be the price for loving this man.

Too damned bad. Dark, light, or gray, I wasn't going to stop.

IX: Ambush (Tank)

"What the fuck's wrong with him?" I stood over my aching brother, handing Emma my knife to cut open his shirt.

She wasn't listening to me, and I didn't blame her. She was too busy bent over Moose, feeling for his pulse. His big head lolled back with a vacant stare. Nothing came outta his mouth but, "no, no, no…"

Moose was a heavy dude, even by my standards. Took me and Stinger together to lift him off the floor and onto an empty table. His old lady, Connie, was right by his side, fanning his sweaty face. Same as his teen daughter, Becky, close to being a woman in her own right.

Make that a *very* worried young woman. Poor thing was sniffling, on the verge of tears.

"Dad! Stay with us!" She leaned to his ear, pulling on the collar of his cut.

There was a huge crash on the empty table next to us. The prospects dumped Emma's tray of medical supplies next to her, and she dug through the mess for the stethoscope.

"Watch where you're going with that shit," I warned. "Our brother doesn't need any more shocks in his state."

Smokey and Stone both mouthed apologies. Em had his shirt torn open now, pressing the cool metal circle to his chest, right above his gut. The whole party came to a dead stop with everybody gathered around us. I made damned sure they kept their distance. Nobody but officers, Emma, and family were allowed at the table.

"I don't understand," Emma said, shaking her head. "Heartbeat seems fine. A little fast...nothing erratic."

Moose's eyes snapped open. Creepy as shit, like something had crawled up inside him and taken control. His thick arms reached up, grabbed her shoulders, breaking away from his family.

"Nurse...it hurts like fuck...I –"

Another crash behind me. I spun, and my jaw almost hit the fucking floor.

Blaze was on the ground, rolled up in a fetal position, clutching his stomach. Saffron screamed, ran forward, and was on him in a second.

"Baby, what's wrong?"

Adrenaline ripped through my system. I turned to Stinger, only to see the VP struggling to hold himself up next to Moose, his hands pressed tight to the table. He was hunched over, and he looked at me as he lost control, dropping to his knees.

Fuck! Fuck, fuck fuck!

More screams and commotion in the crowd. Reb went down, and so did several girls who'd come to party with the single brothers. Marianne flopped down on the floor, cursing like a banshee between her teeth.

Emma looked panicked, but she stayed at Moose's side, desperately taking her measurements, asking him questions. I went to Blaze, pushed my way through Saffron's hold. She pulled back reluctantly, gripping his hand with white knuckles.

"What the fuck's happening, Prez? What's wrong?"

"Ah…my goddamned guts…bastards are on fucking fire…"

Poison. It had to be. There wasn't any fucking room for coincidence with brothers and whores dropping like flies.

But where the fuck was the source?

For a second, I had a horrific worry there was toxic gas in the air. I stepped over Roller, twitching on the floor. He vomited as soon as I was through, loud and gagging. Fuck, as much as I wanted to make sure he didn't choke on his own puke, I had to get the doors open.

I ripped open the doors and windows in bar, eager to get fresh air in here, and then came back. Moose and Blaze were looking paler by the second, the pain in their guts contorting their faces like Halloween masks.

Only the prospects and a few girls were still standing, gawking over all the sick. I rushed up to Smokey and Stone.

"What the fuck happened out here while we were in our room? It's not the air, or we'd all be dropping by now.

Where the fuck's the food and drink, and where did it come from?"

Stone shrugged. "Picked up everything from the store and the bottle shop, same as always."

"One difference," Smokey said. "Package from Cassandra came this afternoon. Twenty big bottles. There was a little note attached. Stone and set the shit at the bar and Saffron cracked it open, started serving it..."

Fuck! Well, that explained why the only ones who'd dropped were the ones who poured that shit into their system. But why the fuck would the mother charter send poisoned whiskey?

I ran to Emma. She was struggling with a bottle, funneling some vile black shit into Moose's mouth.

"He needs to barf this up," she said. "They all do. Jesus, there's so many, Tank. I need help." She reached for her phone and started to dial.

"It's poison, babe. Some shit in the whiskey. What do you need? Is there an antidote?" Fuck, I couldn't hide my worry. I knew all about toxins in the military, but I wasn't a fucking doctor. Didn't have a clue how to cure it.

Poison was one thing we'd never dealt with in this club, and now we had at least a dozen cases twitching on the floor, way too many for Em to handle alone.

"Just keep them breathing. Help them vomit when they need to. Get some water flowing into their systems. Damn!" She tore herself away from Moose and moved to Blaze. "I just don't have enough hands, or enough supplies. I need Linda..."

I stood up, snapped my fingers. Relaying Emma's orders to the prospects, we worked like the devil to make sure nobody went unconscious. I kept Sangria off Marianne and told a few other transient sluts to do the same. Even pulled in Alice from the corner where she sulked.

The girl was wide eyed and freaked out as fuck, but she did her job. She figured out real fast I was calling the shots, with zero tolerance for any bullshit.

She made the rounds, checking just about everybody except Stinger. For some reason, the bitch wouldn't get close to him. If it weren't so goddamned serious, I would've smiled, thankful Em and I had left that cat and mouse game behind.

Several brothers wretched. We tried to guide them away and keep them from choking as they expelled the crap from their systems in buckets. The whole clubhouse was gonna stink like bad whiskey and putrid medicine for a long time after this mess was cleaned up. But it was a small price to pay if everybody made it out safe.

I was helping Reb steady his knees when an old woman and two young guys walked in. The woman stopped. I looked up, and saw they were all decked out in uniforms with the hospital logo.

Fuck! Recognized the old woman as Em's supervisor, the same chick I'd put in her place a few months ago.

"Where's Emma?" she asked, a smile pulling at one corner of her mouth. "Don't worry, Tank. I'm here to help, not give you shit."

I nodded. She was speaking my language. I pointed her over to Em. Relief swelled with this crew rolling in, several folks who knew what they were doing.

Soon, everybody was on their way to being stabilized. Emma and the medics were still hard at work as I walked through the area.

"Damned good thing you called me when you did," I heard Linda say to Em. "Another half hour without the right care, and some of these guys would've been heading for comas..."

Shit! Was it really that close?

I hoped like hell my brothers were gonna be okay. Hoped just as much whoever the fuck had done this was gonna pay.

I couldn't get my mind off the poison. I couldn't stoop over and heal like everybody else, not more than the basics, anyway. The demon inside me wanted to solve this shit the way I knew best.

I had to find out who the fuck sent it here. It couldn't have been North Dakota. Soon as I found out the truth, they were gonna get a bullet through their fucking brains, even if I had to do it alone.

"Show me this whiskey shipment." I grabbed Smokey by the shoulder as he was tending to a whore.

He looked at me, nodded, and passed the metal pan for collecting her puke to the healthy girl next to him. Smokey led me to the bar and pointed to an open box.

Several empty bottles sat next to it, and a couple more that were half-drained. The shit looked normal, sweet and unassuming in all its amber glory. I picked one up, turned it over in my hand, squeezing the neck tight.

Unscrewed the cap and sniffed. Smelled the same as it should. The sinister shit was all hidden inside it, just as downright evil as fucking with a man's booze.

"It's not from Cassandra. No fucking way Throttle sent this shit unless he didn't know it was poison. Where's the label that says it's from mother charter?"

Smokey leaned past me and dug through the box. A second later, he produced a flimsy card with CONGRATULATIONS written on the envelope. I pulled out the folded card and opened it, a cheap thing with a watercolor on the front depicting a grinning bearded man on his bike.

A message was scrawled inside in thick black ink:

We'll all be seeing each other real soon, brothers. Hell doesn't wait for badasses like us. Drink up on us for a job well done!

And keep wearing those patches proudly. Nobody goes to their grave without one.

We're all cool now.

No name underneath it. As if the red flags weren't big and bright enough, that one punched me in the fucking face. Throttle never would've sent shit along without his signature and title. Plenty of inventories and manifests on the shipments passing through Missoula on their way West proved as much.

I crumpled the card in my fist, letting the words roll around my skull. I must've been grinding my teeth like an animal because Smokey's question sounded like it was coming through a wood chipper.

"What is it, Sarge? If it's not from mother charter, then…?"

"There's only one motherfucker I remember telling us 'we're cool.'" I paused, feeling the rage gathering inside me like a storm. "Go out to the garages and start prepping guns. Tell Stone too. I'll be out soon. We're gonna pay the Pagan Rams a visit. Satan just took me by the ear and appointed us chauffeurs to haul these assholes down to hell. Need to move soon, before those fuckers take off for Grizzlies' territory. Go!"

Smokey nodded and walked off to find his fellow prospect. If those boys lived through the night, then they'd sure as hell be patched in. No doubt about it.

Before I did anything else, I grabbed the half-depleted box of whiskey bottles and stepped through the safety exit. I slammed the fucking thing down near the dumpster out back as hard as I could. A thorough check told me all the bottles were shattered, leaking the rest of their toxic contents onto the cracked pavement.

Back inside, I searched for Blaze.

The whole damned clubhouse looked like it had been turned into a sick ward. Men and women were laid up on the tables, thin sheets over a few, moaning and rolling on their sides before puking tar into the buckets their caretakers held out.

I clenched my jaw tight. Those fucks were going to pay bad. Nobody who attacked a Devils' clubhouse walked away alive, and these assholes were so fucking cowardly they'd done it without showing their faces.

I found Blaze near the back. Saffron and a paramedic stood next to him. His old lady was cradling his head, wiping the sweat off his brow. Christ, the boss never looked so damned sick and pale.

"Tank." His eyes focused on me, as if from another world. I came closer.

"He'll be okay in a few days," Saffron said. "That's what they've been telling me. Jesus, I can't believe I served them that crap…"

She closed her eyes. The guilt was tearing her up inside. Blaze gripped her hand tighter. Looked like he was pouring all his strength into it, telling her the guilt was bullshit, even if he didn't have the words.

I leaned in. "You need me, boss?"

"Yeah," he said weakly. "It's the Rams…fucking know it is. Listen! You're the ranking officer while I'm laid up like this…Tank. You need…need to pay them hell for what they've done. Need to…oh, fuck."

Blaze rolled away. Saffron scrambled to hold the bucket out for him as he dry heaved, groaning in pain as his stomach struggled to drain itself.

"Don't worry about this, boss. I'm taking Smokey and Stone. We'll do this club justice. Those fuckers will never leave this state alive."

The young paramedic shifted uncomfortably. He looked at me and blinked, trying to pretend he hadn't heard me plotting murder.

Fuck it. Normally, I would've been more careful with civilians around. But tonight we had to do our club business out in the open, and I'd deal with the aftermath later. Right now, slitting the Rams' throats and laying their ripped up patches in front of my Prez was all that fucking mattered.

"You're doing all you can, Saffron," I said, clenching my fists. "Make sure Emma stays here with you tonight. I'm gonna be out for awhile."

She nodded glumly, stroking her old man's brow as he trembled. It was gut wrenching to see a big man like Blaze laid so low, all because those fucks hit us like the sneaky little shits they were. I was walking away when the realization hit Saffron and she called after me.

"Wait! Tank, you're going with three guys? You shouldn't –"

I was out the door, knowing she wouldn't follow. I wasn't gonna hear it. We both had our jobs. I had to keep going, never slowing down for an old lady who didn't understand mine.

She had to stay at Blaze's side. If I came home in one piece tomorrow, everybody would understand.

Smokey and Stone were geared up and waiting by the truck. I was ready to collect my shit and hop on my bike when I ran into Em, who was coming back inside carrying more shit from the ambulance parked by the gate.

"Tank? Where are you going?" Her eyes shifted back and forth, a worried crease in her brow.

She knew. Fuck, maybe there was one old lady I had to answer to after all. Not that she was gonna stop me...

"Gotta take care of the fucking trash, babe. Stay here. Stay safe. Make sure my brothers get well."

I tried to keep it short and simple. Fucking dummy. I should've known by now my new old lady wasn't that kinda girl. I should've known better, shouldn't have been surprised when she grabbed at my cut while I tried to walk past her.

"How can you go alone?" she demanded "You'll get yourself killed! Don't you think the men who did this are expecting you?"

"I've got two guys," I growled. "Those old fucking goats won't do shit except run. They had to go behind our backs to fuck up the club like this because they know they've got no chance in open combat. They won't stand up to a head on collision. Now, let go, babe."

I tried not to look at her. But it was fucking impossible when she had dying stars in her eyes, fear overtaking her to the point where the blue zip bag in her hands started to shake. I reached for them and put my hands around hers, steadying the tremors.

"Tank...I've got a really bad feeling." She looked up. The look she gave me said her heart had split and sunk to her knees. "Can't you wait? Just a few more days for the other guys to get well?"

"By the time I do that, these assholes could be hundreds of miles away. Need to go now, and catch their asses, if they haven't already beat it. I'll come home fine. I promise, babe."

Smokey and Stone were waiting in the truck. The engine snorted to life, idling in park, ready to help me introduce the Rams to Satan's Scythe.

Fuck it. I wrapped her tight and threw my lips against hers. I kissed hard, deep, more passionate than I thought was possible. I kissed her harder, fiercer than all the ways my tongue fucked her mouth before everything went to hell tonight, reassuring as anything could ever be.

Devotion. Promise. Love.

Everything I owed her was in that kiss.

I'll come home safe, babe, I thought. *Don't you fucking doubt it. I'm not gonna go anywhere 'til the Rams are laid out dead and my club's got its revenge.*

"Tank..." She whispered my name as I pulled away, but I wasn't listening to anything else.

It was time to go. Emma stood on the step next to the door, watching sadly the whole time I strapped on my helmet and started my Harley. Her soft worried face lingered in the mirror as I drove. Then the prospects followed, pulling the truck behind me and blocking her out.

I had to strike the assholes who'd done this dead. If things had gone just a little bit differently, it could've easily been Em and me on the floor, twisting and puking our guts out. Fuck, if we'd fallen, the whole damn club would've been laid up worse.

My biggest hope now was that we weren't too late to kill. The Pagan Goatfuckers already had several hours to piss in our faces and flee. In the ice cold darkness, I stared at the shadowy road, squeezing the handlebars tight, making my knuckles go numb. It was all I could do to relieve the stress 'til we arrived at their evil fucking clubhouse.

If they were gone, so be it. It was never too late to kill. I was gonna find 'em wherever they were. I'd hunt their asses across the damned continent if that was what it took to put lead in their skulls.

In this life, a man lives by one cardinal rule: anybody who fucks his brothers doesn't get the chance to fuck them a second time. Our enemies end up fucked, broken, deep in an isolated grave, and forgotten before they can think about a second strike.

We pulled up to that shithole right at the witching hour. The damned place was pitch black, without so much as a neon sign lit up outside. Dead silent too.

Fuck. I had a sick feeling we were too late. Those motherfuckers had taken off, probably as soon as they'd dropped the poison whiskey off in Missoula.

Still, I wasn't walking away without searching the grounds.

Smokey and Stone parked the truck next to my bike and got out, guns ready. I walked toward them, straightening the vest I'd thrown on over my cut before heading out.

"Looks empty. I'm going in to see what's cooking before we do anything else. Stay by the truck and lay down suppressing fire on anything that moves and isn't me."

They both nodded, taking up their positions near the hood, rifles pointed at the clubhouse. I walked, slow and alert, eyeing the dingy place through the darkness for any sign of creepers ready to pop out and put a bullet between my eyes.

Took a good look through both windows before I tried the door. The bar area looked totally dead, just as dark as the rest of the place, except for a low blue light shining behind the dusty bottles.

Shit. I'd forgotten how loud the shitty old door was when I pushed it open.

No joke, the place was like a haunted fucking house as I made my way through it, careful not to make more racket on the old wooden floor than I'd already created. I raised my nine millimeter and pointed it down the hallway leading to the room where we'd found Alice and Mickey's body.

Nothing.

It was so silent the gunshots outside sounded like the end of the world when they started. I whirled, cursing my ass while I went running back to my boys.

Smokey and Stone were pinned down. The fucks were in the woods, shooting at the ground from the fucking trees.

Shit, shit, shit.

I wished like hell I'd packed the night vision goggles before I left. The prospects were yelling at each other, eyes bright in the darkness. Nothing like facing the reaper to make a man fire on all circuits.

I did my damnedest to aim for the trees on sound alone, tracing the angle of the shots that kept hitting the ground near the truck. My brothers were inexperienced, too green to pop up for more than a quick shot that went fucking nowhere.

I aimed for one crop of trees and fired. The clip I unloaded told me something found its mark when I heard a man screaming, jabbering in the trees like a hurt gorilla. The shots and screaming stopped. Then something heavy hit the ground, snapping several branches below it.

The creaking wood behind me sounded like the noise in the woods. I didn't realize what was happening before the heavy black cylinder rolled to a stop against a chair, just a couple inches from my foot.

I turned just as the fucking thing exploded. It went off like a bomb, bright as lightning nailing me right in the eyes. Thought it was a bomb at first, but a real one at that range would've snuffed out all my senses in a heartbeat. I'd be too dead to hold another thought in my brain.

Fuck, I was still alive, wasn't I? Even with the whole world going white and green?

I was in one piece. Everything except my eyes and ears ringing. Flash grenades were the only thing that could do that.

Firing into the direction where I thought the flash bang came from didn't do shit to clear my vision. I stumbled on a table and lost my damned direction. Then some asshole pushed me and I hit the floor.

My fucking clip was empty and I couldn't see shit to reload. Not that it mattered.

The green and white burn in my vision left by the stun grenade flashed to red, and then pitch black, as soon as some bastard cracked me in the head. I wondered if I'd ever see a damned thing ever again, and then I wasn't able to wonder about anything at all.

X: Not Without My Hero (Emma)

I was next to useless after I came back inside, watching Tank and the prospects set off for God knows where. I tried to go back to tending sick brothers and their girls. Thankfully, their detox was past the critical stage where real harm could be done.

Everybody who'd been poisoned had thrown up several times, and now all they could do was lay on the table with an IV in their veins, waiting for the feverish pain left by the toxin to fade. I was checking on Stinger when Alice slunk by, going out of her way by several feet to avoid the VP.

"Hey!" I shot to my feet, flattened my hands on her back, and gave her a push. "This man needs some you, and there's only so many of us. Help me out!"

She flushed, ashamed or insulted. I wasn't sure which. Didn't care either.

"Take this cool cloth. Hold it to his head. Make sure he doesn't pull that needle out of his arm." I reached for the tube going to the bag of water hanging over his head, giving it a gentle tug.

The raven haired girl followed my orders reluctantly. I watched closely to make sure she wasn't bullshitting me. After a minute, she was cooperating, a tiny hint of concern in her eyes. More than what should've been there just because I'd called her out.

"There's something else I need to know…" I waited for her to meet my eyes.

"What?" Her lips twitched angrily. "I'm doing what you asked. I won't let anything bad happen to him…I'll stay with him the whole night if I have to. What else do you want?"

"I need to know about that place where the Pagan Rams had you locked up." She opened her mouth to whine about her memory again, but I cut her off with a jerk of my hand. "Don't tell me about your amnesia. I know you had your right mind when the guys found you. Where was it?"

"How the hell should I know? I barely know where this stupid town is here." She looked away, brushing the damp cloth gently over Stinger's forehead.

"Huh? Alice?" Stinger cracked his eyes and groaned, only for a second. Then he slumped on the table again, collapsing back into his weakened haze.

"Shhh. It's going to be okay," she whispered.

Damn it all. Tank was worrying me sick, but my inner bitch softened a little to see her acting human toward the man who couldn't hide his raging crush.

"Tell me anything, Alice. Anything will help. How long did it take to get to this clubhouse after they picked you up? Do you remember?"

"Maybe an hour." She shrugged.

I took a deep breath and tried to calm down. It worked. We went back and forth for a good ten minutes before I figured out the place was about an hour northwest, somewhere near the Idaho border. The hellhole where Tank might be fighting for his life had to be off I-90 between Haugan and Saltese.

Satisfied, I left her to tend Stinger and stopped by Linda, who'd set up a little command center in the infirmary. She didn't ask what I was doing until she saw me grabbing syringes from the medicine bin.

"Those won't be very useful treating all these poison cases."

I looked up, but never stopped packing. "I'm going out. I have to see Tank. He's gone out and I'm afraid he's hurt or…"

I closed my eyes. I couldn't bring myself to say the worst word in the lexicon. Nothing would ever kill that giant, gorgeous man. It couldn't. I refused to believe it.

"Isn't this something you should leave to the professionals?" She moved to the door, trying to block me as I started to walk toward it. "I mean, I'm trying to help you out, Emma. I don't want you running off and getting hurt."

I only stopped when we were a few inches apart, the bag I'd packed thrown around my shoulder. "If you had one chance to save Red, wouldn't you have taken it?"

Her face twitched at the question. Linda looked torn. She smoothed her scrubs, lips tight as she shook her head. Sighing, she stepped aside, freeing my path.

"You know the answer. And I won't stand in your way when you put it like that. Just...please be careful, Emma. You take your phone and call at the first sign of trouble. I'll get the cops out there ASAP."

"No need," I said, pushing past. "I'll be back in a few hours to check on the guys."

I walked out. I couldn't spend another second talking sense, or it might've changed the crazy, irrational urge I had to get to my car and drive into the darkness.

Tank and the prospects had been gone for more than an hour. It was past three o'clock. Not even the rising sun would give me any comfort on the long, dark drive.

Only picturing him would do that. If there was anything I could do to help, however remote, then I had to do it.

And if everything had gone wrong and Tank was never coming home, then neither would I. They'd bury me with him in the wilderness.

Fear and anger pulsed through every nerve as I gripped the steering wheel, leaving Missoula's dim lights behind, roaring into the mountainous darkness.

God no. I wasn't letting him end up like Linda's Red. He'd kill me if he knew what I was doing, but he'd already given so much to keep me safe, so much time wasted without his lips on mine.

Whatever lay ahead, it was going to claim us together. I'd either be coming home safe with Tank in the morning light, or neither of us were coming home at all.

I instantly regretted not grabbing a gun when I pulled up the long gravel road to the Pagan Rams' clubhouse.

The first thing I saw was the truck. The bullet holes were obvious in my headlights. Just a little bit ahead, Tank's bike lay on its side, tipped over in the dirt.

Something terrible had happened here.

I rolled down my window and listened. My heartbeat was going a trillion ticks a second, senses on alert like never before, ears straining to hear *something* but dead silence.

After almost a full minute, I swore I heard a man cough. It was faint, not very far ahead of my car.

Carefully popping the door, I stepped out, touching the ground lightly so my shoes wouldn't make too much noise. Instinct made me keep my head down as I walked, looking for life signs. The battle here looked like it was long over, but I couldn't shake feeling invisible guns aimed at my head.

I was almost past the truck when I heard the another cough. I whirled and screamed as a man's hand reached for my foot from underneath the truck.

I fell. Pain rocked through my hip when I hit the hard ground.

Idiot! I was flat on my ass, desperately trying to roll away from the nightmare hand wrapped around my ankle.

I was still rolling when I saw the wide, familiar eyes staring at me. My butt touched the cool grass on the other side and I leaned forward for a better look.

"Smokey?"

He held one finger to his lips, intense and ominous. His lip ring jiggled back and forth.

"Yeah. I got Stone under here. He's hurt."

That got me moving. I was on my hands, starting to crawl. When I stuck my head underneath the truck, I saw Smokey's bigger body shielding his fellow prospect, trying to stem the bleeding wound on his leg with a torn scrap of shirt.

Stone grunted and blinked his eyes. The pained expression said the bullet tore him deep, probably to the point where he couldn't walk without help.

"How long has he been like this?" I asked, reaching into my bag.

"Good solid hour. Ever since Tank disappeared inside and we got ourselves ambushed. The fucks were in the trees. We killed at least one of 'em, but the others dropped my brother. Surprised they didn't finish the job when I pulled him under here. They all disappeared after that, more concerned about Tank than us."

Shit. My heart sank. I looked up and stared at the clubhouse door. It was hanging on its hinges, cracked open, a yawning cavern with nothing good inside.

"Okay," I whispered. "Just hang on. I'll help you move him, and then you're going to get him home to Missoula. Linda or one of her friends will be able to do him justice better than I can..."

That wasn't necessarily true. My need to save a human life gnawed at me, but finding out what the hell happened to Tank chewed me up a hundred times worse.

I uncapped the syringe and steadied its needle near Stone's muscular arm. One shot in the veins would soothe the pain and make him loopy, easier to move. It was a powerful sedative.

"Fuck," Stone growled. "Just keep some pussy ready, baby. Tight and warm..."

I blinked. He was staring right through me, blasted out of his mind.

Smokey forced a smile. "Fuck you, brother. You can think about getting your dick wet again when you're all healed."

I motioned for Smokey to grab his free arm while I took the other. We pulled at the same time, hauling him out onto the dirt. From there, the bigger, stronger man took over, lifting his leaner brother into his arms.

The truck was unlocked and I grabbed the handle to load him inside. We shifted the seat forward, creating just enough space so he could lay down.

"Make sure he keeps breathing. He's lost a lot of blood, but I'm confident he'll be good for the ride. His pulse is in a good range." I touched his neck one more time, double checking what I'd discovered beneath the truck.

He nodded and scrambled into the driver's seat, waiting for me. I looked at him and cocked my head.

"You have a handgun, don't you?"

I needed something small and easy. One look at the huge rifles they were hauling told me I didn't have a clue how to operate them. The kick on those things alone would send me crashing to the floor.

"Huh? What do you need that for? You're coming home, aren't you, nurse?" Stone's voice was strained.

I shook my head furiously. "I can't. Not until I know Tank's okay. He's the reason I came out here."

The prospect's face was tight. "I better check with Blaze or Stinger. Sorry, Emma, but they'd never let you go in there alone...the Rams are still prowling around. Got a bad feeling nothing good's happened in the clubhouse. He's been inside too damned long."

Damn! Hearing him say what I knew made my heart slap my ribs. There was a good chance he'd been killed – I had to face it – even if it wasn't enough to make me run. I had to find out. I had to see him again, alive or dead. I had to keep my promise.

Now, I was pissed off. I slapped the side of the truck and stood on my tip-toes, glaring at him through the open window.

"Look, all the officers are down sick. Blaze put Tank in charge before he left. Unless we know Tank's been incapacitated, there's nobody who's going to tell me what I need to do. Certainly not you, prospect." I used his title, hoping it would drive home the point. "I'm going in one way or another. It'd be nice to have a gun for protection, but if you're not going to cooperate…"

I shrugged. Stone's cold eyes threw ice on my hot face. The glint in his eye said he thought I'd lost my mind. Finally, he broke the glacial stare and looked at his brother bleeding in the back, gritting his teeth.

"Fuck. All right." He leaned over, jostling the glove compartment until it opened. "You know how to use one of these, right?"

The nine millimeter sat in my hands like a rock. I turned it over gingerly, trying to keep my composure as I got used to its deadly weight.

Jesus. Never thought I'd have to learn how to shoot like this…

"I know enough," I lied. "Now, hit the road. The sooner Smokey gets help in a clean environment, the better. I'll call as soon as I find Tank."

He nodded. I stepped back as he rolled up the window, and then began backing out, refusing to give me a second glance on his way.

We both had our orders. His were tied to the club, the whole brotherhood that was the Prairie Devils' MC. Mine was bound by my heart's irresistible pull, fiery devotion to the one man who mattered most.

Okay. Let's do this. Do it for him, I thought, gathering my courage.

I crept toward the broken building. There were shells and torn scraps of ground closer to the clubhouse's entrance. Out near a crop of trees, a big red splash spilled from the forest. I paused for a second, and noticed the lifeless human body next to it, barely concealed by the brush.

Swallowing hard, I pressed on, knowing full well that might be how I'd find Tank. Hell, it might be the way somebody else would find me when I left this place.

The clubhouse stank. I tip-toed inside it, trying not to choke or cough at the dank must rolling up my nostrils. The stupid door yowled like an angry cat on its hinges when I gave it a shove.

There were no signs of life inside. Just terrible, deadly silence.

I stepped forward, walking past a dirty bar. Several chairs had been overturned. I wasn't sure if it was a scuffle or just the natural state of this place.

A shredded plastic tube lay on the floor. It looked like a flashlight had exploded and left a tiny scorch mark on the wooden panel. I poked it with my toe, unsure what it was.

There was only one way deeper. A long dark hall led back toward what looked like several rooms. I took a deep breath, clenching the gun in both hands to keep from shaking.

I wanted to call his name so badly, just one little whisper. But if anyone else was in here, then it might easily lead to my doom.

I never got the chance to yell for Tank. An earsplitting scream ruptured the grim silence, high and feminine. Then there was a single gunshot, so loud it was like a rocket going off in the room up ahead.

"That's what you get for fucking up our scheme, bitch," a gruff voice said. "It would've worked without your bullshit! You're worm food, same as this fucking Prairie Pussy."

The gun's metal felt hot and sweaty in my hands, resonating with my energy, my fear. I raised it and peeked around the corner, ready to fling open the door.

The strangers were armed. They had to be talking about Tank. Relief shot through me when I realized he was alive, but who knew if that would last.

I had to do something!

Surprise was all I had on my side.

The door was slightly cracked, but not enough to see without shoving it open. My fingers shook as I gripped the doorknob, ready to throw it wide, guns blazing at anyone who wasn't my man. In one jerk, it flipped apart and banged on the wall, and I burst in, aiming for the chest of the first man I saw.

I couldn't afford to stare at the gory mess on the bed he was standing over. I just fired, and watched as blood rained on blood, a thick red blossom bursting square in his chest.

"Reaper! Fuck!" The gruff voice I'd heard earlier took one look at the man I'd shot and roared before his body hit the floor.

Two men charged toward me. I swung the gun, but was horrified to see Tank between us. He was chained up in a chair, hands bound behind his back, and apparently knocked out. He didn't stir at the commotion.

I was so shocked to see him I made my worst mistake: hesitation.

The assholes knocked me flat before I could get off another shot. The man was on top of me like a grizzly bear, his flabby belly suffocating me. His partner tore the gun from my hands.

"No!" I yelled as the one tool I had to end this was ripped away.

"Jesus fucking Christ. Not another bitch to kill. We already had our quota of girls," the leaner man said.

"Shut the fuck up, Socket. Sooner we get this over with, the better." The big man cupped my mouth.

I screamed into my hand, and then screamed louder on the inside when I realized nothing would come out. His gaze was ruthless. Murder twitched in the deep black pools of his eyes when he stared at me.

Behind them, Tank groaned loud and moved his head. I could barely make out his face over the man's shoulder, but I saw him regain consciousness.

Our eyes met. His gaze electrified the instant he realized it was me.

"Emma!" He lunged, rocking the chair so hard they both went crashing to the floor.

Skinny man turned. "Shut up, asshole! We told you to keep your fuckin' mouth shut and we're not gonna say it again."

I closed my eyes as a savage kick nailed Tank in the head. I knew it must've put him back into a coma, or maybe worse, because he wasn't struggling anymore.

No, no, no…Jesus no.

Fat man smiled. He put a thick hand around my throat and squeezed, choking off my breath. My eyes spun, and stopped on his chest. I noticed a PRESIDENT tag a lot like Blaze's beneath the name BLOCK.

"You two know each other? Maybe our luck's looking up after all." His fingers tightened on my throat and I gasped, struggling for air. It wasn't coming. "Calm down, you fucking cunt. We lost two good brothers today, plus an old whore we had to put down for doing a half-assed job. Killing you and this gorilla strapped to the chair won't bring back Gutter or Reaper, but it'll sure as shit make us feel better before we blow this fucking place for good."

I fought hard, but he was too heavy. I'd been without air for too long. My whole body was tingling, going numb and dark, fuzzy like my vision.

"Socket! Leave that asshole alone and help me the fuck out. Throw Ruby's corpse on the floor. Let's get this bitch in the bed." He leaned low, planting a sickeningly long kiss on my cheek, and then biting me there.

I yelped in his hand. With all my might, I forced my knee up his thigh. It didn't feel like I'd even touched him, but he jerked. Then he steadied.

I'd hit him. Not hard enough. Fat man grunted like a pig, reaching for his crotch.

"Fucking slut!" He lifted me up by the throat and something going a hundred miles an hour slammed into my face. I realized it was his hand through the blinding pain.

"Cunt tried to bust my balls," he growled to his partner. "What a dumb bitch. Come on, Socket. Get her up there. The only asshole getting his nuts split today is gonna be the piece of dogshit lying on the floor. We'll let him wake up to our come leaking out her dead pussy. Leave his ass just enough time to suffer before we shoot him in the guts and light this goddamned place up like a fire pit...these Prairie Pussies aren't getting shit. They've ruined my fucking club, and I'll make damned sure I ruin theirs too when the badges find the burned stockpile out back. We'll make sure they know it belonged to those assholes, same as Mickey's daughter."

He laughed. The sound blended into the noise of fluid splashing the floor. I wasn't sure if it was Socket splashing gasoline all over the place or just the dead woman's blood flowing faster. Her neck seemed broken, tilted at an unnatural angle.

Fuck. I'm sorry, Tank. I tried, I tried, I really fucking tried.

My brain panicked, shuddered, and started to shut off. Regrets weren't going to save our bodies from these animals. I hoped there would be mercy somewhere for our souls.

Then the pain flared again, sharper than before, yanking me into a darkness too thick for love and mercy.

XI: Balance (Tank)

Emma! Emma!

I had to check three times to make sure my fucking eyes were all there. Yeah, they were really open, staring dumb at the assholes shifting something around on the floor.

Fuck. My guts churned when I realized it was the dead whore, leaving a long bloody trail across the floor as they dragged her to the wall.

Hearing her skull split beneath the bullet was what woke my ass up the first time. If I didn't wake up to a gunshot, then I had to be dead. Too many years working for Uncle Sam and the Devils internalized that fucking sound like a rooster going off.

Same as Em's voice. I knew her softest whisper and her loudest scream like my own heartbeat, but now I wasn't hearing anything at all.

I turned my head, shallow and slowly so the fucker's wouldn't notice.

Shit, where was she?

Her arms and legs were hanging limp when they lifted her up. All my bones ached like I'd dropped off a moving truck, but nothing hurt worse than seeing that evil fucking goat haul her onto the bloody bed.

My Emma. My woman. My baby girl.

All tangled up in my *worst fucking nightmare* with two motherfuckers who'd signed their death warrants the instant they sent poison to my club.

The old bed creaked as Block rolled on top of her. His hands were on her tits. He cupped them both and his knuckles went white, hard enough to hurt. Socket was at her feet, grabbing her ankles to spread her legs apart.

"Get her fucking pants off. Come on, hurry. Let's fill this bitch up and bleed her out so we can hit the fucking road. Surprised I can make my dick work at all after this all this horseshit today..."

Emma's head lolled. She whimpered, half-conscious, registering the grotesque pain the monster had inflicted on her precious face.

I saw red. Crimson, volcanic, crazy fucking red.

Never knew how the fuck I hauled my ass off the ground, but I did. I took off like a screaming missile, howling as I plowed into the skinny asshole from behind, knocking him against the wall so hard he bounced back across the room. He tripped on the whore's corpse and fell face down in her blood.

I tried like hell to break my damned chains. The shit was rusted, and I knew I'd do it if I just got the right angle for impact.

Block screamed and ducked, flattening himself on Emma's body and narrowly missing the chair as it flew over the space where his head used to be. It hit the wall and bounced, flinging me forward with it. I jerked back at the same time it hurtled forward, savagely pulling on my restraints.

The fuckers broke with several inches to spare, still strapped to my wrists. Something loud cracked in my arms. It should've hurt, but I was too fucking drunk on mad, killer rage to register pain.

Socket was up on his feet again, stumbling around, desperately trying to wipe his fucking face. The dead chick's blood blinded his stupid ass. I charged him again and rammed my head straight in his guts.

Didn't stop 'til I had him against the wall, wrapping my chains around his waist, shaking his brittle fucking spine like a ragdoll. I slammed the fuck into the wall again and again and again, the darkness inside me smiling when I heard his bones crack.

He grunted one last time and dropped, a mess of shattered ribs and fucked up organs. His gun clattered on the floor.

I was reaching for it and praying like hell Block wouldn't have time to shoot when the bullet went off. Fucking thing roared right past my ear, one inch away from putting me down for good.

Emma screamed, awake from the hellish commotion. So did Block.

I turned, untangling my chains and trying to raise the gun. Wasn't easy with my arm all fucked up. Fire blistered from my shoulder blade right up to the socket, making it damned near impossible to point at anything.

Come on, dammit! Just one more move for Em. Put these cocksuckers down for good.

Emma and Block were all tangled up. He was trying to choke her, but not very well. With a cowardly yelp, he rolled off her and crashed to the floor when my gun swung toward him. Then I saw the syringe jammed right in his chest, dangerously close to the heart.

Emma. I grinned, wondering what the fuck she'd shot into his veins.

I didn't even hesitate. I stepped up, forced my shitty arm to work, and pulled the trigger. Fire ripped up my head, raging hellfire lashing every inch of my body. But not as much as the molten lead I pumped into his skull.

My ears were so wild with pain they didn't register the blast. When I looked down again, Blocks' nasty fucking face was destroyed, one eye obliterated, his skullcap gone from the two rounds I planted there.

Emma was off the bed. Her hands wrapped around my waist weakly, reaching for my arm with the gun in hand.

She knew I was fucked up. The other fuck against the wall was barely breathing. He'd bleed out internally sooner or later, yeah, but I wasn't taking any fucking chances. The last Rams' appointment with Satan's Scythe was way fucking overdue.

"Let me help," she whispered, pressing one hand on my back to guide me forward.

I didn't squeeze the trigger 'til I had my gun against his head. I spread myself out to shield her from the blood spatter. Skull, brains, and hot lead buried itself in the wall. Socket slumped, finally returned to the hell his ass crawled out of.

My hand seized. The gun clattered on the floor. I couldn't grip shit in my fucked up arm anymore, my nerves turned to pure fire. Emma put her little hand over mine and then gently ran her hands up my shoulders, nudging me toward the door.

I could barely feel it, but fuck if having her there, safe and mostly sound, didn't feel good.

"We made it. They're all dead. Let's go home. Steady…steady…"

How the fuck did she do it? The girl had just survived certain death and defilement, and she still whispered into my ear like a damned angel, airy and sweet as the first day I saw her.

I had to stop and lean on the shitty bar several times on the way to her car. Started to blubber about the prospects when we got outside, but she stroked my shoulders again, telling me they were fine.

It wasn't 'til I was lying in her backseat that my eyes focused again. She got in and started her engine, pulling away from this nightmare for good.

"I'm so fucking sorry, Em. You never should've come for me. I can't believe how close you came to –"

"And you shouldn't have gone by yourself. We're both alive and in one piece, aren't we, Tank? You saved me."

"Yeah, babe. You saved my ass too." It felt so fucking weird to say it, but she had a point.

Her face was messed up in the mirror. The bruises those fuckheads left were starting to show, and it made me want to kill them all over again. Yet, she was all there beneath it all, safe and beautiful as the Em I knew, the Em I'd pledged my soul to.

"Fuck, babe. We've suffered enough shit to keep doing this. I get it. I really do. Don't let me talk about leaving you again. Slap me right across the fucking face."

She laughed, perfect and bright as the first pale sunlight spilling onto the car from over the mountains. "You're not going anywhere, Tank. An old lady stays at her man's side through thick and thin. Once you put your brand on me, it's never coming off. Never. I don't care how many times we fuck up, freak out, and just screw off. You're the only man I'll follow to the ends of the earth."

Inside my fucked up brain, the fire in my arm was making things hell. But here, with her, it was total heaven.

The worry squatting on my chest all these months like a goddamned two ton elephant was gone. Whatever else this shitty episode had done, it pried open my fucking eyes.

Now, I couldn't unsee it: Emma was right, and she deserved to be here, right by my side.

Having her brought balance to my crazy, top heavy ass. I'd never have it any other way again.

One Week Later

Blaze twirled the gavel in his hand. I gritted my teeth. Only a few more hours 'til I'd be able to move my damned hands like that again. The sling locking up my arm was coming off today.

He looked right at me and pointed. "Tank did the heavy lifting here, but it's club business, and all the brothers deserve to know."

He looked like a judge. Well, a heavily tattooed judge who pumped iron and wore leather with the dirtiest fucking mouth any courtroom had ever seen. Appropriate, though, since he had my fate right in his fucking hands.

It was my ass on the line, but I could feel every other brother in the room tensing up with me.

"The DA's office took the bait this morning," Blaze said. "ATF signed off on it too as soon as they got the guns into their possession. Said the shit we pointed them to at the Rams' clubhouse was the biggest haul of heavy weapons since they busted some cartel down in Texas a decade ago. Mickey's loot just saved Tank a prison sentence."

Fuck! I slumped in the chair, sucking in a heavy breath. All the brothers chuffed. Their eyes were on me. There wasn't space to crowd around me all at once and slap my back, so they showed their appreciation in a different way.

Their fists hit the table in pairs, loud and wild, booming thunder that shook the fucking rafters. Blaze and

Stinger were the last ones to join in, their thin, constrained smiles giving way to full on shit eating grins.

"Welcome home, bro. This time, for good." Blaze extended a hand to me and the biker applause tapered off.

I took it. Squeezed that man's hand harder than anybody's since I was discharged from the Army.

"It's not just Tank who's off the hook here, boys," Blaze said, turning back to the rest of the brothers. "Throwing the Feds a fucking bone should deflect the heat for awhile. But that doesn't mean we get sloppy. The rogue agent Tank killed and nearly went to prison for won't be the last asshole who comes sniffing around this club – especially with Throttle wanting to step up the shipments before Jack Frost settles in for good."

Several brothers flexed their fists, a sign of irritation. Everybody was wound so damned tight lately the whole club was gonna explode if we didn't catch a fucking break.

Whatever. Blaze helped my ass out, and I was gonna stand behind my boss. He made the tough calls because he needed to. Not because they let him run a damned popularity contest.

"The Rams are dead. Every last one of them. With nobody left to patch over, this territory's all ours, Devils' land through and through. We shouldn't have any more distraction. If there's anything good that came outta this shitstorm, it's that. I'll make sure those shipments move onto Seattle, smooth as whiskey." I locked eyes with Blaze, and he nodded, showing his appreciation.

Stinger cocked his head. "You got a point, brother. I'm not gonna say there's a silver lining in shitting my guts out for three fucking days after that crap went through my system, but you're right about getting things on track."

"All things considered, we're pretty friggin' lucky to be around for more shits at all, brother." Moose leaned back in his chair, hands folded on the back of his big head. "I thought it was a heart attack soon as I went down."

"You scared the fuck outta everybody when you caved like a fucking mammoth," Reb laughed. Moose shot him a dirty look. "Hey, bro, I'm just fucking with you. Everybody here got a piece of it except Tank and the prospects. I skinned my throat barfing this crap too."

"It's hard to believe a simple mistake's the reason why we're all here, breathing and bullshitting," Blaze said. He looked at me. "Emma's friend said we would've been gone before anybody treated us if that shit was concentrated just a little more."

I shrugged. "Like I said when we first debriefed, we'll never know what the fuck happened there. Don't know if the whore did us a solid intentionally because she hated their asses that much, or if she was just so blazed out of her mind she couldn't follow through on her idea. All I know is she didn't bat an eye while they beat her up in that fucking room where I was tied down. When I woke up, half her head was gone, and the rest is history."

"History," Blaze repeated. "We won't forget it, but we're not gonna fixate on any bullshit in the past neither. Right now, I'm all about the future. This club's been through pure hell, one goddamned thing after another ever since we started this charter less than a year ago. Doesn't mean we stop doing what we do best, bros. We live free, we have our fun, and we grow our family when the time's right. We got better times ahead. I feel it in my fucking bones."

Blaze's stare was intense. I nodded along with several other brothers, hoping like hell he was right.

"We got my wedding in Reno coming up. Our white hat businesses are starting to boom. Plenty of money and Jack to go around, and for now, no more assholes to worry about." He smiled. "It's as good a time as any to add a few new bros to this MC."

"Been a long time coming," Stinger said.

"You're damned right. Per the Devils' charter, I'm calling a formal vote on giving Smokey and Stone their patches. These two have proven themselves twice on the big things recently, and lots of little shit before. They're bad enough and smart enough to think for themselves, but they know how to take orders too, the same as everybody else in this club." Blaze paused.

I raised my good hand that wasn't in the sling. "Seconded, Prez. Let's vote."

The boys did their job. If they hadn't been there to help my ass out, things might've gone differently for me and Em at the Rams' shitty clubhouse.

Blaze already had a damned good idea how the vote was gonna go. He was so confident he called it for both dudes, and the ayes rolled out unanimously.

"Okay." Blaze's gavel slapped the wood with a loud clap. "Roller, go bring those two in. Stinger, help me get these ready."

The Prez stood up, walked to a box behind him underneath the MC's flag, and grabbed the two new cuts. Roller stepped outside and came back a minute later, holding open the door.

Smokey slowly wheeled Stone in. He wasn't as lucky as me in his first big gun fight, and he'd be in that chair for a few more weeks according to Em.

The prospects moved slow as molasses. All the brothers suppressed their snickers. Even I fought down a big fat smile. They couldn't see shit with the thick black hoods over their heads.

Both those boys were shitting their pants. I could tell just by looking at the way their chests were moving, taking big breaths, wondering if they were gonna be their lasts.

"Up there at the head of the table," Roller said, as coldly as he could manage. "The Prez wants a word with you."

He gently pushed on Smokey's back. The prospect's hands were shaking on the handles for Stone's wheelchair. The man sitting there kept turning his head back and forth, even though he couldn't see shit, no doubt wondering if it was gonna the last time he moved his face while it was intact.

"Stop," Roller said, as soon as they were a couple inches from the Prez and VP.

I rocked my fucked up arm gently in the sling to keep from laughing. Moose nearly lost it and buried his face in his hands, pulling on his beard to stifle the chuckles.

"This is where you've ended up," Blaze growled. "Both you assholes. Go ahead and think you can hide from the devil, bros, but don't you think for one second you're gonna hide your shit from me. Everything you've done...*fuck*. It's time you bros got what you deserve. Long overdue. Every fucking inch of it."

Even through the tight hood, I watched a huge lump slide down Smokey's throat. Blaze spread the cut in his hands, turning it around so they'd be greeted with the patch first. Stinger did the same.

"Roller." Blaze paused, licking his lips. "Remove their hoods and let them pay their respects to Satan."

Grinning, Roller reached for their throats, pulling on the cords there to loosen the tight fabric. In one quick jerk, the hoods were off.

The two prospects stared at the grinning devils on their new leather like idiots. I couldn't contain my smile anymore, remembering how the club razzed my ass when I earned my patch. Everybody went through this shit, but it was always unique.

"Congratulations, brothers," Stinger said. "You've both earned these patches with all the voting rights and privileges they're entitled to."

"Yeah. Congrats." Grinning at last, Blaze shoved the cut he was holding forward at the same time as Stinger.

"Now don't let both your heads swell up so damned big they sweep you off your fucking feet."

Everybody laughed. The two new full patch brothers turned their cuts over in amazement, and then shed their old prospect leather to don the new skins with full patch colors.

Blaze and Stinger took their seats. Any church session where a brother was patched in was a good church session. Still didn't compare to having Emma wrapped around me, though.

We'd been cooped up in the room for over an hour, and I was starting to get anxious. Blaze must've sensed as much because he slapped the gavel to call order with everybody laughing and congratulating the new brothers.

"All right. Unless anybody else has any pressing shit we need to wrangle with today, I'm gonna bring this to a close so we can saddle up for the pig roast tomorrow night."

Heads nodded enthusiastically. Everybody had something to do now that we were getting deeper into autumn. Half the men were tuning up their bikes, and dudes like Moose had family shit to tend to. Smokey and Stone just wanted to hit the town and show off their new patches.

Me? I wanted Emma. Soon as that gavel knocked, I was heading straight for her sweet ass, and I wasn't gonna stop 'til it was in my hands.

Blaze waited. Nobody raised a peep. The sound I'd been waiting for clapped as wood smacked wood.

I slid out of my chair and met Blaze's eyes.

"Today's the day you're getting that fucking thing off, isn't it?" He pointed to my sling.

"Yeah. Heading over to have Em do it right now, boss."

"Good. You're gonna need that hand free for getting your brand on her." He grinned and pressed a friendly hand to my shoulder. "Don't let your old lady walk around another day without it. Show everybody she's fucking yours."

"I'm putting it there if I can't even sign my own fucking name, boss. No doubt about it." I took another step forward, then stopped and looked back. "Gonna put a nice ring on that girl's finger one day soon too. Same as you and Saffron."

Blaze laughed and I beat it before he could give me more shit. On the way out, I saw Stinger standing near the door, talking to Roller.

"Found this before we turned that shithole over to the Feds," he told the VP. "Thought you should have it."

Stinger snatched the small card from Roller's hand. I only caught a glimpse, but it looked a lot like a driver's license. The dark haired girl in the portrait couldn't be anybody except Alice.

Blaze was walking over, right behind me. They flashed him the license and I stopped for a few more seconds to stare. Yep, it was her, all right.

"Fuck, Prez. Do you see this shit? She's got Mickey's blood. Maybe a niece…maybe his own fucking daughter.

Shit, I have to get this to her." Stinger started to march, but Blaze reached out and caught him by the shoulder.

"Give her some space, bro. She blew this fucking place early this morning. Couldn't tell you where."

"She needs to know!" Stinger growled, his face going dark.

"Only if she wants to. Look, this club's nursed too many fucking strays back to good health in the recent past. The bitch made it crystal-fucking-clear she wanted to forget whatever the hell happened. Pretty sure she wants to forget our asses too. It's not your place to chase her down and shove things in her skull she's not ready for."

Stinger pinched his fist, completely covering up the license. "You know what? Fuck this, Prez. Fuck it all. And fuck her too!"

I stepped aside as Stinger stormed past. The VP nearly ripped the door off its hinges. Blaze looked at me next, quietly seething.

Fuck it was right, just not the way Stinger meant. I turned and headed out the door before I got drawn into any more drama.

It didn't seem like the VP and his new obsession were ever gonna have a happy ending, but then it looked the same way with Emma and me for a long fucking time.

Not my problem. Not my drama. Alice and Stinger would write their own fucking ending.

Everything I needed for the rest of my days was waiting in the infirmary. And I needed her *now*.

My brain fought almost as hard as my dick when I saw her. Shit, how the fuck did she manage to look so damned good in her scrubs?

When I cracked the door, she was bent over, filing some medical stuff away. My cock jerked instantly, straining in my fucking jeans.

I hadn't had so much as a blow in the past week since the blowout with the Rams. Tonight, she was all mine, and I was gonna show her tight pink pussy how bad I missed it.

Emma squealed when I came up behind her. She was deliciously small next to me. Thank God it wasn't hard to pick her up with one arm and pull her in.

"I see you're excited to get that thing off."

"Babe, you don't have a fucking clue. Let's do this." I plopped down on the stainless steel table while she retrieved the scissors.

I was horny and excited as fuck. Had to ignore the persistent yapping voice in the back of my head that was worried. Sooner or later, my luck would run out. I was gonna take a beating one day that wouldn't be so easy to heal from. I never knew if my body was fixed 'til it was doing what it was supposed to.

Her smile reassured me. I shook off my bullshit doubts as she gently undid the straps and cut away the excess. The thing popped off.

So did my fucking arm. When I heard that deafening click, I thought for sure I was fucked. I waited for a firestorm shooting up my brain, except it never came.

"It's just the bones settling," she said. "Try to move it."

I reached out. My fingers tingled a little. The muscle was slightly sore, but the rest of it seemed okay.

Hooking it around her back, I spread my hand, guiding it down to her ass. My good hand crept around and did the same. Fuck, I'd break chains forever just for one more squeeze of what she had hanging on her hips.

Emma giggled and fought me as I pulled her close, yanking her shirt up with my teeth to plant these lips on her warm, naked belly.

"Change into something else and come with me. I'm gonna make sure my arm's working again once and for all. Meet me in my room in five minutes. Unless you'd rather have me help you get undressed?"

She laughed as I stood up, still holding her tight. The girl's bashful streak was there in the bright red splotches filling up her cheeks. I loved that fucking innocence, but I loved the way she melted and let me do things no other man would ever do to her even more.

"Okay! Okay!" she yelled when I cupped her ass again. "Keep your hands to yourself for a few more minutes. I'm coming."

I turned and walked out, heading for my room. It was hard as fuck to keep my smile from spilling off my face.

By the time she came in, I had all my tools laid out. Emma closed the door behind her and folded her arms, looking at it curiously.

"Take off that shirt and lay down. Let me know where you want this. You're gonna get it today one way or another." I looked up, studying her for any sign of fear or doubt. "You nervous?"

Emma snorted. "After what we just went through together? I think I can handle a little needle, Tank. Besides…"

She stepped up, sleek and sexy, rubbing against me like a cat looking for affection. "I'm kinda excited to get my first tattoo. I want it right here."

Emma turned, exposing her neck. It was a perfect place. Pale, smooth, virgin. She rarely ever had herself buttoned all the way up either, and the whole damned world would see it.

"You sure you got nurse's outfits high enough to cover that shit?" Long as she wore it around all the brothers and out in public, I was happy. I didn't think she'd do it at the hospital, though.

"Linda won't give me any crap. And the day she leaves and some new asshole does is the day I start looking for another job. Being an old lady takes priority, Tank." She reached for one hand and squeezed it. "Everything else is second to you. I wouldn't have it any other way."

I smiled. "Lucky me. Now, take off that shirt. Last time I ask before I give it a pull."

She obeyed. A minute later, she was flat on my bed. I was damned glad I'd be cleaning that fucker up soon and sleeping somewhere else. It would do for this purpose.

I started slow, praying my bones and muscles weren't hiding any new imperfections. It was all in the brain first and foremost, bringing the design I wanted to life. She insisted before that I should do whatever the hell I wanted, as long as it looked pretty.

First, I inked an outline of a black rose, a long thorny stem forming a circle. Flames danced along the borders. Not even fire could contain the insane fucking energy I had for her, and I made sure she knew it as soon as I went to work the inscription.

She twitched beneath me. I paused, taking a breath. "You okay, babe?"

"Yeah. Except okay's too weak a word for this." She sniffed, happy and overwhelmed.

I smiled to myself. This was gonna be the best damned ink I ever did.

It took another half-hour to get everything just right. She laid there like a good girl, a living, breathing, beautiful canvass for the needle and my own damned passion.

She didn't move much when I drew the needle gun away and turned it off. "Ready to have a look?"

I gently helped her up, reaching for the mirror on my nightstand. It hit me the same time she gasped.

"Oh my God. It's so damned...*real*, isn't it?" Emma smiled.

PROPERTY OF TANK, PRAIRIE DEVILS MONTANA MC was inscribed in the fire and thorns. It nearly matched my own designs, a good start with plenty of room to expand later on as she desired.

"There'll always be shit outside us threatening to burn our asses down or draw blood. I chose the thorns and flames as a reminder. But what's important is right inside that loop, babe. There's nothing stronger than that brand, nothing that's ever gonna reach in and fuck apart how hard we've fought to get here." I reached for her hand, pulling her up off the bed, swinging her tight to my chest.

"Tank..." Christ, she was so fucking beautiful, whispering my name and narrowing those *come-fuck-me* eyes.

"I don't need to tell you the brand on your skin and the one on the cut I'm giving you soon is just a reminder when I'm not around. When I am, I'm gonna show you how deep this goes, deep as my blood and heavy as my goddamned soul. The brand you really need to feel is in these lips."

She leaned on me, standing high on her toes, begging for a kiss. Damned good thing too because I was all out of flowery words. My cock was hungry, and he'd reached the very limits of how long I could keep him restrained.

Emma and I shared a long, hot, sultry kiss before I pushed her away and took her hand. "Come on. Let's get the fuck outta here. Need to show you the rest of what these fingers can do."

She came along, the spring in her pulse telling me she was as horny as me. Just the way I wanted my girl. *My old lady.*

I got her on my bike and helped fix her hands snug around my waist. I was still grinning like a fucking idiot as we took off through the gate, nestled close to ward off the icy mountain air.

She was half-way to heaven, but I was gonna send her the rest of the way there. I had one more surprise waiting for her a few blocks down the street.

XII: Eternal Flame (Emma)

With Tank, there had been so many firsts. I couldn't believe I'd met him as a clueless, broken, too-good-for-my-own-good girl.

Look at me now, I thought, fingering his belt as we rolled through Missoula.

I was on this Harley, and I was loving it. My hands were wrapped tight around my tattooed hunk, a badass who'd killed for me, taking life and death and love in his hands. My neck itched, a pleasant reminder of my first tattoo.

Jesus, what would the next few years bring?

I didn't have a clue. But whatever it was, I was ready, damned ready to be the best old lady this man could have.

Lost in all my dreams and the rock hard temptation beneath my hands, it took me a minute to realize we were lost. My heart pattered. I wondered if he'd taken a wrong turn? This was the other end of town, far from my neighborhood.

"Tank? Where are we going?"

"One more minute and you'll find out, babe. Be patient."

I pursed my lips, wanting to pout. It was bad enough just touching him like this without laying into him. Well, two could tease.

I brushed my hand lower as we slowed and rounded the next block. My hand brushed the edge of his huge cock again and again. Tank's breath hitched. His hard abs jumped beneath my curled hand.

I laughed.

"Bad girl. Bad fucking girl. You're damned lucky you've got a lotta good to make up for the naughty." He grunted as I reached lower and squeezed. "Fuck! Less than a minute, babe. Keep your fucking hands to yourself before I run this bastard off the road. And it'd be a real tragedy to get fucked up going less than twenty miles an hour."

He wasn't kidding. We slowed way down as the bike roared into a neighborhood. It was a lot cleaner and neater than my ratty old rental's place.

My confusion only deepened when he pulled up a steep driveway attached to a gorgeous house on a wooded lot. It was *much* nicer than my rental – hell, nicer than Mom's place. Even had the proverbial white picket fence around it, the only thing separating the thick forest, a strange living contrast of wild and order with the woods.

"Thought I'd show you my new place," he said, stepping off the Harley and offering me his hand.

"Really?" I undid my helmet and jumped off. "Where'd you find the time?"

"The MC's always got connections. Realtors too." He punched a button on a remote in his hand and the garage door opened.

The old truck he barely used when he wasn't on his bike was parked inside, and he already had the beginnings of a nice tool setup inside. Tank squeezed my hand tighter, leading me to the door inside.

"Come on. What I really need you to see is on the kitchen table."

The house was pretty amazing. My eyes danced around the high vaulted ceilings and the new wooden floors. The kitchen was a dream. Just staring at the counters and all the new appliances made me want to learn how to cook for him here.

"What's this?" He let me go as I approached the table, reaching for the neat scrap of paper.

It was a title. His name was there, just like I expected. But when I looked below it and saw EMMA GALENA, I nearly fell over.

I swooned. Laughing, he reached out and caught me, gently plucking the paper out of my hands and laying it on the table safely.

"Place is light on furniture," he said. "Figured you'd wanna pick that out yourself. I got all the basics for us. We can start cleaning your place out later this month, soon as you give notice and –"

I couldn't talk. I couldn't even listen. All I could do was throw myself forward, clawing at his neck, smashing my lips to his.

It took Tank a few hot seconds to process the reaction. When he did, he kissed me back, squeezing me tight and pressing me to the wall.

Our tongues did all the talking for the next five minutes.

God, he was divine. His manly scent rolled off his cut, one more temptation for the fire, one more familiar, sweet thing to cling to in the freshly painted house.

"Upstairs," I moaned, as soon as I could move my lips off his. "Let's christen this place right…"

Tank grinned. "If right means fucking your brains out, then yeah, sounds like my kinda plan."

I flushed, hot and overwhelmed. The happy surprise and lust crashing through my system was dizzying, stronger than any shot I'd ever knocked in my belly.

Tank wasn't gonna wait for me to steady. The world spun as he threw me over his shoulder and ran toward the long staircase. I laughed and beat playfully on his back, admiring the ridges of his ass moving below, the same strong hips that would soon be pistoning his cock deep inside me.

No more teasing. No more wait.

As soon as he let me go, I started to rip off my scrubs, followed by my bra and panties. Tank mirrored me. When I looked up again, he was naked. Jesus, I'd never get tired of seeing those wicked tattoos covering his granite body.

He stepped forward with fire in his eyes, one hand on his cock. "Lay back and spread those pretty legs, babe. My tongue's been missing that pussy nearly as much as this dick."

I took a few steps back. Tank grabbed my wrists and nudged me down faster. I crashed backward on the mattress as he kneeled on the floor, burying his face between my legs.

The laps came in broad, wet, swirling waves. My muscles tightened in tune to every jerk of his tongue, wet and mad and wild. Every lick spread me open, parted me deep. His tongue shoved its way up through my velvet, tasting my cream before it darted up and focused on my clit.

He replaced his tongue with his fingers, eager and stroking deep inside me. His lightning focused on my nub, forcing horny fire deeper up my womb while he fingered me rough. The wet contrast of his mouth and his calloused hands was too much.

My brain didn't know what to do.

No, that was a lie. It dropped deep into the lava pool surging up inside me, sinking like a stone.

"Tank! John! God. Damn. It!" My breath hitched along with everything else.

His tongue laps spiked higher, faster, shallower. I came, trying to growl out his name a second time, but the orgasm stole everything. My breath, my voice, my everything belonged to him just then.

He controlled my pleasure the same way he reached in and filled my whole fucking life. And I surrendered with a purr and a moan.

When a woman finds a man *worth* giving herself to, she gives herself completely. Then and there, I gave it all to Tank, my old man, my badass, shuddering through my spasms far longer than I thought possible.

He gave me one minute – exactly sixty seconds – to collect my breath before he moved up. He came up my belly kissing, covering me with his huge body, pressing down on top of me.

"I'd say this fuck is special because it's the first one in our new house. But babe, I'd be lying through my teeth." He paused, swishing his tongue against mine for a deep taste before he continued. "Every single fuck with you is special, Em. I don't care if I bust my nuts inside you ten thousand times – and I will. I'm never gonna take it for granted, *never* gonna get sick of it, *never* gonna stop dying happy when I feel your pussy wrapped around my dick. I'm never gonna stop loving claiming what's mine, showing you what real love and lust can do in every inch of this hungry fucking cock."

His sweetness punched me along with his vulgar spice. Before I could answer, he decided to ratchet up the heat. Fondling my breasts, he gave them one more good squeeze, then flipped me over. His hand slid up my neck, careful to avoid the new tattoo settling in my flesh, grabbing a fistful of blonde hair.

"Ease your sweet cunt back on this dick, baby girl. I'll race you to the fucking finish line."

My body took over. Thinking was done. I couldn't do anything but feel as I followed his guiding hand, settling on his cock with a loud moan.

Tank gripped my hair and started to fuck. He mounted me deep, thrusting between my legs. His free hand alternated from my nipples to my thigh, always squeezing and pinching and plucking, fanning the fire lit by his insane cock.

The little metal bead in his swollen head rubbed me just right. All the blood flow drained below my waist and then shot up my skull again in one savage burst. His pierced cock needled me just perfect, a stark raving friction I'd never stop coming to.

God, he needed to come with me. I needed his fucking come.

I clenched my pussy as hard as I could, just as the convulsions began. Somehow, I kept my hips swaying, crashing back into him again and again, matching his thrusts.

Hot surprise gurgled out his throat. "Oh, fuck, babe. Emma. Fuck. Fuck. Fuck!"

Curses exploded into growls. He pinned me down on the mattress, holding his dick inside me as it swelled. Hot seed shot into my belly, spasming and filling my deepest spaces, jerking and twitching again and again.

We were one. Finally, irrevocably, forever one.

His heartbeat matched mine, and so did the guttural pleasure in his throat. I didn't stop coming until he softened. He stayed inside me a good long while, running his hands over my flesh, kissing me more tenderly now that the fever had passed.

"Dammit, babe. Don't know whether to lick you some more or haul you up on my lap and spank that ass raw." He grunted, seriously rolling the options in his head.

I smiled, rolled, and looked at him, running one sleek leg up his flank. "Why not both?"

His smile started thin as always, but then he lost it. Tank broke into a full blown grin and laughed, just the biggest, meanest, hottest badass you could imagine chuckling like a happy, mischievous boy.

"I didn't fucking doubt it before, but now never will: you really are my old lady, Emma. Now 'til the day I'm dust."

Pressing my thighs together, I arched my back and purred happily, loving what he'd left inside me. Soon, there'd be more. And one day, it would get me pregnant, fusing us together in the deepest way a man and a woman can join.

I couldn't wait.

They say big things come in small packages. But with Tank, it was all enormous, everything from head to toe to heart. And I had a whole crazy life ahead just trying to hold all his huge surprises.

Thanks!

Want more Nicole Snow? Sign up for my newsletter to hear about new releases, subscriber only goodies, and other fun stuff!

JOIN THE NICOLE SNOW NEWSLETTER! - http://eepurl.com/HwFW1

Thank you so much for buying this book. I hope my romances will brighten your mornings and darken your evenings with total pleasure. Sensuality makes everything more vivid, doesn't it?

If you liked this book, please consider leaving a review and checking out my other erotic romance tales.

Got a comment on my work? Email me at nicolesnowerotica@gmail.com. I love hearing from my fans!

Kisses,
Nicole Snow

More Erotic Romance by Nicole Snow

KEPT WOMEN: TWO FERTILE SUBMISSIVE STORIES

SUBMISSIVE'S FOLLY (SEDUCED AND RAVAGED)

SUBMISSIVE'S EDUCATION

SUBMISSIVE'S HARD DISCOVERY

HER STRICT NEIGHBOR

SOLDIER'S STRICT ORDERS

COWBOY'S STRICT COMMANDS

RUSTLING UP A BRIDE: RANCHER'S PREGNANT CURVES

FIGHT FOR HER HEART

BIG BAD DARE: TATTOOS AND SUBMISSION

OUTLAW KIND OF LOVE

NOMAD KIND OF LOVE

SAVAGE KIND OF LOVE

SEXY SAMPLES: SAVAGE KIND OF LOVE

I: Three Nights (Saffron)

They say it only takes one night to change a woman's life. For me, it was three, each more savage than the last.

Deep in the darkness, forced to wrestle with dreams and desires and nightmares, a girl finds out what's really important really damned fast. And when it's all over, there's no more doubt.

Scars don't lie, and neither do hearts.

Three sunrises later, I knew I'd never know uncertainty again.

Three nights. Three vicious, unforgettable, pitch black collisions with life and death, love and hate. Three nights to mold me into what I was always meant to be.

I still think about the last one the most.

Starting with the way the sick, soulless bastard held the knife to my throat, digging in so deep he drew blood. His words echoed like a lion's growl in my ear. Distant and distorted by fear, but unmistakably dangerous.

"I see you've made your choice, baby doll. If you're not gonna tell us what we need to know about your boyfriend and his Prairie Pussies, then I guess we'll do things the hard way." He paused, his stained teeth shaping a smile. "Lucky for you I like it hard."

"Kill me now. You're a dead man either way," I growled.

The knife relaxed its deadly pressure on my throat. His other hand tangled itself deeper in my hair and jerked, twisting my face to his, just the right position for a grotesque kiss.

I'd bite his lips if I had to. Only one man's skin belonged on mine, and I wouldn't forget it, no matter how hopeless this battle was.

Evil excitement flickered in his dark eyes, mingling with surprise. He stopped just short of planting his kiss and getting my teeth ripping at his lip.

"Kill you? No, dolly, I'm in no rush. Not until I've torn you up and sent you home to Blaze with plenty to remember me by. Gotta fucking burn some sense into you, make you give up what you're holding behind that pretty little face. And then – maybe then – I'll put you and the rest of those Devil cocksuckers out of their misery..."

My mind usually blanks at the sound of my belt coming unbuckled in his dirty fingers. Then everything becomes a mess, a deafening chaos like the world itself ending.

The fire consumes everything. My pants drop, and he lowers his cigar, letting it linger so close to my skin I can feel the heat.

"What the fuck is this?" He rubs tenderly near my hip, tracing my tattoo. "My, my. Pretty flowers for a pretty lady. It's nice to have a target. Hold still, doll. Those flowers can't do much screaming, but you sure as hell can…"

Did I really live through it?

Hell yes. This night, and so many more.

Nobody ever said becoming an old lady to the biggest badass in Montana was easy…

Never in a million years did I expect to end up on the stage, shaking my twenty-four year old bare ass for grubby dollars.

At home in Missoula, I was Shelly Reagan, a college dropout who couldn't even get a damned job stocking shelves. Here in Python, I was Saffron, the most popular dirty dancer since June did her last act on the stage before taking on the manager's role.

Rolling my hips and wearing nothing but a fuckable smile paid the bills a lot better than shuffling around a grocery store. It wouldn't have been so bad, except for the fact that everybody I'd grown up with knew who I was and what I did.

Everybody except Mom, of course, and she was my only friend left since the others took flight. Same as it had been since my older brother Jordan went West after our family's last explosive fight.

A working class girl does desperate things in a recession with a disabled mother and a big brother missing in action. The dollars were all that mattered.

Dollars and drinks, maybe. At least Pink Unlimited's drinks were free to dancers, and the managers were nice.

My supervisor June was a stone cold bitch on the outside, but deep underneath, I could tell she cared. I stayed on her good side by doing my job and making money for the Prairie Devils' new strip joint.

I think she respected me for not whining and creating worthless drama like the other girls.

It was a good gig, until the night when I ran into a giant in leather out back.

I was trying to breathe in the fresh mountain air when the bike came roaring in. He rode an older Harley, and it snorted an oily, greasy stink into the narrow parking strip, mucking up my lungs.

So much for break time! I thought unhappily.

I tried to ignore him, but I couldn't when I saw him coming right for me. June always said to leave the guys sporting patches alone. I knew enough about MCs not to question her advice. Didn't have any trouble drawing the line between their club business and ours, just like the boss said.

"You work here?" he asked, eyeing me up and down.

Men ogling me wasn't anything new. Still, I wished I'd at least thrown on my pants before going out here instead of the flimsy robe we wore to cover up when we weren't dancing.

"Nope. I just like to stand out here half-naked."

I should've known. Sass never got me anywhere, and it wouldn't tonight.

The man pushed closer, corralling me against the wall with his gut. His huge leathery hands slapped the brick, poised on both sides of my head.

Jesus, can't you take a joke?

"Let's try this again, bitch. You give me a serious answer this time. This is strike two, and I don't do three."

He smelled drunk. This wasn't at all how the Prairie Devils who owned this place were supposed to be. Then I noticed his patches for the first time.

They're different. Is this a support club?

"Yeah, I'm on my break. How can I help you, sir?"

Stuffing the sarcasm wasn't easy. Unfortunately, not knowing who this stranger was or what he wanted didn't leave me much choice.

"Need to speak to your boss. Got some cash to pick up, and it better be ready. Take me backstage so I can get the hell out of this dump." He looked down and his eyes feasted on my cleavage while I wondered how to answer. "Fucking Devils. Fucking whore."

My eyes narrowed. I ignored the leering and studied him instead. I'd seen the Prairie Devils guys a few times, and their patches weren't like this. They definitely didn't have a strip going up the side of their jackets that said GRIZZLIES MC.

Uh-oh.

How could I be so damned dense to miss it? The Grizzlies had terrorized towns in the Flathead area for at least a generation.

The reeking alcohol rolling off him suddenly smelled like trouble. So did the greasy bandage tied tight across his head.

He pushed past me and grabbed for the back door. I caught up, gently tugging on his sleeve. He swore when the lock caught.

"Open this fucking thing. Right now!"

"You can't go in there! If you have a message, I'll pass it along. Manager's instructions. I'm sorry, we've all got our rules and it's what I've been told to –"

He spun, a nasty twitch in his lips pulling at his unkempt beard. His fist was like taking a brick to the face. Everything turned to giant red stars, exploding in a fiery ring around my socket, anchoring around my poor eyeball. I fell.

It took me several seconds to realize he'd punched me in the face. Then several more to look up, crying at the pain.

The same fist hovered in mid-air. I rolled into a ball, afraid he was about to beat me to death. He stuck out his finger instead.

"Pass this along: if we don't get our fucking money, the deal's off. You can tell that asshole Maverick and his whore that they've got twenty-four hours to cough up what's owed, or else our whole charter's gonna pay them a visit."

I tried to remember the threat, but the stars blossoming in my skull wouldn't let me. They swelled bigger, brighter, ten times more painful.

The roar of his bike was the last thing I heard before I blacked out.

I woke up chilled to the bone. Must've been out well past break time.

The sharp fire in my head was gone, replaced with a steady throb. I threw my hands against the wall and used it to help myself up, wincing when I touched my eye. New pain howled fiercely through the tender flesh around my socket, so sharp I thought I'd faint again.

"Shit...need help," I muttered to myself.

My brain was barely functioning. My legs switched onto auto-pilot and carried me inside, fumbling for the key card to the back entrance in my pocket. Never knew how I got it in and opened the door half-blind and consumed with agony, but I did.

June flipped out when she saw me. It was the first time I'd truly seen her surprised. Ironic, because that night was the last time I saw her.

I mumbled something about a stranger hitting me in the face, and she helped me over to a vending machine. For the next half hour I had a cold can of root bear on my face and Sandy at my side. Some other badass showed up and June had to step away, leaving me with the other girl to make sure I didn't have a seizure or something.

My boss and the beast in leather approached a little later. Jesus, I was scared, begging him for protection. I couldn't go home tonight. Not after this.

He granted my request to spend the night at the clubhouse. I had to wait it out until I could go home in the evening, just like normal. Mom wouldn't even notice if I was gone longer than usual, though I wasn't sure how I'd hide the bad eye.

Ice cold metal nipped at the pain in my skull. It wasn't a proper ice pack, but it did its job. Numb twilight buzzed around my brain when I felt a heavy hand on my shoulder.

I flew out of my chair and would've hit the floor if Sandy wasn't standing by to catch me.

"Jesus, Mister! Can't you see she's a little jumpy? A hello would be nice!" Sandy sounded pissed, ready to lay into him. But her words melted when she raised her head and took a good look at the man.

"Maverick sent me. See this patch?" He tapped the VP tag on one breast.

I felt Sandy nod.

"Means I'm here to help your friend stay safe from the assholes she really needs to worry about. Same patch that writes your check too," he growled. "Let me see it..."

A powerful hand tugged at my arm, quick but gentle. I struggled to my feet, opening my eyes for the first time in awhile.

I couldn't make out much more than a tall silhouette with broad shoulders, medium length hair, and some serious stubble on his face. He took both my hands, steadying my feet, drawing me into him.

"Fucking shit, my bro never said it was this bad." He shook his head with a snort. "Those fucking bears are gonna pay big time. Can you walk, baby?"

I groaned incoherently. Thought I could, anyway. Maybe I just wanted to be away from bikers so badly right now I convinced myself of the impossible.

"That's okay," he said, softening his voice. "Slow and easy. Come to papa. I'll get you home safe and put some real ice on that shit."

His powerful arms went to the small of my back, and then the whole world turned upside down. My stomach lurched at first, adjusting to the movement. I realized I was floating.

He was carrying me outside, careful to avoid jostling me too much. I let my head slump to his leather clad shoulder, wondering what I'd gotten myself into.

Should've just asked to be taken home. Do I really want to be at their clubhouse if something's going down between two clubs full of men like this?

A resounding NO rattled in my head. Too late, though, because we were already out in the darkness.

Going home wasn't much easier. Mom was sure to lay into me if she saw my eye, and then I'd have to explain how I'd gotten nailed at a strip joint she didn't know I was working at. All while I had the brutal headache throbbing behind my eyes too…

Big mistake. Everything.

Every part of me screamed I'd made a mistake ever taking this job. Beneath the cool and sexy mask I wore to make money, I wasn't cut out for this life, not for the violence and crime, and probably not even for shaking my tail.

God damned bikers! If their drugs and scuffles hadn't trashed this town in the first place, maybe there'd be more real jobs.

Anger pulsed through me. I had a feeling an MC had something to do with Jordan up and disappearing too. He'd talked about going West and joining up to ride since he was eighteen. Three years later, all signs said he'd actually done it.

It was easy to hate the men on bikes who roared around like they owned the fucking planet.

Except for right now, when the tough guy carried me so sweetly to his truck, tucking me into the seat and fastening my belt. What little I could see through my bad eye said he didn't look like the brute who'd thrown his fist at my face.

Didn't smell like the same either. This man had a different scent altogether, rich and earthy and soothingly masculine. He smelled *strong*, without giving off the nauseating musk I often picked up in the strip club after a full night passed with way too much testosterone swirling through the stuffy air.

"What's your name?" I whispered, wondering if he could even hear me as he slid into the driver's seat and started the truck.

"Name's Blaze. I'm VP of the Prairie Devils in this area. No need to bore you with more details than that.

You just lay your head back and enjoy the ride, woman. You're safe with me."

Look for Savage Kind of Love at your favorite retailer!

Printed in Great Britain
by Amazon